T0375175

THE
FIRST
DAY OF
SCHOOL

THE FIRST DAY OF SCHOOL

JOHN MUDZYN

THE FIRST DAY OF SCHOOL

iUniverse books may be ordered through booksellers or by contacting:

iUniverse
1663 Liberty Drive
Bloomington, IN 47403
www.iuniverse.com
1-800-Authors (1-800-288-4677)

ISBN: 978-1-5320-6621-4 (sc)
ISBN: 978-1-5320-6611-5 (hc)
ISBN: 978-1-5320-6610-8 (e)

Library of Congress Control Number: 2019901600

Print information available on the last page.

iUniverse rev. date: 02/11/2019

REALIZATION

I didn't realize that it happened;
All I know is that it did.
I think about all the time I wasted
Trying to keep it hid.
I thought it was over,
Gone in a flash.
Finally, I realized
For a lifetime it would last.
I didn't realize when it happened
How gently it arrived.
So deep, so innocent, so pure—
It did indeed survive
Through tears derived from hate and shame,
Clouds of darkness, full of rain.
I thought the storm would never stop
Because I was told to deny what was in my heart.
No matter how hard I tried,
It came down to this:
The love that came so gently
Grew so strong from that kiss.

Elliott ran into the house, rushed upstairs, and jumped into the shower. He had gotten to the gym late that afternoon and didn't realize the time. Earlier, he had made plans with three friends to spend Friday night at their favorite bar. After trying on three or four shirts, he finally decided on a yellow tank top that looked perfect with his new shorts. After all, it was still 104 degrees outside, which was typical for a late July evening in Phoenix. Elliott wanted to look good in case he met Mr. Right that night.

As he waited outside for the Uber to arrive, he texted his friends to let them know that he was on his way. The bar was already crowded when he arrived. It was a retro seventies disco night, and the bar was pulsating with Thelma Houston's "Don't Leave Me This Way." He waited in line at the bar to buy a beer and then met up with his friends. They exchanged hugs and quickly turned their attention to an extremely sexy-looking man who was standing alone at the bar. His friends couldn't stop looking at the guy, who seemed to know they were talking about him. Asked if he thought the guy was hot, Elliott replied that he wasn't his type. That's when the conversation and attention turned back to Elliott.

One of his friends said, "Nobody seems to be your type."

"Elliott, you've had three different boyfriends in the past six months," another piped up, "and none of them turned out to be good enough."

Elliott just smiled and said, "I guess I've just been waiting. I'll know when I finally see my Mr. Right."

They ordered another round of drinks. As the server was handing Elliott his beer, Elliott's attention turned to the door. He couldn't quite comprehend what he was seeing. He stood there, staring toward that door.

One of his friends asked him what was wrong, but Elliott did not answer. When he began to realize what he was looking at, the bottle of beer slipped out of his hand and crashed onto the concrete floor, which caused the beer to explode in a spray of foam.

CONTENTS

CHAPTER 1

Growing Up

Elliott grew up in a small, conservative, solidly Republican town in northeast Ohio. He lived with his family in a modest home on Maple Avenue. Elliott's parents, who some called leftover hippies, owned and operated the only pizza shop in town. His parents smoked a little weed on weekends, and they were extremely lenient in raising Elliot and his older sister, Becky.

Elliott's father, a quiet, gentle man, had inherited the pizza shop from his parents. Dan always encouraged his children to think outside the box and look past the obvious.

Elliott's mother, an extremely outgoing woman, was the face of the restaurant. She could always be counted on to give her customers a welcome feeling and a great meal. Although her given name was Margaret, she preferred to be called Peg. She loved wearing loud-colored, loose-fitting dresses and was never seen without a white flower in her long brown hair.

Peg and Dan met at the Woodstock Music Festival. Although the Age of Aquarius had come and gone, they still believed that freedom of expression—along with open, honest discussion—was a better alternative than the, "Only for me, what's in it for me?" social rhetoric that was coming from the administration in Washington.

Peg always strove to allow her children to express themselves openly—even though some of their opinions were contrary to social acceptance. Dan was more central in his political philosophy, but he fully supported Peg in going against the grain and allowing their children to think for themselves. They never imagined that this independence of thought would not be enough to help their son navigate the various storms that would blow through his young life.

The First Day of School

The summer flew by in a flash. Suddenly, it was Labor Day, and the new school year would be starting the next day. Elliott attended a small Catholic grade school and would be entering seventh grade. Becky would be a freshman at the larger public high school.

On the last day of summer, Elliott was concerned that his school uniform from the previous year would not fit him properly. He had grown considerably over the summer and was nearing six foot tall. He was not as athletic as some of his classmates, even though he looked athletic. He was self-conscious about the braces that covered his killer smile.

On an ordinary summer day, he would be at the pizza shop, helping his parents clear tables and wash dishes. Peg and Dan allowed him to take this last day of vacation off to prepare for his first day of school. Elliott begged his mom, who also had the day off, to take him to the mall to buy a new pair of pants and white shirt. Elliott wanted to look perfect on his first day of school.

While walking to school, Elliott met up with a couple of his classmates, and the three of them marched off toward the building that would be their prison for the next nine months. They wondered out loud who their teacher would be. They hoped it would not be Sister Mary Bennett, the Enforcer, as the students called her.

Arriving at school, the boys were relieved that they had dodged a bullet. Their teacher, Sister Mary Therese, was new to the school.

As Elliott entered his classroom, he noticed how young Sister Mary Therese looked. He thought that she was a way too pretty to be hidden behind that nun's habit. He introduced himself with a handshake, found his assigned desk, and waited for the rest of the class to arrive.

When all the students were seated, Sister Mary Therese announced that a new student had recently moved to their town. She opened the door and motioned for the new student to come in. He was introduced as Jeffery. Jeffery was an extremely athletic-looking young man. He looked handsome in his new school uniform, and his dark hair was cut just right.

Jeffery's father, William, was an up-and-coming conservative Republican who was running for Congress and needed to move into that congressional district. William rarely talked to Jeffery besides to give instructions or opinions. He tried to portray an image of conservative and moral tranquility. He insisted that his wife and son never strayed from that perception.

William was to be addressed as William—never Bill. He insisted that his son was called Jeffery and not Jeff. Jeffery's mother, Laura, was a devoted politician's wife, and she rarely smiled. She also had a fondness for vodka and tonics. Laura was never seen without her hair perfectly styled, and she always wore the finest fashions of the day.

Jeffery seemed quiet and intimidated. He introduced himself to the class and mentioned his passion for football. He shyly told them that he hoped to make it to the pros one day. As he walked to his desk, Elliott couldn't stop looking at him. He became fixated on Jeffery's piercing brown eyes, which appeared to sparkle as the sunlight from the windows shined across his face.

Sister Mary Therese excused the class a few minutes early to make sure they made it to the lunchroom on time. Elliott sat down next to his friends, and as he began to eat his lunch, he noticed Jeffery sitting alone.

Elliott asked his friends if they would move over and invite him to sit with them. Their response was typical of seventh grade boys, telling Elliott that there was no room at the table. "Let the new guy sit alone."

Elliott picked up his lunch tray and walked over to the table where Jeffery was sitting. "Would you mind if I sit here and join you?"

Jeffery smiled and said, "No, I would not mind. Please have a seat. Thanks for coming over."

Elliott introduced himself, and the two boys began to talk. At first, it was small talk. Elliott described the ins and outs of the school. He also explained who was cool and who to stay away from. As the lunch hour progressed, they forgot to eat, instead, telling each other as much as they could about themselves.

Elliott asked, "Do you ever go on campaign trips with your dad?"

Jeffery replied, "Not often. I only have to go when my father needs another perfect family photo for the news. That is the only time he wants me around."

The two of them wanted to continue talking, but the bell rang, signaling them to head back to class.

When school ended, Jeffery waited for Elliott in the hallway. His mother was going to pick him up, and he needed to wait for her outside.

Elliott mentioned that he lived down the street and walked.

Jeffery shyly asked Elliott if he would wait with him until his mom arrived.

Elliott was more than happy and answered, "Yes."

The two of them sat down on a curb and continued their conversation.

Jeffery said, "I think that is way cool for you to be able to work and talk with your parents. I could never do that with my parents. They are always too busy to bother with me."

Elliott said, "Would you like to hang out at the pizza shop on Friday? I would like to introduce you to my family. Also, it would be a terrific way for you to meet some classmates. Everyone hangs out there on Friday evenings."

Jeffery accepted the invitation.

As they waited for Jeffery's mother, Elliott's smile became brighter.

Jeffery's eyes sparkled like diamonds in the afternoon sun.

Jeffery's mother was an hour late, and Elliott was amazed at the new Cadillac that pulled up. He laughed out loud, comparing the car to his parents' four-year-old Ford.

Jeffery said, "My father thinks that showing off the best of everything is the only way to win an election."

Laura did not get out of the car or roll down the window. She just blew the horn. The boys waved goodbye, and the first day of school ended with the boys smiling that they have met. For reasons they did not yet understand, they both felt like they would be together for a long time. That first day of school was a good day.

Introductions

During school on Friday, Elliott and Jeffery made plans to meet up at six. The restaurant was crowded, as it always was, on Friday evening. Elliott was talking with his school friends, laughing and halfheartedly helping clear the tables.

Becky was answering the phone and writing down takeout orders. She liked the job because it allowed her to flirt with Luke, a twelfth grader who drove the delivery van on weekends. Every time Luke returned to get the next order, he would smile and tell Becky that she was the best-looking order taker in town.

Peg called Elliott over and said, "What's up tonight?"

Elliott confessed that his new friend was supposed to be there that night. "Mom, would it be all right if I take the night off and hang with Jeffery?"

Peg smiled and said, "Yes, that it will be okay, but only if you don't act embarrassed when you introduce Jeffery to me and your father." She gave him a swat on his butt and said, "Have fun, kid."

Becky overheard this conversation and said, "Why do I have to work while Elliott gets the night off?"

Peg looked at her, gave her a grin, and winked. "That's because you are my favorite daughter."

Becky dropped the subject.

It was well past six thirty, and Jeffery had not arrived. Elliott was disappointed. When Jeffery finally walked in, Elliott smiled and walked over to greet him. He introduced Jeffery to Peg, Dan, and Becky.

Becky looked Jeffery up and down and turned to a friend. "He looks much hotter than any seventh grader I have ever known."

After a few minutes, Jeffery asked Elliott if they could go outside. "I have something I need to tell you in private. My parents were fighting, and they didn't have the time to drive me into town. My father told me that he didn't believe that these were the proper people I should be seen with. I snuck out of the house and rode my bike here. I really wanted to be here with you tonight."

Elliott was concerned that Jeffery would be in trouble when he got home.

Jeffery said, "Don't worry about that. My father will be busy with his campaign, and my mother will probably be passed out by then. Will you please start calling me Jeff instead of Jeffery? I like that name better, but my father forbids me from using it. He always says that Jeff is not a proper way to be introduced."

Elliott was confused, but he said, "Sure, sounds good to me."

Before they walked back inside, Jeff confided to Elliott that it was the first time he felt completely comfortable sharing details about his home life.

Elliott flashed his beautiful smile and said, "Don't worry. I am here for you."

Back inside, Whitney Houston's "All the Man I Need" was playing.

Jeff smiled and said, "I love this song."

Elliott said, "I like it, but I prefer to listen to Madonna."

One of their classmates yelled, "Madonna sucks."

Elliott laughed and said, "It doesn't matter. I love her."

Jeff got into a conversation with some of the boys about football, and Elliott continued his discussion about Madonna with other classmates. One by one, parents came to pick up their young teenagers. Soon, Jeff was the only one still there.

Elliott asked his mom if she would drive Jeff home.

Peg replied, "It is way too dark and late to be riding that bike home. Get into the car. I will be there in a few minutes."

On the drive, another Whitney Houston song was playing on the radio.

Elliott asked Jeff if he wanted Peg to turn it up.

Jeff replied, "Oh no! I don't want to bother her. Besides, she won't do it."

Elliott asked his mom to turn up the radio, and she reached over and cranked up the tune.

Jeff said, "I can't ever touch the radio in my parents' car—let alone ask them to turn it up. They would just tell me to shut up. My street is coming up on the right. Be careful because the street sign is difficult to see at night."

Jeff lived in the affluent part of town with large houses and impeccably manicured lawns.

When they arrived, there were several cars in the driveway.

Peg asked, "Why are all those people here at this late hour?"

Jeff said, "I guess they are working on my father's campaign. They won't even notice me walking in." He thanked Peg for the ride home.

She told him that he was welcome anytime to their home and restaurant. "But if you hang around too much, I may put you to work."

Jeff smiled. "I would like that very much."

On their way back home, Peg said, "We like Jeff, but be careful because his family is in a different league. It appears that Jeff has some serious issues going on at home."

Elliott said, "I think Jeff is lonely and needs a good friend. I feel good when we are together, and I want to be that friend. By the way, Mom, thanks for driving Jeff home."

Peg smiled and said, "No problem."

Stronger Bonds

As the school year progressed, Elliott and Jeff became as close as friends could be. Rarely would you see one without the other. Even though they came from worlds apart, they had a lot in common. Both had started first grade a year late. Two weeks before the start of first grade, Elliott fell out of a tree and sustained a serious concussion. Peg and Dan, after consulting with the doctors, decided to keep him out of school until the start of the next school year. Jeff started first grade a year late because William thought it would be beneficial to hold him back so that he would be older and more mature and stand out from the rest of the class. They often joked that by the middle of their senior year, they would be eighteen and the older statesmen of their class.

Jeff was turning into an extremely handsome young man. Puberty had also been good to Elliott. He had stopped growing at six feet. His braces had finally come off, which resulted in an even brighter smile.

Jeff's father was elected to Congress in the fall and started spending more of his time in Washington. Because Jeff was in school, his mother only traveled to DC on weekends and school holidays.

Jeff hated those trips. He often confided to Elliott that he wished his father had lost the election. "These trips take me away from my friends when they are all hanging out and having fun on weekends."

One day, Jeff took a chance and asked his father if he could stay at Elliott's home for the weekend.

William vetoed the idea immediately and said, "You need to begin cultivating new friendships in Washington. That will be the only way for you to get ahead in life."

Jeff said, "You could have just said no."

Before his father could respond, he was summoned to a phone call and walked away. Politics always took priority over Jeff's needs. He was beginning to understand that it would always be that way.

When Jeff was in Washington, his parents always paraded him around. It was as if they needed to convince everyone that they had the perfect American son. They insisted that he attend all political gatherings and parties with them.

At one gathering, William introduced him to the crowd. "This is Jeffery, my up-and-coming football hero son and future congressman."

Jeff wanted to walk out of that room, but he smiled and answered as he was instructed to do. The longer those trips continued, the more he missed Elliott.

Willian never stopped telling Jeff that Washington was where he needed to be for his own good.

Laura never intervened, and she focused on being the proper congressional wife.

At a boring party, Jeff found an empty office and called Elliott. They talked for quite a while, and Jeff told Elliott how all the food was horrible and how phony everyone was.

William walked in and demanded to know who Jeff was speaking to.

Jeff knew that his father didn't like Elliott, and he said he was talking to a classmate about football.

"Perfect. I thought you were talking to that little brat Elliott. I don't understand why you want his kind for a friend. I would prefer that you don't hang around him anymore."

When his father left the room, Jeff said, "I miss you."

Elliott said, "I feel the same. I also miss hanging around with you."

Neither one yet understood what it was, but they liked the way saying it made them feel.

Lonely Summer

As the school year was nearing the end, the boys had to face the reality that Jeff would be in Washington for the next three months.

William continued his daily harassment. "I don't know why you want a friendship with that little brat. He and his family are not people who can help you advance in society. You need to make friends here in Washington." William arranged for Jeff to join a summer football team at an upscale private school.

Jeff was somewhat happy to be able to play the game he deeply loved, but after a few weeks, he wanted the summer to be over. He wanted to go home. He had many things he wanted to share with Elliott, and he wanted to hear all about Elliott's summer.

Elliott spent the summer helping his parents at the pizza shop. He had become withdrawn. He missed his friend. He would take his time walking to work. During these walks, he would think about Jeff and wonder what he was up to. His greatest fear was that Jeff's parents would insist that he stay in Washington. They would never see each other again. Elliott lost interest in hanging around his other friends during this summer.

Peg tried to talk to him about his feelings, but she got very little feedback from her son.

He would only tell her that everything was all right. "I wish everyone would stop asking me if I am okay."

Dan said, "Elliott is in the process of becoming a teenager. This is an extremely tough time for every young boy. We need to be patient and ride out this storm of male puberty."

Peg hoped that's all it was, but she felt there was more to it. Elliott was beginning to struggle with a deeper emotion that he still didn't understand. She knew she had to be patient and make sure her son knew he could always confide in her.

As summer vacation came to an end, Jeff's parents demanded that he enroll at that private school and remain in Washington, which resulted in a huge argument.

William said, "You will do as you are told."

Jeff felt like a trapped animal that was being backed into a corner. For the first time, he shouted back at his father. He grabbed the school enrollment papers from William's hand, tore them to pieces, and threw them on the floor.

William slapped Jeff's face.

Jeff looked his father directly in the eye and shouted, "I hate you, and if you make me stay here, I will run away."

Laura was making her afternoon cocktail in the next room. She said, "I would prefer to go back to Ohio for a while. I will take Jeffrey with me for the remainder of the school year." That seemed to be the only way she could defend her son without having to admit it.

William walked out of the room without answering.

Jeff glanced at the torn-up papers on the floor. He kicked them around and held his stinging cheek. He felt the accomplishment of defying his father and the hatred of William's slap. He noticed his mother looking at him from the other room while sipping her drink. She never said anything to him. He had so much that he wanted to talk to her about, but he was beginning to realize that she would never be someone he could tell his deepest feelings.

Reacquainted

Back in Ohio, Jeff and Elliott spent the first few days getting reacquainted.

Jeff said, "I almost had to remain in Washington for the school year. My father had everything arranged for me to stay there. It was only because I fought back that he agreed to let me come back to Ohio."

Elliott said, "I had a feeling something like that would happen. I am so glad you came back."

During those first few days, Jeff couldn't stop looking at Elliott. He was amazed at how mature Elliott looked. He mentioned to Elliott that he should think about joining the high school football team next year.

Without hesitation, Elliott said, "That's your game—not mine. Trust me, that will never happen."

Jeff ran his hand down the side of Elliott's face and said, "When did you start shaving? You must be getting old along with me."

Elliott loved the way Jeff's hand felt as Jeff slid it slowly down his face. Elliott wanted to change the subject, but before he could, the bell rang.

Everything seemed to be getting back to normal, and when they talked, they looked each other directly in the eye. Every time they realized it, they quickly turned away.

Eighth grade went by faster than the previous year did.

As summer vacation was approaching, Elliott feared that Jeff would have to leave for the summer. They would be entering high school in the fall, and Jeff had already been accepted to play on the football team. He would have to start practice early in the summer and would not be able to go to Washington.

William said, "You can stay if you make the varsity team and become the quarterback. If not, you will have to go back to Washington."

Jeff tried to explain that his position on the team would not be his decision. "It will be up to the coach—but I think you already know that!"

"That's the deal. Live up to it—or back to DC you go."

On the last day of school, when both boys arrived at the pizza shop, Jeff told Peg about the ultimatum.

Peg said, "You go and be the best you can on that team. I don't think you know how good at football you really are. You might just become the quarterback." She winked at him and added, "We are all rooting for you, kid. Never forget that." She threw him a dish towel and apron and smiled. "Help me clean the tables."

He got up, hugged her, and said, "I would love to help you."

When Laura came to pick him up, Jeff said, "I enjoyed working and helping this afternoon."

Laura said, "I don't think it is proper for a son of a congressman to be seen working in a low-class pizza place."

Jeff said, "It isn't a low-class place. Don't ever refer to it that way again!"

Laura said, "You need to keep quiet." Jeff wanted to pull the steering wheel and cause his mother to smash the car. Instead, he thought about the fun he had helping Peg that afternoon. All he wanted was for his mother to tell him she was happy that he had an enjoyable time. Deep down, he knew that would never happen.

CHAPTER 2

High School

The first day of high school was a totally new experience for both boys. It was the first time since they met that they would not always be in the same class.

Elliott was in awe when he realized that this school was tremendously larger than his previous school. He became anxious at the thought of navigating the maze of hallways to locate his locker and classroom assignments without his best friend at his side. That new experience would be his alone.

Jeff had been at football practice since early summer and had already walked the halls and been given the grand tour by his coach and teammates. He had no apprehensions and fit in without any problems. Jeff also had something else in his favor. He was now on the football team and a congressman's son, which elevated him to a higher hierarchy within the student body.

On the first day, they only saw each other in passing in the hallway.

Jeff was walking and laughing with a group of teammates and only gave Elliott a slight glance. Everyone wanted to be friends with Jeff. He was no longer the new boy.

Elliott found his way to his classes without much difficulty, and he was relieved to hear the final bell. He waited outside in case Jeff showed up after school, hoping they could hang out for a while.

Jeff was practicing on the field. He was determined to become the quarterback—even if he had to practice all night long. He wasn't going to let William win.

Elliott's World

As the days passed, Elliott felt betrayed by Jeff and his newfound popularity. He continued to struggle with his deep feelings but refused to admit to himself what the root cause of those feelings was. He began developing new friendships. These new friends had different interests. They were not football jocks, and they were interested in things like the drama club. Elliott was apprehensive about joining the club, but with a lot of persuasion from his parents, he decided to give acting a try.

One of the students in the class was named Darlene. She was outspoken and never hesitated to give her opinion—even if she wasn't asked to give it. Darlene preferred to wear jeans, untucked shirts, and a baseball cap. She seemed happiest just being one of the guys.

The drama teacher tried to allow the students to develop their own acting skills. He often had them read lines in front of the class. After he wrote all the students' names on pieces of paper, he would randomly pull out two names. The two students would read for the class.

One afternoon, the teacher picked Darlene's name and asked her to pick out another name from the box. Looking at the name, she said, "Elliott."

Elliott realized he could not get out of it and slowly walked to the front of the classroom. He and Darlene were instructed to rehearse their lines in the hallway, and when they were ready, they would deliver their lines to the class.

Darlene tried to take charge of their rehearsal and kept interjecting her way to recite the lines. She was extremely forceful with her opinions and kept pointing her finger at Elliott, demanding that he did it her way.

Elliott grabbed her finger as she was hitting his chest and said, "You need to settle down. Don't point your finger at me. You can read your part any way you want, and I will do my part my way—or we can combine our techniques and show the class that we worked together."

Darlene said, "Dude, don't ever tell me to settle down."

Elliott said, "All I want is for us to do a decent job—nothing else."

She agreed to calm down and listen to him. When they finished reading to the class, they received a loud ovation and an excellent job from the teacher.

After class, Darlene approached Elliott and said, "I thought you had a lot of guts to talk to me that way. No one ever talks back to me."

Elliott laughed and said, "Perhaps it was time someone did. Look at us—we did a fantastic job together."

They didn't know their interaction was the beginning of a lifelong friendship. As the days passed by, Elliott began sharing details about Jeff and telling her about all the fun they used to have together. He was extremely careful to stay one step ahead of his thoughts and not divulge his true feelings for Jeff.

One afternoon, they were hanging out after school. Elliott mentioned that he had stopped to watch Jeff's practice the day before. "Jeff noticed me standing behind the fence and gave me a smile. He kept looking over at me, so I decided to leave and not cause any further distraction."

Darlene grabbed his shoulders and looked him in the eye. "I understand what you are trying to tell me. Just say it. You will feel better."

Elliott teared up and poured his heart out. He shared all his feelings he had kept to himself for so long. He explained how the feelings were like a tapestry filled with every emotion from love to hate and anger to shame. "I need to accept that Jeff and I are moving in different directions." He asked if she would help him move forward instead of looking at what was in the past.

Darlene said, "I have to deal with my own feelings I have for other girls, and that is why I understand where you are coming from."

They hugged for a long time, each feeling some sense of relief. Elliott made her promise that she would never disclose to anyone what he confided to her. He promised he would do the same.

Darlene said, "It is time to forget about that spoiled, rich football jock. Look at the facts, Elliott. When was the last time he called you and wanted to hang out? You are not part of his so-called A group of jocks and cheerleaders—and neither am I."

Elliott said, "I know. You're right, and I am beginning to realize the same thing. I just can't get rid of these feelings I have for him."

She said, "Those feelings will pass. And one day we might look back and laugh about all of this."

He said, "I hope you're right."

Jeff's World

Football had quickly become the center of the universe for Jeff. Because all his free time was spent at practice, he didn't socialize as he used to on weekends. Jeff seldom saw Elliott, and when he did, it was only in passing in the school hallways. He harbored a deep resentment toward his father and had made up his mind that he would become the best football player without any help from William. He was also questioning his deep feelings for Elliott, which seemed to never leave his conscience. It was becoming evident to him that their friendship had always been more than just a friendship. He found himself on a narrow tightrope, balancing his family situation, football, and Elliott. He was afraid that if he dared look down, he would fall, and his entire life would crash down around him. He decided to make football his top priority and hope the rest would somehow work itself out.

Even with his newfound popularity, Jeff was an extremely lonely young man. At night, he would stare at the ceiling or cry, thinking about Elliott. He was afraid they would never be more than just friends.

As time progressed, he became totally engrossed in trying to become what he thought everyone wanted him to be: the most popular guy in school. He wasn't going to allow himself to fail. He would not let anyone view him as weak. In the process, he started to lose himself. He was slowly becoming what he hated the most: his father.

At practice, one of his teammates said, "Hey, man, you need to slow down. You are acting as if you're trying to win an election or something.

Chill out, dude. You're becoming annoying." He realized the guy was right. How did this happen? He began reevaluating his priorities, especially his feelings for Elliott. He still needed to prove himself on the football field. That took top priority. He had no intention of moving to Washington if he failed.

The First Game

The first game of the season was about to happen. Jeff's attitude improved, and along with his natural talent, it helped him land the quarterback position. That did not sit well with one of his teammates, Larry. He thought he should have been named quarterback. Larry thought the only reason Jeff made it was because his father was a congressman.

Jeff said, "Shut your fucking mouth."

Larry said, "Jeff, watch your back. I promise I will get even with you one day."

On Friday, the school held a massive pep rally. The rival team had beat them four years in a row. During the rally, Jeff was the center of attention. With all eyes on him, he seduced the crowd with his wit and good looks.

Elliott and Darlene were in the gymnasium with the rest of their class.

Darlene nudged Elliott and said, "See what I mean? He loves all the attention. He is eating it all up. He has not even looked over here at us."

Elliott didn't say anything. He just kept looking at Jeff.

When the rally was over, Jeff was summoned to the principal's office. His father had flown in from Washington with a couple of congressmen to watch the game. William stopped by the school to ensure that an arrangement was in place for him to address the audience during the game. He would never pass up an opportunity to brag about all his accomplishment in Congress. As he was looking over the program, he said, "Why is the program printed with your name as Jeff instead of Jeffery?"

Jeff answered, "Because my name is Jeff."

William yelled, "It's Jeffery."

Jeff looked at his father and said, "Jeffery has been gone for a long time. Where the hell have you been?" He then turned and headed back to class.

Back at his desk, he smiled and thought back to the time he asked Elliott to start calling him Jeff. He wanted to find Elliott and tell him what had happened. He hoped that he would have the opportunity to tell him all about it. For now, he had to keep all his thoughts on the game.

Before William left, he demanded that the school make a public apology at the game about the misspelling of Jeffery's name.

That evening was extremely warm for an Ohio October night. Jeff knew that a lot was riding on this game—for the school and for him personally. It was going to be his big opportunity to shine.

Peg and Dan gave Elliott and Becky the night off. Peg knew Elliott had been struggling about Jeff and thought it would be beneficial for her son to watch him play.

Elliott decided not to go to the game, but after plenty of harassment from Darlene, he gave in. It took him all afternoon to decide what to wear to the game. He settled on a new pair of jeans and his favorite yellow sweater.

Darlene said, "You are probably the only one who has to plan what to wear to a damn high school football game."

William arrived, shook hands, and posed for photos with his fake smile. As the team was walking out, he walked onto the stage. "Stick with me and the Republicans. We are the only ones who can save your children from those who believe that living an immoral lifestyle is okay. Together, we will do this in the name of God."

Jeff could not believe what he was hearing.

William called Jeff up to the stage and introduced him as Jeffery, the star of the team.

Jeff wanted to crawl under the stage and hide. How could his father single him out from the rest of the team? As embarrassed as he was, Jeff managed to say, "I am only one part of a talented team." He asked the rest of the team to join him on the stage.

William was livid.

Elliott wished he could run up and pull Jeff off the stage.

Darlene said, "Wow. That congressman is a weird dude."

A fat guy sitting next to her told to keep her opinions to herself.

She said, "Fuck off. Have you ever heard of the First Amendment, dude? Probably not if you're defending that asshole congressman."

Elliott grabbed her arm and led her to another section. "Let's watch the game from here."

The game was not going well for Jeff. He fumbled the ball once, and the other team was up by seven points.

When the fourth quarter was about to begin, Jeff looked over toward the bleachers and saw Elliott. For a couple of moments, he stared at Elliott. He noticed how much Elliott had matured. He thought Elliott looked sexy in his tight jeans and yellow sweater.

Elliott, noticing how Jeff's eyes were shining from the field's overhead lights, gave Jeff a huge smile and a thumbs-up. Jeff kicked a field goal, and his team went on to victory.

The crowd jumped up on their feet with an ear-piercing yell.

Jeff looked around and noticed that he was alone on the field. His team had run up to the stage to take a photo with William and the other congressman. William never looked at his son, and Jeff declined to participate in the picture. He was heartbroken.

Jeff frantically searched for Elliott, finally locating him by the gate. He grabbed Elliott by the arm and asked if he would wait for him while he changed out of his uniform.

Darlene said, "I will be at the pizza shop."

Jeff changed, and they walked to the pizza shop

Jeff told Elliott that he missed him deeply. "I am beginning to realize that my new friends only hang around me because of my position on the team and because of who my father is. They are a phony bunch of assholes. Look how they ran up and kissed my father's ass. Before the game, my father wanted nothing to do with them. I was the one who called them up onto the stage. They think he cares about them? If they only knew the truth."

Jeff put his arm around Elliott's shoulders and said, "Remember that first day of school way back then? Sometimes I wish that day had never ended. I am glad we had that day."

Elliott told Jeff that he missed hanging out with him. He wanted to tell Jeff more and felt that Jeff wanted to do the same. Instead, they both kept walking, keeping their thoughts to themselves. Jeff kept his arm around Elliott's shoulders until they reached the restaurant.

Jeff's parents didn't say a word to him when he arrived home. There were no congratulations for winning the game. They never told him they were proud of him. He didn't get a hug or kiss from his mother. He was happy and proud of his performance, but he was angry at his team for abandoning him on the field. He hated his father for the way he conducted himself at the game. *Why can't Mom just hug me and tell me she is proud of me?*

He wished Elliott was in bed with him. He liked the way he felt when he put his arm around Elliott as they were walking to the pizza shop. He wanted to hold him and whisper all his secrets to him. He knew that could never happen because of the world they lived in—and because of who his father was. He was all alone, despite all the privilege around him. The only comfort he had was when he was with Elliott. He wondered why that was considered so wrong.

As Elliott lay in bed that night, he became aroused while thinking about how good Jeff would feel next to him. With every stroke, he kept picturing them kissing. The thoughts scared the hell out of him. He understood that he could never disclose his feelings to Jeff. He felt trapped and alone, wondering why it was happening to him.

A Mother Always Knows

The morning after the game, Elliott was thinking about why Jeff put his arm around him last night. *Was Jeff trying to me something? Perhaps he has deeper feelings for me. Was he just reaching out to an old friend? Should I call Jeff and divulge my own feelings? Perhaps it is all just hope on my part—and nothing more.*

Peg was sitting at the kitchen table and asked Elliott what was bothering him.

Elliott didn't answer.

Peg lit a joint, took a couple of hits, and passed it over to Elliott. "You are reaching adulthood. Let's have an adult conversation. Take a couple of hits, relax, and then we can talk. I will start. I already know what you want to tell me. I can tell you what that is, but you need to be the one to say it first. Saying it will make it reality, and that is what you need to go forward with your life."

Elliott took a hit and began to cry.

Peg did not say a word.

Elliott admitted for the first time, out loud, that he was gay. "I have known for most of my life. I want to apologize to you, Dad, and Becky for bringing shame to the family. I want you to know that I have tried my best to hide these feelings. I have reached the point where it is too hard to do that anymore."

Peg said, "You must never be ashamed of who you are. Your dad, Becky, and I will go on loving you—as always. I am your mother, and I will do anything I can to protect you and your sister. I can't shelter you from everything you will face in your life. I wish I could tell you that your life will be full of happiness and joy and that no one will be there to hurt you, but I can't tell you that. You are entering an adult world in which being different or going against what is perceived as normal comes with risk and some hate. You can choose to live your life as a victim, hiding in society's shadows, always complaining that it isn't fair that you were dealt this hand, or you can go forward, hold your head up, and not be ashamed that you are who you are. No one can change that. You can be proud and show the world who you are and find the happiness you deserve. It won't be easy for you. Some people who you thought were your friends will turn away from you. Others will point fingers and talk about you. If you accept yourself, I know you will be able to navigate through all this and find the answers you are looking for. That was the first thing you needed to say. Now tell me the other thing that is bothering you. Remember, I already know what that is—now it's your turn to say it."

Elliott said, "Jeff."

Peg said, "What about Jeff?"

"I am in love with him. I can't stop thinking about him. I have felt this way since the first day of seventh grade. I don't know what to do. If I tell him, will that end our friendship? On the other hand, some of the things he says to me sound as if he feels the same. I am so confused."

Peg handed the joint back to Elliott and smiled. "It feels better to say it, doesn't it? This one, only you can figure out. You know Jeff better than anyone, but you need to be extremely careful. Jeff has a very different situation and relationship with his parents. If he feels the same, he may need to keep that a secret—even from you. His father is extremely intimidating, and Jeff may be afraid of him. If it's meant to be, then it will happen when the time is right."

Elliott said, "Jeff and I would sometimes sneak some of your stash when you weren't home and smoke it."

She smiled and said, "I know."

He said, "I love you. What is there to eat? For some strange reason, I am hungry."

Peg reminded him that it was almost time to open the restaurant and he needed to get his butt in gear.

Elliott began analyzing things differently. He felt fortunate to have parents like Peg and Dan. He wondered how this conversation would have gone if he had William and Laura as parents. He called Darlene and explained that his mom already knew he was gay.

Darlene started laughing and said, "Mothers are always the first to know—even before us."

The next morning, Peg asked Elliott if he could take a small box to the church and give it Sister Mary Therese. It was full of their old school uniforms. She was donating them to help those who couldn't afford to buy new ones. Sister Therese would be waiting for him. When he found her, she took him aside and mentioned that she understood that he and his mother had a serious discussion yesterday. She told him that his mother called her because she was worried about him.

Elliott felt embarrassed that Sister Mary Therese knew about him.

She said, "It's okay. I figured out a long time ago that you could possibly be gay. Even though this is against church doctrine, it isn't against my beliefs. Many of the church's teachings are out of date, and the church isn't always the expert about what God is thinking." She gave him a hug and assured him that as long as he was a good person, found ways to help others, and believed in God, he would find his way. She reminded him that she would always be there for him. She told him to never be afraid to talk to her.

He didn't tell her anything about Jeff. He figured that she probably already knew. He thanked her for being so up-front with him.

Jeff called Elliott that evening, and they talked about school, the game, and hanging out at the pizza shop. Jeff said that he was happy they had hung out together.

Elliott was careful not to mention anything about his conversations with his mom and Sister Mary Therese.

Jeff said, "You sound different. Are you okay?"

Elliott said, "Everything is good. In fact, it's been a great few days."

The Play

Elliott navigated through the next few days, contemplating how he needed to proceed with Jeff.

Jeff was still hanging with the in crowd, and Elliott thought he was wrong thinking that Jeff had any feelings for him. He said, "Darlene, Jeff thinks his new friends are phony assholes. Just look at how he acts. He has all of them eating out of his hand as if he is God—and he seems to love all of it. Looks like Jeff is beginning to follow his father's examples, using every opportunity to impress the crowd."

When it became obvious to Elliott that Jeff was escaping into a different world, he heartbrokenly made the decision to never tell Jeff about his true feelings for him.

Ninth grade held so much promise for these two young men at the beginning, but it had become a foundation for a wall that was being built to conquer and divide them. Elliott and Jeff knew their lives were changing, and neither one knew how to slow it down.

By the start of the new school year, Darlene was the essential element in Elliott's life. He relied on her to keep him grounded and focused. He wanted an escape in tenth grade and decided acting would be an opportunity. He remained in the drama class, which resulted in him being cast in the school's production of *Our Town*.

Elliott secured the lead as the stage manager, and Darlene would get to play opposite him as Emily Webb. The two of them rehearsed for three weeks. On the night of the first show, Elliott began having doubts that he would get through the production without forgetting his lines. He understood that his part was the glue that held the storyline together and moved the play from beginning to its end.

The director put his arm around Elliott and assured him that what he was feeling was what every actor felt at the start of a show. He told Elliott that he was a natural and would impress the audience.

Darlene grabbed his hands and said, "Look, dude, your part is as important as the quarterback of a football team. The play goes as you go. Get your ass on that stage and give them hell."

The only word Elliott focused on was quarterback. He thought about Jeff and how he led his team to all those victories. He looked at Darlene and said, "This is my ball game, and I am going to give them all I have tonight."

As the curtain opened, Elliott walked onto the left side of the stage. He was ready to take the audience on a journey. Before he recited his first line, he visually scanned the audience. It seemed like the entire school was there—along with half the town. He noticed his mom and dad and Becky. Sister Mary Therese was sitting a few rows behind his parents. He smiled when Peg turned her head slightly, so he could see the red rose in her hair. Peg always wore a white flower, saving a red one for special occasions. Peg gave him a large grin and winked. Elliott's heart sank when he didn't see Jeff. *How could Jeff do this to me? This performance is as important to me as his damn ball games are to him. The hell with him. He is a carbon copy of William, only thinking about himself. Since they won the game last night, it must have been more important to go out with his team to party and celebrate.*

Elliott kicked a winning goal that night. He shined on the stage as did Darlene and the entire cast. The audience gave them a standing ovation.

At one point during the show, Peg excused herself to use the restroom. As she approached the main door of the theater, she noticed Jeff sitting all alone in the corner. It was as if he wanted to be invisible to everyone on the stage. Peg, not wanting to make this more awkward than it already was, simply gave Jeff a hug and thanked him for being there. She mentioned that she and Dan were giving a party for the cast at the pizza shop and that he was welcome to join them. She smiled and never told anyone about seeing Jeff in the theater. She knew he had his reasons for not wanting to be seen, and she respected that.

Elliott hurried down into the audience and caught up with Sister Therese. He said how much it meant to him that she came to see the show.

Sister Therese said, "I would not have missed it for anything. I have never forgotten the first day of school. You walked up to me in the classroom, extended your hand, introduced yourself, and welcomed me to the school. No student has done that since then."

They laughed, and she asked how everything was going.

He said, "I think I am on the right track, and I'm glad I found some joy with the drama club." He thanked her for being there.

The cast party was fun and loud. To Becky's amazement, Luke showed up to surprise her and ask her out for the next weekend. Becky let out a scream when she saw Luke walk in.

Elliott walked past them several times and teased her by making fake kissing sounds.

Peg and Dan focused their attention on preparing the food in the kitchen. It was Elliott's party, and he was the host. For the first time in several months, he was having fun.

When one of the students asked Elliott if Jeff was coming, he answered, "Jeff is busy with the football team."

Darlene said, "This is beneath Jeff. He would rather hang with the elite football players and good-looking cheerleaders."

Elliott was beginning to believe that Darlene was right. He understood that he was losing someone special in his life. He was beginning to realize that it was out of his control. Jeff was starting to forge his way in a different direction. Elliott felt there was no room for him in Jeff's life anymore. He never forgot what his mom told him the night she drove Jeff home.

Jeff went home alone after the play, careful that he would not be seen leaving. He knew the night belonged to Elliott. Elliott had found a new life for himself—along with new friends—but that didn't erase the feeling of loneliness that formed in the pit of his stomach. As he stared at the ceiling, he thought about how good Elliott looked on that stage and how proud he was of him. He fell asleep that night crying.

Holidays

After *Our Town* concluded its run, Elliott became withdrawn—even though he had amazed his many new friends in the play. Darlene kept him grounded and provided a much-needed friendship. The holidays were approaching, and Elliott and Darlene spent much of the week before Christmas at the mall. They were searching for the perfect gifts for their families.

Darlene didn't know if her mother wanted to celebrate Christmas this year. Her parents had spent the past year and a half fighting in court, which left Kathy angry and hurt. Her father had moved to Florida with his new girlfriend, and he had very little contact with Darlene.

While hanging out at the pizza shop, Darlene talked to Peg. "I want to make sure my mom has a good Christmas."

Peg was aware of all that had gone down and felt sorry for Darlene. She saw a young girl who had many personal obstacles in her life.

Later that day, Peg invited Kathy and Darlene to spend Christmas with them.

At first, Kathy declined, but after a few minutes of persuasion, she accepted. "But only if I can bring a dish to share."

Darlene went to Elliott's house and gave Peg a hug.

Peg noticed that Darlene had tears in her eyes.

Christmas turned out to be one of the best Darlene and Elliott had in years. Dan and Elliott went out and bought an eight-foot blue spruce. Becky and Elliott decorated it with all the traditional ornaments that had been handed down by their grandparents. Kathy brought an unbelievable sweet potato casserole that was topped with what appeared to be an entire bag of marshmallows. Peg spent the day roasting a turkey and teaching Becky and Darlene how to make all the side dishes. Elliott set the table with his mom's best china.

Becky invited Luke, and whenever Elliott and Darlene were alone, he would say, "Isn't Luke gorgeous?"

Darlene would snap back, "Hands off—he belongs to your sister."

Dinner seemed to go on forever. No one was in a hurry to leave the table. They shared enjoyable conversation and laughter. Peg told stories about the family, and Kathy showed pictures of Darlene when she was a baby. After dinner, they all sat around the tree and opened gifts. Dan made sure that the wineglasses were kept full, even allowing the kids a glass or two to toast the holiday.

Later that afternoon, Elliott disappeared into his room. Darlene found him sitting alone on his bed, holding a small gift-wrapped package. He said, "This was supposed to be a gift for Jeff. We saw it a long time ago when we were at the mall. It is a gold chain that was displayed in the window of a jewelry shop. Jeff kept looking at it and wanted to buy it. He decided not to because he knew his father would not approve. His father doesn't believe that a real man should wear a necklace. I went back to the mall the next day and bought it. I still have a tough time trying to forget about Jeff, and if I take the gift back, it would make everything seem so final."

Darlene said, "Put the gift back in the drawer. You never know what the future will bring."

Jeff's parents took him to South Florida for the holidays. William was eyeing a run for the Senate and thought it would be beneficial to accept an invitation from a major Republican donor. "This will be the perfect time to discuss campaign strategy." The condo on South Beach was decorated with a white plastic Christmas tree, a few red ornaments, and white lights. It appeared that the tree was been pulled out of a box and hurriedly set up prior to their arrival.

For Christmas, William, Laura, and Jeff drive up to Palm Beach to have dinner with the donor at an exclusive country club resort, Mar-a-Lago. Jeff noticed how ornate the place was. It crossed his mind that whoever approved the décor must have been on drugs.

Laura wouldn't stop saying how beautiful the place was.

Jeff looked at her with disgust and thought, *What a kiss ass she is.* The people sitting in the dining room were all dressed up and looked extremely uncomfortable. There was almost no conversation going on at those tables. Everyone seemed to be focused on looking as proper as they could.

The servers were taking their time to accommodate the guests by delivering the food and mixed drinks. The young man assigned to wait on Jeff's family was from Cuba. Jeff and the server made eye contact several times throughout the day. Jeff thought that the guy was hot, and he was glad to have something to focus on—other than those who were sitting at his table.

Dinner consisted of warm dry turkey, cardboard-tasting stuffing, lumpy mashed potatoes, and sweet potatoes that ten minutes earlier were probably still in the can. Jeff wondered if there was a McDonald's nearby that he could walk to. He ate very little of the tasteless food and was glad the portions were extremely small—even though the prices on the menu were outrageously high. The only thing that seemed to be in abundance was the alcohol, and Laura took full advantage of it. At one point, Jeff hurriedly switched his empty water glass with his mom's full glass of vodka, and he spent the rest of the afternoon sipping it and slowly developing a vodka buzz. Laura never noticed; instead, she just called the server over and ordered another one.

Jeff's father and the donor spent the entire dinner discussing the upcoming campaign. They rarely acknowledged the others at the table. Jeff stared at the rich donor talking to his father. The man appeared to have a strange shade of makeup on his face. Even though his face was orange, his hands were white. His hair looked as fake as the rest of him. Jeff wished that he could be as far away from there as possible. He longed to be back home and for his life to be as it had been.

He kept thinking about Elliott. He knew Elliott and his family would be enjoying a beautiful Christmas, and he wished he was there sitting next to him around the tree. That evening, after they arrived back at the condo, Jeff went into his room and sat on the bed. There were no gifts to be opened and no happy family conversations. His parents had not even wished him a merry Christmas. It was all about politics, and he knew that it would get more intense in the coming months.

Jeff picked up the phone and dialed Elliott's number. He just wanted to hear Elliott's voice. When Becky answered, he heard laughter and Christmas music in the background. He hung up without saying a word. He couldn't wait until the holiday was over.

CHAPTER 3

High School and Reality

With the holidays over and a new year beginning, everyone seemed to be getting back to a somewhat normal existence—except for Elliott. His parents had promised him that he could get his driver's license. He had anticipated that day for as long as he could remember. It would give him independence and be another step toward adulthood. Darlene took charge and helped him study the driver's manual. She made sure he knew that book inside and out.

Elliott enrolled in the school's driver's education class and spent one afternoon a week with the instructor, driving various roads around town. On the morning of his test, he woke up early. He hurried his dad through breakfast and said, "We can't be late can't be late. It won't look good."

Elliott was extremely nervous because it was April 1, and he didn't want it to be a fool's day for him. He took the test in his dad's old Ford, and the instructor watched his every move. There was very little conversation because Elliott needed to keep his mind on the driving. The instructor was a young and handsome officer, which intimidated Elliott more than the driving. Elliott passed the test and was awarded his first driver's license.

Dan said, "Take the car by yourself to get back to school. I remember how excited I was when I got my first license. My dad let me take the car to school. I want you to enjoy this day as much as I did."

When Elliott arrived at school, lunch was beginning. As he made his way to the cafeteria, he kept looking down at his new license. He ran into Jeff. It had been an eternity since the two of them had talked, and Elliott felt a bit awkward.

Jeff was smiling and almost laughing. He said, "I saw you walking, and I purposely stepped in front of you. I thought that would be the only way you would stop."

They both stared into each other's eyes.

Elliott said, "Look, Jeff, I just got my driver's license."

Jeff said, "I am so happy for you." He reached over and gave Elliott a hug. It was not a normal hug like a grandmother or aunt would give; it was a deep, tight hug. Jeff whispered, "I am proud of you, and I miss you."

They tried to overcome the awkwardness of the situation since they both wanted to tell each other so much. Jeff said how good he looked, and Elliott messed up Jeff's hair, complimenting Jeff on his new haircut.

Darlene approached them and said, "Both of you, after school, pizza shop—and you better both show up."

Elliott said, "Both of you, parking lot, after school—I'll drive!" He flashed a big smile.

Darlene jumped into the back, and Jeff sat next to Elliott.

Jeff said, "You're driving way to slow."

Elliott said, "This is my first day driving, and it wouldn't look good if I got a ticket today."

Without realizing it, Jeff placed his hand on Elliott's knee and kept it there for the entire trip.

Elliott loved the way it felt and didn't say a word. He wished that Jeff would move his hand up, but he felt embarrassed that Jeff might notice how excited he had become. When they arrived at the pizza shop, Elliott turned off the car, looked at Jeff, and smiled.

Peg greeted them with a smile and said, "It's nice to see you again. I hope you won't be a stranger. The three of you must be hungry. You want sausage or pepperoni?"

Darlene offered to help Peg in the kitchen, and the boys started catching up on school and what classes they liked and which ones they hated. Jeff explained how terrible his Christmas was in Florida. They started laughing and kidding around—just as it used to be.

They agreed to spend more time with each other.

The Catalyst

Tenth grade ended on a good note. Jeff and Elliott were spending almost all their free time together. Peg worried that her son would end up getting hurt and never stopped asking him how things were going with Jeff.

Elliott assured her that he and Jeff were in a good place. He said, "If being friends is all it can be, then so be it."

Jeff's father was in full campaign mode, traveling the state from one end to the other. The election was in November, and William was not going to let anything stop him from being elected to the Senate.

Football practice would start in early August, which allowed the boys to hang out with each other.

For his birthday, Elliott's parents gave him the old Ford.

The two young men had a freedom they had never experienced before. Jeff was extremely happy that his father was so preoccupied with the election and that his mother was spending most of her time by his side. He was disappointed, however, when neither of his parents wished him a happy birthday.

On the day after the Fourth of July, Elliott drove over to Jeff's house to spend the day swimming in Jeff's pool.

Laura had come home from the campaign trail early that morning. She was planning a poolside luncheon with a few influential wives of Republican leaders. The boys couldn't get out of there fast enough.

As they drove around, Jeff said, "Let's go hiking in the new state park and see what William brags he managed to get done."

They stopped at McDonald's, bought a few bottles of water, and headed to the park. Only a few people were there. The trail snaked along a deep ravine that was covered with trees and brush. At the bottom of the ravine, the creek was running fast and unusually deep because of recent rains.

The boys began teasing each other, guessing who the fastest runner was.

Jeff playfully punched Elliott's arm and said, "Let's run to that rock up ahead."

They started running, and Elliott tripped on a root. As he fell, he grabbed a sapling.

The sapling broke, and Elliott fell into the ravine.

Jeff thought Elliott was playing around, but when he heard the loud splash, he knew it was real. Panicking, Jeff raced to the bottom, franticly trying to locate Elliott. He thought Elliott might have drowned. He jumped into the water, and after a few minutes, he found Elliott near the bank, holding onto a tree branch. Jeff maneuvered through the strong current and managed to get to Elliott.

Jeff started crying and yelled, "I thought I lost you. I thought I lost you. You scared me. I can't lose you. I love you. Don't you feel something when we are together? I have felt this way ever since we met. I know it's wrong to have these feelings, but I can't stop them." He pulled Elliott closer and gave him a kiss that Elliott could only imagine in his wildest dreams.

They were both in tears, and Elliott kept hanging onto Jeff. He told Jeff that he was not hurt and that he loved him so damn much. "Yes, Jeff. I feel it too. I always have. This scares the hell out of me. All I know is that I like the way I feel when we are together."

They stood in the water, kissing and holding each other, for several minutes. When they finally found a way up the bank, they sat for a moment. When Jeff was sure that Elliott was not seriously hurt, they began to look for a way back up to the trail. After a few minutes, they collapsed onto the tall river grass. They were soaked from head to toe.

Jeff took off his wet T-shirt and then helped Elliott take off his. Within minutes, they had taken everything off. They stared at each other's naked bodies and began kissing each other. They touched each other in places where they had never touched before.

Jeff sat on top of Elliott, and his touch felt like it was hot candle wax dripping all over his naked body. Jeff imagined his body melting into a hot lava, flowing straight through him and on to Elliott. With their eyes fixated on each other, they exploded into a sensation they hoped would never end. They collapsed into each other's arms.

Jeff said, "I have been waiting for so long to tell you how I felt. This can't be wrong. It just can't be wrong. I have realized for a long time how much I love you. I am so scared that you don't feel the same for me."

Elliott sat up and said, "I am so much in love with you. I can't imagine my life without you. I am also scared. What will others say if they know about this? I know we are in this alone, and we have to be so damn careful."

Jeff said, "I wish I had all the answers." He put his hands around Elliott's head and told him that whatever happened going forward, they would be in it together—and would find their way together. They kissed again, put on their wet clothes, and made their way back to the car.

It was done. The secrets, the hurt, and the confusion were over. They both knew how they felt for each other. They also understood that would never be able to go back to being just friends. They both knew they were more than just friends.

On the drive home, there was very little conversation. Everything that needed to be said was told through their actions on the river grass. Jeff kept his hand on Elliott's knee for the entire trip. Elliott dropped Jeff off at home and then went on to his house. Since no one was home, he wouldn't have to explain why he was soaked.

He stood in the shower and thought about what had just transpired. He felt as if a weight had been lifted off his shoulders. He wanted to shout out to the world about Jeff and himself, and he wanted answers. He didn't understand why two people in love could be so wrong in the eyes of society. Reality hit, and he knew it would have to remain a secret. *With all the hate in the world, how can this be wrong?* He hoped that, in his lifetime, he would be able to express who he was and who he loved without any fear and shame.

Jeff arrived home and was not even noticed by his mother or her guest. He went upstairs and sat in his room. He still felt Elliott's touch all over his body. He knew that Elliott loved him. He had never felt as completely happy as he did at that moment. He also understood that they were on a dangerous path, especially when it pertained to his father. It would never be accepted by the Republican party. He and Elliott would have to be so careful. They could not allow anyone to ever suspect what they were doing or how they felt for each other. It would be a rough road if they weren't careful.

Adjustments

Their lives had become a maze of emotions in the days and months after their revelation to each other in that park. The both intensely knew that what had happened, and what they said to each other, was a genuine reaction to what had always been deeply rooted in their souls. Also, they accepted that it was not an improper show of their affection. However, the reality was that society would never tolerate this behavior. It would be judged as a reprehensible transgression of morals. They made their pledge that their devotion and endearments to each other would remain their secret, never to be disclosed.

August arrived, and Jeff started football practice. His parents were on the campaign trail since the election was only three months away. Arrangements were made to bring Laura's mother up from Florida to watch over Jeff. His grandmother and mother were carbon copies of each other. The only difference Jeff could see was that his grandmother preferred gin over vodka. Laura made sure the house was stocked with an ample supply of the beverage. She insisted to be called Patricia, never Pat, and absolutely never Grandmother.

She has been divorced from Jeff's grandfather for several years. Jeff knew almost nothing about his grandfather. Whenever he asked anything about him, he parents always changed the subject or offered very little information. All they ever said was that it was best that he wasn't in their lives anymore. Patricia had very little interaction with Jeff or his friends. She showed no desire to know what his interests were. She could have stayed in Florida because Jeff was navigating his time alone.

Intensifying Jeff's fear of disclosing his love for Elliott was the fact that his father was running a campaign based on political interpretation of family values and Christian morals. William's campaign was receiving millions of dollars from religious organizations. The more money they gave, the more William pledged that if elected to the Senate, he would do everything he could to keep homosexuals out of the military and fight to keep marriage between a man and a woman. At campaign stops, he never failed to mention his all-American football star son and how close they were to each other. Jeff considered that the biggest of all the lies his father campaigned on. After all, he and his father barely had any positive interactions. Jeff also thought it could be the reason his mother drank as much as she did.

Elliott worked almost every day at the restaurant. He had a different outlook on life. He cherished the times he and Jeff spent together. He was comfortable telling Jeff his deepest secrets and loved hearing Jeff tell his. He accepted the fact that they were both in it alone, but he felt a deep sense of loss in not being able to share his love with the world.

Elliott and Jeff met up whenever possible, and they became experts on how to locate discrete places to get together. One afternoon, while they were driving around, Jeff said, "Hey, let's go to my house. Patricia has gone out shopping for the day, and she is meeting friends for dinner this evening." He smiled at Elliott. "Think about it—we will be all alone in that big house."

When they entered the house, Jeff said, "Please close your eyes. I will lead you up the stairs." When they arrived at the destination, Jeff said, "Okay—open your eyes."

Elliott looked around and realized they were in Jeff's parents' bedroom. He became instantly aroused. He started kissing Jeff harder and deeper than he ever had.

Jeff tore off their shirts and tossed them across the room.

Elliott took off his shorts and kicked off his shoes, causing them to land on Laura's dressing table. Elliott pushed Jeff onto the bed and positioned himself on top. He took charge of every detail, bringing Jeff to the verge of explosion several times.

Jeff did the same to Elliott.

When they were ready, the love inside them erupted into a hot sensation that seemed to cover every inch of their sweat-drenched bodies and the sheets on the bed.

Jeff led Elliott to his parents' shower, and they stood in the hot water until steam covered every inch of the bathroom. When they were fully dressed, Elliott said, "Should we change the sheets?"

Jeff smiled and said, "Hell no."

As they walked down the stairs, they realized Patricia had come home early. They froze, hoping she hadn't heard them.

Jeff whispered, "We need to be quiet and get out of the house before she spots us."

John Mudzyn

Patricia walked by and said, "Where the hell does your mother keep the tonic? She knows damn well I can't drink my gin without it. I should have stayed in Florida."

Jeff sighed and said, "It is in the garage. I will go get it." He brought back three bottles of tonic and said, "Here are a couple of extra—in case you run out tonight."

She said, "Put them over there."

Jeff and Elliott jumped into the old Ford and laughed all the way back to Elliott's house.

Every expression of love needed to be hidden in the shadows, away from society's prying eyes. It hurt them deeply when they saw straight classmates on dates, walking hand in hand, or freely exchanging kisses in view of everyone. They understood there was no other choice for them. They hoped that it would be different someday, but for now, they had to play the hand that was dealt to them.

Elliott had Darlene to confide in, but Jeff had nobody, which bothered Elliott deeply. Jeff took his frustrations out on the football field. Out there, no one could beat him or judge him unfavorably. He used his talent as an outlet. Every time he scored a touchdown, he would laugh out loud. He wished everyone knew a gay boy had just led them to another victory.

Two Worlds Collide

The summer of realization came to an end, and it was another first day of school. Elliott would pick up Jeff in the morning, and the two of them would make their way to class. Unlike the past couple of years when they rarely saw each other during the school day, they had several classes together. Jeff still had football and devoted most of his time away from his classes to practicing.

Elliott spent that time hanging out with Darlene. They hadn't seen much of each other during the summer and had a lot of catching up to do. Elliott talked to her in vague terms about the summer and Jeff.

One afternoon, as they were walking to Elliott's house, Darlene said, "I have figured out what you are not telling me. You and Jeff did it, didn't you?"

Elliott tried to change the subject, but Darlene persisted with the questions.

Elliott finally cracked and said, "Yeah, we did it—almost every day. He loves me."

She gave him a high five and told him to be careful.

Elliott made her promise that she would never tell anyone—not even Jeff. "This must stay our secret."

She assured him that she would never betray his trust.

The homecoming game was two weeks before the election. The dance was the evening after that game. Elliott and Jeff could go because they were juniors, and only eleventh and twelfth graders could attend. They talked about the dance, and Elliott urged Jeff to go. "As the quarterback, you will be expected to go. It's like your duty to be there."

Jeff said, "The only way I will go will be if you also go."

Elliott smiled and said, "You mean as a couple?"

Jeff replied, "Yeah, right. Wouldn't that stop the show if we walked in arm in arm?"

Elliott would ask Darlene, and Jeff would ask a friend of his, Brittney, to go with him. The girls readily accepted the invitations and began the ritual of looking for dresses and everything that went along with that.

Darlene was uncomfortable shopping for a dress and asked her mom to help her out.

Elliott and Jeff spend an entire Saturday shopping for the perfect tuxedo and shirts. They decided on black suits. Elliott selected a lavender shirt, and Jeff chose a white one.

On Friday night, Jeff led the team to another victory.

Jeff's father couldn't pass up the opportunity to hold a campaign rally at the game. William and Laura arrived back in town, and after the game, William stole the limelight away from his son. This time, he had Laura on the stage with him. William sent word to Jeff that he needed to change out of his uniform, put on the suit and tie they brought for him, and join them on the stage. Jeff told the messenger to shove the suit up his ass. He refused to change, and he joined them on the stage in his muddy, grass-stained uniform.

Laura was appalled. When Jeff tried to hug her, she recoiled and stepped away from him.

William gave Jeff a look that could kill and introduced him as Jeffery. Jeff walked up to the mic and said, "Hi. My name is Jeff."

William whispered, "Jeffery."

Jeff spoke directly into the microphone and said, "As I have told you before, Jeffery hasn't existed in a long time—so get over it." He walked off the stage and met up with Elliott at the pizza shop.

Jeff said, "I'm glad I walked off, and next time, I will not even go up there. I just can't understand how these people can't or won't see past his lies. The more he lies, the higher his poll numbers go. He can take his religious moral majority and go straight to hell."

Elliott reminded Jeff that they had haircut appointments at ten in the morning. "I will pick you up at nine thirty. Afterward, we can have lunch at the mall. That will give us enough time to get home and get ready."

The morning of the dance, Elliott said, "You know my mom and her picture taking? She wants all of us there so she can take a few photos. I am sure Kathy will probably be there and want to do the same."

Elliott had trouble getting ready and was frustrated because he didn't like the way the shirt looked. "Mom, why does this always happen to me?"

Peg said, "Because you are too fussy about the way you look. The shirt looks good. Just relax." She snapped a few pictures of him.

When it was time to pick up Darlene and Kathy, Dan stepped in and went to pick them up.

Darlene seemed extremely uncomfortable in a dress and heels, but she looked very pretty. Her lavender dress matched Elliott's shirt perfectly.

"Only for you," Darlene said. "You are the only one I would wear this ridiculous outfit for. This dance better be worth it."

When Jeff and Brittney arrived, Jeff was taken aback at how handsome Elliott looked in his tux. Elliott wanted to kiss Jeff. He knew Jeff was going to be the best-looking guy at the dance. Pictures were taken, the parents wished the four of them good luck, and off they went.

They sat together for dinner, mingling with the other students and admiring how everyone looked.

After a couple of dances, the girls excused themselves to go to the restroom. Elliott saw it as an opportunity to go outside for a few minutes to get some fresh air. He said, "We will meet you back at the table in a few minutes."

There were several other students outside, hanging near the front door. Some of them were smoking.

Jeff said, "Lets walk toward the back of the building to get away from the smoke."

Deciding to take advantage of the darkness, Jeff gave Elliott a long kiss. They didn't realize that two of Jeff's teammates were smoking some weed in the dark. They witnessed the kiss and how Jeff kept grabbing Elliott's ass—and how Elliott didn't resist.

At the door, Darlene and Brittney were looking for them.

Jeff said, "Sorry. We started talking and lost track of time."

The four of them rejoined the dance. Jeff earned an award for being the most outstanding player on the football team. As he walked up to accept the award, one of his teammates, Larry, who had witnessed the kiss smiled at Jeff and said, "Don't get used to always being the hero. Next year, I will be the quarterback. You can count on that."

Jeff smiled and said, "Good luck. I look forward to the competition."

When the dance was over, they stopped at McDonald's and hung out for a while, then drove the girls home.

Jeff said, "Larry is always getting in my face. He is pissed that he was passed over for quarterback. He is a sore loser. I wanted to punch him in his ugly face tonight. Maybe next time I will." Elliott pulled into Jeff's driveway, and when they were sure that they wouldn't be seen, they kissed. "Thank you, Jeff, for persuading me to go. I had a wonderful time."

Darlene called Elliott later that night. "Thanks, dude, for a nice evening."

Elliott said, "You didn't call me to just say thanks, did you."

"Not really," she replied.

"Come on," he said. "What's bothering you? I know you better than you think. Where is that direct, outspoken Darlene I used to know?"

She said, "Don't misunderstand me. I did have an enjoyable time, but I am sad and somewhat angry. As the four of us were dancing, I looked at you and Jeff. I started thinking that you and he should have been dancing together. I should have been able to be there with a girlfriend. It isn't right that we couldn't do that. Are we cowards? We had the opportunity to make a statement tonight—a statement to show everyone who we really are. I understand why we couldn't do that, but I still feel cheated."

Elliott said, "I feel the same way. I think we would become targets of hate and violence if we dared to make a statement like that. I certainly don't want to, and I know you don't want to finish our last two years of high school being hated. We will figure it out. Hang in there, girl."

Monday Morning

On Monday morning, Elliott picked Jeff up for school. When they walked in, they immediately realized that something was wrong. Friends and classmates stared, and pointed at the two of them, and whispered derogatory remarks. A few made fake kissing sounds.

In English class, one of Elliott's supposed friends, who he had known since grade school, picked up his chair and moved to the other side of the classroom.

When the first class was over, Darlene caught up with Elliott and explained that it was coming from two football players who were jealous that Jeff was quarterback. "They were standing behind the building at the dance and saw you and Jeff kissing. They are telling everyone that both of you are fags."

Elliott started to panic. *How can this be happening?*

It was even worse for Jeff. The entire football team went to the coach and informed him that they refused to share a locker room with Jeff. They were uncomfortable undressing in front of a "queer."

Larry approached Jeff and laughed in his face." I told you once to watch your back, you stupid fag. Glad you didn't listen to me. Guess I will be the new quarterback after all."

Jeff punched Larry in the face, causing him to fall on the floor. "How does it feel to get punched by a fag?"

The coach reported it all to the principal, and Jeff and Elliott were summoned to the office.

The principal said, "Is all of this true?"

Elliott tried to deny it.

Jeff said, "It's true. Even if we deny it, the damage is already done." They were told to go home for the remainder of the day. The school would decide what to do next.

They drove around for most of the day, talking and trying to understand the impact it was going to have on them. It was late in the evening when they arrived at Elliott's home. The first thing they noticed was Jeff's parents' car in the driveway. They knew it this was not going to be good.

They walked into the house, and Peg was standing in the doorway between the kitchen and dining room. She looked sad. She motioned for them to come in.

Laura was sipping a drink and crying in the dining room. William was pointing at Dan and yelling obscenities. He looked like he was on the verge of having a stroke, and Peg asked him to calm down.

William said, "Shut the fuck up."

Dan grabbed William by the arm and told him to leave. "I don't care who you are. No one talks to my wife that way."

William refused and kept yelling at them. "You people don't understand who I am. I will crush all of you."

Peg hugged Elliott and refused to let go, but Laura never got up from her chair. Peg tried to give Jeff a hug, but William grabbed her arm and said, "Keep your filthy hands off my son!" He then demanded to know if all of it was true.

Elliott started crying and tried to answer.

William looked at him and shouted, "Shut your mouth, you faggot, you little queer. I am asking Jeffery, not you."

Jeff said "Yes, it is all true—and I am not sorry that it happened."

William slapped Jeff across the face. "You have a filthy mouth. I should slap you again."

Peg said, "I will not tolerate any kind of child abuse in my home. Get the hell out of here before I call the police!"

William yelled, "Go ahead and call them, you stupid bitch. If you think that they will believe you over me, then you are fucking crazy!"

Dan pushed William against the wall and yelled, "I don't care who you are or who you think you are—nobody talks to my wife that way. Take your fucking ass and get out of my house. I won't need to call the police, you will—after I am finished beating the shit out of you. Now get out!"

William caught his breath and said, "Tomorrow, Jeffery will leave for Washington. He will be enrolled in a private school there—far away from here. I have already instructed the school here to announce that Elliott is the one to blame for all of this. Jeffery just got caught up in his little scheme."

William walked over to Elliott, looked him in the eye, and said, "If you ever try to contact Jeffery or he tries to contact you, I will make sure that the authorities come to this house and search it for drugs. You will be surprised about what they will find. I hope you understand what I mean. I will get pleasure watching as your parents are hauled off to jail. If that happens, it will ruin them and their pathetic pizza shop. Believe me, I can and will do it. Don't push me any further. I will not let a little fag like you ruin my election to the Senate." He snapped his fingers at Laura and pushed Jeff toward the door. Before the three of them walked out, William yelled, "Don't forget what I just said!"

As they drove home, Jeff sat alone in the back seat. He knew that anything he said would only anger his father more than he already was. It all came down to one purpose: winning the election.

Laura remained silent. On the worst night of his life, Jeff received nothing but hatred and silence from his parents. He was scared and lonely. He didn't have anyone he could confide in. His world as he knew it ended that night.

CHAPTER 4

The Aftermath

Elliott was staring into the darkness. It was two thirty, and he had not been able to fall asleep. He kept replaying what had happened and trying to understand how things could have spiraled so out of hand. Could he have done something to have stopped it? More importantly, should he have allowed them to get to this point? Every question was greeted with another question. This was his fault, he knew it, and he had to live with the consequences.

He didn't go to school in the morning and spent most of the day in his room. He felt like he was dealing with a death, and it was one of the first steps to process the loss. That's how Elliott spent his first day without Jeff.

Jeff didn't say a word to his parents on their way home from the confrontation. He felt as if he had been kicked in the stomach. For the first time in his life, he fully understood that his father only regarded him as a political pawn, part of a chess game in which the prize was always the election win. He was defeated. He kept trying to understand what was so wrong. He and Elliott loved each other, pure and simple—why was that so damn wrong? He wanted to jump out of the car and run back to Elliott, hold him, and tell him everything would be okay. Deep in his soul, he knew that could never happen. He could never put Elliott or his family in jeopardy. His father would not hesitate to carry out his threats.

The next afternoon, Jeff and his mother were on a plane to Washington. He was going to a place he hated and into a future in which he could only see darkness. As he watched his mother give to the flight attendant one demand after another, he wished she would just talk to him. He didn't even care if she yelled at him. All he wanted was for her to see that he was deeply hurt. Instead, Laura ordered another drink, closed her eyes, and fell asleep. That was Jeff's first day without Elliott.

Elliott didn't want to talk to anyone on that first day, but Darlene rushed over to see him anyway. "Thanks for coming, but there is no way you can understand what I am going through."

She said, "I understand that you are in trouble. I always thought we had a close friendship and friends come to friends in time of crises. Fuck you. I was just trying to help." She left without saying goodbye.

Instead of going home, Darlene went to the pizza shop. It was not open yet, and the door was locked. Darlene stood in front of the door and cried.

When Peg opened the door and let her in, Darlene said, "I tried to talk to Elliott, but it only turned out badly."

Peg said, "I am sure Elliott appreciated you stopping by. We all need to be patient."

Darlene said, "Why did this have to happen? This should be the happiest time of their lives. Instead, they are miserable."

Peg hugged Darlene, "Please do not give up on Elliott. He will come around."

The trip from the airport to Jeff's parents' home was just a quiet as the plane ride. When they arrived at the house, Patricia was yelling at someone over the phone. William was campaigning, and Laura just poured herself a drink and disappeared into her bedroom.

Jeff went up to his room, picked up the phone, and started to dial Elliott's number. He needed to hear Elliott's voice and talk to him. Before he finished dialing, he remembered his father's threats and hung up. He threw his backpack on the floor and cried himself to sleep. He was scared and lonely and didn't like what he saw ahead for him.

Elliott's New Normal

On the first day back to school, Peg said, "Elliott, you need to be patient. There will be some students who will not hesitate to show their prejudice and anger toward you. After all, the school also lost their star quarterback, and you will be blamed for that. Please take your time and understand that these kids are products of their parents' and their churches' prejudices. It won't be an easy day for you. Try to use the anger and hurt you feel to possibly change someone's perception in a positive way. This will be the best way for you to move forward."

It was not an easy drive to school. There would be no laughing and teasing each other in the car, and there would not be Jeff's hand on Elliott's knee as he drove.

When Elliott arrived at school, he wasn't sure if the paranoia was just in his mind, but he soon realized that everyone had their own version of what had happened. There were stories going around that he drugged Jeff and then molested him. Another story was that Jeff was the instigator, and he even propositioned some of his teammates for sex. A few of Elliott's teachers didn't even look at him. His drama teacher took him aside and said, "Stay strong. This will pass." Elliott didn't care what everyone was saying. He laughed when he heard the stories. Only he and Jeff knew the real story, and that was all that mattered.

After the lunch period, he entered the restroom to wash his hands before his next class. As he was standing in front of the sink, a group of his classmates grabbed him, dragged him over to a stall, and shoved his head in the toilet. They held him there for a few seconds, pulled him out by his hair, and said, "This is what we do to queers. It's a good thing your boyfriend has left the school. If he was still here, he would have needed an ambulance to get him off the practice field."

When they left, Elliott was shaking while trying to dry himself with paper towels.

A student in the next stall heard everything and ran out to report it.

Several teachers and the principal demanded that Elliott disclose the names of the students, but no one asked Elliott if he was hurt. Elliott refused to answer them. If he snitched, he would be an even bigger target.

Peg and Dan were called and came to school.

Dan said, "Where the hell are the police? Why haven't you called them?"

The principal said, "There is nothing we—or the police—can do. Your son refuses to identify who did this. Even if we knew who did this, they would probably say that Elliott made a pass at them. That is why they reacted that way. It will be his word against theirs. Unless Elliott wants to pursue this, we will consider this matter closed."

Peg said, "We will take Elliott out of this school and enroll him in another one. You people seem to think that this kind of bullying is okay. How dare you tell us that there is nothing you can do." Peg also informed the principal that they would no longer provide free pizzas for the pep rallies as they had done since Becky was a freshman.

Elliott said, "No, Mom. I am not going to leave. If I do that, then I will be hiding for the rest of my life. Jeff and I did nothing wrong. If I run away from here, then I will be admitting that we were wrong. I will be okay. I know that I need to watch my back."

Dan said, "If anything like this happens again, you will not know what hit you. I will report this to every news outlet in the state. You will have so many organizations investigating what is really going on here. Trust me—it will not be an enjoyable time for you!"

For months, Darlene did her best to keep Elliott grounded and focused on the future. Elliott was always vigilant about who was walking beside him. He never went into the restroom alone. He had to adjust every aspect of his school routine.

Slowly, the criticism toward him subsided—except for one. Those who he thought were his friends since grade school stopped talking to him, and they even stopped going to the pizza shop. One of these so-called friends requested that his seat be moved to other side of the room in English class. He didn't want to sit next to Elliott. That was the most hurtful to Elliott.

The drama club provided an escape. Elliott felt safe and not judged in that environment. Elliott was now living his new normal. When he was alone, especially at night, he still felt the winter chill deep inside. It was always there—no matter how normal his life became. Through all this adjustment, Elliott was grateful that he had his parents and Darlene to confide in.

Jeff's New Normal

Jeff was driven to his new school on that first day by a driver. William demanded that Jeff should be chauffeured as the other students were. Jeff received no words of encouragement from his parents. His mother only said, "Remember who you are and make sure you don't embarrass your father." Jeff thought that this was strange. He knew who he was, and his parents were trying their best to make him deny it. In the back of the limo, Jeff reminisced about sitting in Elliott's old Ford on their way to school. His left hand seemed out of place because there was no knee to rest it on.

Jeff's new school was the opposite of his old school. First and foremost, it was exclusive all-boy preparatory school. Everyone was required to wear a uniform that consisted of dark blue slacks, white shirt, red tie, and dark blue blazer with the school's insignia patch on the right sleeve. The only deviation to the uniform was with the color of the tie. The party that held the White House dictated a red or blue tie. There was no individuality, and everyone looked like robots walking down the hall.

Every student had a place in school as well as in society. These young men were the products of the most important people in Washington. They were sons of congressmen, senators, and cabinet members—and there was even a grandson of a former president. No longer would he be able to socialize with classmates from normal American families. There were no factory workers' children or children of housekeepers in the student body. What was most obvious to Jeff was that there was no one there whose parents owned and operated a pizza shop.

The one ray of light for Jeff was that the school's football team that was taken extremely seriously by the parents and alumni. It was not too late in the season for Jeff to join the team. When school ended, Jeff sat outside, alone, and waited for his ride. Not one student asked if they could wait with him. It was the beginning of Jeff's new normal. He wasn't a hero to anyone in this environment—he was just another face in the crowd.

The next few weeks saw a flurry of activity within the school. Election Day was fast approaching. Most of the students had parents who were running for election or re-election. Every day, limousines would pull up to the school to pick up students who were summoned for final election family photos. With every car that pulled up, Jeff hoped it was not his turn.

One afternoon, his luck ran out. His father wanted a family photo taken of them back in Ohio. Because William would not allow Jeff to travel back to their home state, arrangements were made to have the picture taken in Washington. Jeff was picked up and driven to a warehouse. When he got out of the car, he noticed a large stage set up with a massive background picture of an Ohio farm. Laura, Patricia, and William were all waiting for him. After he was up on the stage, he remarked, "Wow, this is fake."

William said, "It isn't fake. It is politics—and you better get used to it."

Jeff rolled his eyes and made a face for the first picture. William shook him and told him to grow up.

Patricia grabbed Jeff's hand and pulled him to her side.

The final photo had Jeff standing between Patricia and his mother—without a smile on his face. The next day, the photo was released to every news outlet in Ohio with a caption: "Your next senator with his all-American family."

Elliott saw the picture on the news. He was fixated on how sad Jeff looked. He also noticed the shine was gone from Jeff's eyes. William and Laura traveled back to Ohio on Election Day to cast their votes, but Jeff remained in Washington. That night, William was elected senator.

Say Goodbye to Junior Year

Elliott knew that he would always be known as the gay guy. He had made peace with that fact. After all, he was the gay guy in school, and he was not going to hide—even if he could. He knew he and Darlene weren't the only ones in that school who were gay. He also knew the treatment and harassment he received after being outed most likely caused any other gay student to remain safe in their closet. He was angry that the school offered no source of counseling for gay students.

Elliott wrote a letter to the school board to ask for better counselors at the school. They never responded to him. They informed his parents that they needed to control their son and to advise him to keep his opinions to himself. Elliott still believed that one day there would be help available to all gay students to allow them to grow into their full potential as proud Americans. Perhaps he would find a way to lead the fight for equality.

That summer, he worked with his parents, hung out with the few friends who didn't abandon him, and contemplated where his life would go from there. Darlene kept telling him to pursue an acting career.

He said, "Look, girl, what kind of an actor would I be? I couldn't even act straight when I needed to—and look what happened with that." He knew his senior year would fly by, and he needed to start making decisions about his future.

Peg and Dan assured him that he didn't have to worry about paying for college. They had been saving ever since he and Becky were young. Becky was married to Luke, and she decided not to attend college. She was expecting their first child, and school was the furthest thing on her mind. Elliott was told that he could apply to any school he wanted to attend. Peg always let him know they would not force him to go to any college. That would be his decision to make.

One afternoon, he and Darlene were driving around. Darlene's father had reached out to her. He wanted her to know that he understood how hard the divorce had been on her. He wanted to make things up and bought her a new car. Darlene was the driver, and Elliott could sit back and relax. Darlene wanted to go to the mall in the next town. She decided to take a different road and drove past the entrance to the state park where he and Jeff had sex for the first time.

Elliott had not been to the park since that day. Elliott started replaying the memories in his mind and smiled. He realized it was the first time in a long time that he thought about Jeff. He became scared. Was he beginning to forget Jeff? He wondered if Jeff ever thought about him. Was he becoming a distant memory for Jeff? He knew he couldn't live in the past, but he still loved Jeff and didn't ever want to forget him. The thoughts concerned him deeply.

Jeff's school year ended pretty much the same way it started. He made a few friends, but seldom would he be invited to any of their homes to hang out. It always seemed that there was some function or another that took priority. Jeff's father spent almost all his time in Washington. Jeff and William had come to a sort of a truce. Jeff slowly curtailed his snide remarks, and William agreed to be more tolerant and slow down his criticism of the things Jeff did. Although it was a short-lived truce, it did give Jeff some peace of mind. Jeff took what he could from William's fake promises.

Patricia's health started to decline, and contrary to the doctor's advice, she didn't put down the gin. By then, there was no need for tonic—just straight gin. Laura would sit on their balcony in the early afternoon and share a cocktail or two with her mother. There never was much conversation between the two women. Laura would sit there until Patricia fell asleep.

One morning, Jeff overheard his parents discussing Patricia. Her health was rapidly declining, and they needed to put her in a home. The next afternoon, two medical caretakers arrived and helped his grandmother into the back seat of a minivan. Jeff's parents never discussed what happened to Patricia, and he never saw his grandmother again.

One evening, William came home and said, "Jeff, because of my connections in the Senate, I was able to get you enrolled in one of the most prestigious colleges in the country. All you need to do is keep your grades up next year and be the hero on the football team."

Jeff tried to explain that he was planning on going to Ohio State.

William said, "That is not an option—and it's not a proper school to be able to excel in football."

Jeff said, "Are you crazy? Ohio State has one of the best football programs in the country."

William said, "Forget about Ohio State. This other school will be a better springboard for a political career." He sent Jeff out of the room. The case was closed.

Jeff went up to his room, sat on his bed, and started to think about Elliott. This startled him because it had been a few months since he thought about him. He wondered where Elliott would go to college. He began to fantasize about how much sexier Elliott must have become. He still missed Elliott very much.

Graduation

Jeff did excel in football that last year of high school. He brought his team to a victorious year. William was delighted that Jeff would be going to college and on his way to a pro football career. Jeff would be on his way to a major political career.

Elliott stayed in the drama class and excelled as Elwood P. Dowd in the school's production of *Harvey*. Darlene played the leading female role and made her character, Veda, as realistic as possible. As quickly as it started, senior year of high school was winding down. Elliott and Jeff would soon be graduating, worlds apart from each other, and beginning new chapters in their lives.

On graduation day, Peg and Dan were as proud as they could be. Becky and Luke arrived with their new son, Mark.

Elliott was fussing about the way he looked in his cap and gown.

Darlene said, "Who the hell cares how you look? After all you have been through these past four years, just take the damn diploma and get the hell out of here. With any luck, you will never have to see these people again."

While the senior class was waiting for their names to be called, Elliott looked around and remembered all the times he had been in the gymnasium with Jeff. He wished he and Jeff could have been together on that day. When he heard his name called, he looked over at his family. They were all beaming with pride.

After the ceremony, Peg and Dan hosted a party at the pizza shop for Elliott and Darlene. They gave him the keys to a new car. Dan took Elliott outside and said, "I am so proud of you son." They hugged, and Dan had a few tears in his eyes.

Jeff's graduation was held in an exclusive Washington country club. He also fussed with his cap and gown, but he didn't have a Darlene to tell him to shut up. He smiled when he thought about Elliott and wondered how they both would have helped each other get dressed for this big day. When his name was called, there was no family there to give him a smile. His father was busy with a meeting, and his mother had a fund-raiser to attend.

When he arrived home, he went upstairs to his room and cried. He opened a dresser drawer and took out a picture he had kept hidden from his parents. The picture was taken one afternoon when they were at the pizza shop. Becky took the picture with her new camera. Just as the picture was being taken, Elliott put his arm around Jeff's shoulders. Jeff stared at the picture for a long time, looking at Elliott's beautiful smile.

He was happy that high school was behind him. Now he could look forward to a life away from Washington, and more importantly, a life away from his parents. Even though he was being forced to attend a school not of his choice, he would be on his own for the first time in his life. All those plans he and Elliott made to go to the same college were just memories now. He fell asleep holding the picture.

CHAPTER 5

College: A New Beginning

College was a relief for Jeff. Living away from home gave him a break from William and Laura. He had been accepted at one of the most prestigious schools on the East Coast. Although this was not the school of Jeff's choice, he reluctantly accepted after William threatened to not pay anything if he didn't go along. Jeff remembered what a classmate of his back in DC once mentioned: "Whether you like your father or not, take full advantage of everything he offers. It will shut him up for a while." Jeff decided he had nothing more to lose. William had already destroyed his world that night back in Ohio. Jeff's majors were communications and broadcasting. If the football career didn't happen, he could fall back on it.

William said, "You need to make political science your major."

Jeff said, "Just because you demanded that I attend this college, it does not give you the right to choose my career. The subject is closed. I will not discuss this any further."

Jeff slowly adapted to college life. At first, it was difficult juggling school and football. With the help of his coach, he found the time to make it work. It didn't leave him much time for a social life. He was glad about that. That was the last thing he needed.

Jeff tried to suppress any feelings toward other men. Although he was extremely lonely, he didn't have any desire to get attached to anyone—and he certainly didn't want another relationship to end like his last one.

Jeff's dad got him into one of the most sought-after fraternities on campus. Jeff lived in a century-old Victorian house that was filled with the finest furnishings and amenities. All the fraternity members were sons of the most influential families from around the country. Jeff thought it was ironic. William worked long and hard to keep secret the fact that his son was gay but arranged for him to live in a house filled with many attractive young men. If William was paying the bills, then that was the way it had to be.

It was difficult for Jeff to constantly be around so many good-looking guys. He was extremely careful that no one ever saw him staring at them. He walked a tightrope, always vigilant to not say anything to cause suspicion to the secret he kept hidden inside. He made a promise to himself that he would never go through what he and Elliott had to endure—even if it meant hiding who he truly was to be accepted into the fraternity.

Elliott enrolled in the community college in Cleveland, which was about thirty miles away. During the week, he stayed in one of the dormitories. On Friday afternoons, after his last class, he would drive home. His parents were getting older, and he needed to go home on weekends to help at the restaurant. He was taking business courses and was considering law school. He was majoring in business law, and he needed to get his associates degree behind him.

Elliott discovered that he could be himself at school. The students who attended were a cornucopia of individuals from a diversity of hardworking families. The students were not pretentious and relished in their individuality. Elliott became more aware of why his parents always strove for their children to be their true selves.

Elliott always found time for Darlene on weekends. He was disappointed that she did not want to pursue a higher education, but he applauded the fact that she was beating her own drum. Darlene had taken the civil service exam a few days after graduation, which led to her landing a job with the United States Post Office. Darlene had a new girl in her life. She met Heather over the summer, and they had been seeing each other ever since. Darlene was beginning to find her way, which made him extremely happy.

Darlene would always say it was time for him to find a boyfriend. "You're not getting any younger, dude. You are a good-looking guy. Don't waste your life waiting for something that will never happen."

Elliott said, "A part of me wants to find a boyfriend, but I am extremely scared—and the pain and scars of losing Jeff still haven't healed completely."

Darlene said, "It's time to get over that spoiled rich boy. If Jeff still feels the same way, why hasn't he reached out and contacted you? You know William's threats were bullshit, don't you?"

Elliott said, "I appreciate your concern, but I am not at that point yet. I hope I will be able to move on someday—just not yet. You were not there when Jeff's father made those threats to my family. You didn't see the hate in his eyes. I did. Trust me—William meant every word of it."

Darlene dropped it for the time being.

The Baptism

Elliott enjoyed spending weekends with his family and friends. Peg and Dan where beaming grandparents, and Elliott was asked to be Mark's godfather.

On the morning of Mark's baptism, Elliott complained that his suit didn't fit right.

Peg said, "Get over it and hurry up. We will be late if we don't leave soon."

Darlene was honored to be asked to be Mark's godmother.

Walking into the church, Elliott saw Sister Mary Therese, and he was delighted to see her. She was the only teacher who totally understood him and his struggles.

Darlene's mom invited Sister Therese to join them for brunch at her house.

Elliott said, "I will not take no for an answer. You can ride to Kathy's house with me."

During the baptism, Mark started crying while Elliott was holding him.

Darlene took Mark, and the baby stopped crying for the remainder of the ceremony. After the baptism, Elliott said, "You handled Mark pretty good. You should consider having a baby of your own."

She smiled at him and didn't say anything.

As he drove back to his dorm, Elliott began to think about Jeff and wondered where he was and what he was doing. He knew that the wonderful day he just had with his family was something that Jeff would never experience with his own family. The feeling of missing Jeff continued throughout his first year of college. Even though he had many new friends, he couldn't shake the loneliness.

Some Things Never Change

In his first year of college, Jeff exceled on the football team and was awarded the team MVP at the awards banquet. Because of all the press coverage, Laura and William attended the banquet. The dinners were part of an intricate system of solicitation for donations that would go to the school's sports program. It was also an opportunity for parents to network their sons and ensure they had the proper avenues to advance their social status.

Jeff's father gave a speech touting his accomplishments in the Senate and praised the school's directors and faculty. He briefly mentioned the football team. When he finished talking, he called Jeff up to the stage for a photo, never once telling Jeff that he was proud of him. The award was only an expectation demanded by William, another step on the social ladder.

Jeff expected his father to steal the limelight, but it still hurt. When the ceremony was over, Jeff left without saying anything to his parents.

What the Hell Was I Thinking?

Jeff ran into a few of his fraternity brothers who were heading out to a party.

They shouted, "Jeff, come and join us. We're heading to an off-campus party. It will be fun."

Jeff agreed and went along with them.

After a couple of beers, some of the guys suggested joining a group of girls at a table across the room. Soon they were all drinking and talking together.

As the evening went on, his fraternity brothers were making plans to hook up with a few of the girls. Jeff became nervous when he realized what they were planning to do. He had never kissed a girl, let alone had sex with a female. He wanted to leave, but he decided that leaving would only raise questions that he was not prepared to answer. Before he knew it, only he and one other girl remained.

He brought over a couple of bottles of beer, and they talked and drank by themselves.

At one point, she said, "I would like to do a couple of shots of whiskey. I noticed one of the guys over there has a bottle. Let's see if he will share it with us."

Jeff went over to the guy and asked if they could have a couple of shots.

The guy said, "No problem, man. If it helps you get laid tonight, the bottle is yours."

Back at the table, Jeff was amazed at how much she could drink. He also had his share of the whiskey and was feeling no pain. As the evening went on, the girl became extremely interested in Jeff. She began running her foot up and down Jeff's leg, stopping slowly at his crotch. She said, "You are so hot. I want to see you without your shirt on." She started unbuttoning the shirt, and she almost fell over. Jeff helped back to her seat and said, "I'll get us a couple of bottles of water. I think we have had enough alcohol."

When she finished the water, she suggested heading back to campus.

Jeff said, "I think I should get you a cab and make sure you get home."

She told Jeff that she wanted him to show her the fraternity house.

Jeff became extremely anxious because he understood what she was leading to. He couldn't think of a way to get out of it. He knew they both had too much to drink, but he could still think clearly enough to know that it would not be proper to leave her there alone.

She yelled, "I want to see where you live. Let's go there now."

Jeff agreed to head back to the campus with her. The fresh air might sober her up, and then he could convince her to go home. Along the way, she started hugging and kissing him. She kept calling him Jeffie and begging him to show her where he lived. "Come on, Jeffie. We can continue the party at your house."

When they arrived at the fraternity, guys were making out with the girls from the party. One of the guys gave Jeff thumbs-up. Jeff was extremely drunk.

In Jeff's room, the girl started taking off her clothes. Jeff reluctantly went along with it.

Within minutes, they were both completely naked.

She started kissing and fondling him. "Your body is so perfect and tight. It's really turning me on." She looked him up and down. "Wow. I am impressed. You have even more to offer than I imagined." She took charge, and they became fully involved with each other.

He said, "I don't have any condoms … so we need to stop."

She smiled and said, "It's your lucky day, Jeffie. I always have a few in my purse."

As they were nearing their completion, Jeff suddenly began thinking of Elliott, the river grass, his parents' bed, and all the other places they had sex. Even with all the alcohol in him, he knew what he was doing didn't feel right. He wanted it to be over and for her to leave. He hurriedly finished, helped her find her clothing, and watched as she left.

He sat on his bed and began to laugh. *What the hell was I thinking? Was I trying to prove something to the world—or to myself?* He didn't even remember the girl's name. He was so angry at himself. He knew it was not the world he belonged in. He needed to start navigating his life in its true direction. He needed to find the world he belonged in. He didn't know how or where to start. Once again, he felt lost and lonely.

A New Boyfriend

Elliott's first year of college was filled with opportunity and discovery. He became involved with a gay organization called Gay Pride. The group's main mission was to educate the community about issues involving gay life. Also, it was a way for them to become more visible to the entire community—not just the gay community. He was impressed with the other members of the group. He felt as if he had taken a huge step forward by getting involved with others like himself. He soon had a new network of friends.

These friends thought like him and understood him. He was excited to introduce Darlene and Heather to the group. They eventually began donating their time to help in any way they could. Elliott enjoyed telling his parents about the group and all the good they were doing. Peg told Elliott not to worry about helping at the pizza shop on weekends.

Elliott said he wanted to help.

Dan said, "You heard your mother. We will be fine. You need to live your life for yourself, not for us."

Elliott reluctantly agreed, knowing he was fighting a losing battle. With his weekends free, he began going out more often with his new friends.

One Saturday night, Elliott was at a party at a friend's house. He was hanging with his friends, drinking a few beers, and listening to the music. Someone tapped him on the shoulder, and Elliott turned around to see an extremely attractive guy smiling. At first, Elliott thought it was Jeff. He had Jeff's haircut and build. He smiled and said, "Hello."

The man's name was Jim. They began talking and drinking together.

Jim said that he had been watching Elliot all evening and thought he was hot and sexy. Before long, he invited Elliott to go home with him. Elliott accepted.

Jim lived on the west side of downtown, and Elliott followed in his own car. Jim's apartment was on the twelfth floor of a high-rise apartment building on Edgewater Drive, overlooking Lake Erie. Elliott was amazed at the view from Jim's living room. They gazed out at the lights from the small boats on the lake. Elliott started to unbutton Jim's shirt, and Jim led him into the bedroom.

Elliott had not had sex since he was with Jeff. He felt nervous and excited at the same time. When they were finished, they exchanged phone numbers and made plans to see each other the following weekend. On his drive home, Elliott thought about how good he felt, but he had the feeling that he had just cheated on Jeff. He knew that it was not cheating, and he knew he liked Jim. He hoped it would be his first step in getting past Jeff.

When he got back to his dorm, he called Darlene and told her that he felt that he had cheated on Jeff.

Darlene said, "Get over it, girl. The only one you are cheating on is yourself if you keep thinking like that. Do you think Jeff is just sitting around and not getting involved with anyone? He probably has a different guy every night. I am positive that he doesn't think he is cheating on you. If you like this guy, then go for it. If not, then stop complaining to me about Jeff. It's your fault if you end up alone."

Elliott said, "You're probably right, and yes, I plan to see Jim again."

Darlene said, "Not *probably* right—I *am* right."

Unexpected Changes

The stage was set. The first game of Jeff's second season was about to begin. During summer practice, Jeff excelled as a first-rate football player. He was selected as the starting quarterback. It was a dream come true. He was on his way, and a pro football career was in sight.

The festivities around campus were intense. Pep rallies and parties were going on all week. It would also be a nationally televised game. The team spent countless hours practicing, fine-tuning every detail of every play they had rehearsed all summer. The atmosphere was escalated to a higher level when several dignitaries and donors began arriving. Many were from Washington, including Jeff's parents. Jeff had little contact with his parents over the summer. Practice had taken up a great deal of his time, and William and Laura vacationed in Hawaii for two months. Jeff had to prepare himself for the criticism that always accompanied his father's visits.

Jeff spent the morning of the game in the locker room. He wanted to go over the plays one last time. As he put on his uniform, he thought of the game in Ohio when he noticed Elliott in the bleachers. He wondered why that memory crossed his mind, but he was glad that he remembered it.

The team had to wait until all the dignitaries finished their speeches. Jeff listened as his father bragged to the crowd that the quarterback was his son. It was another one of William's political stunts. After all, his parents hadn't bothered sending him a card or letter or even calling him while they were in Hawaii. Now he was their cherished son. He said, "What a bunch of bullshit. I wish he stayed home."

The game started out slowly, and neither team scored in the first quarter. In the second quarter the opposing team scored, and then Jeff caught a pass, ran down the field, and scored a touchdown. The game was tied. All eyes were on Jeff as he huddled with his team, going over how they would handle the next play. He would kick the ball and then stay back to ensure they would get possession. He knew the other team would throw in his direction. Sure enough, the ball came flying in his direction, and he caught it. Jeff began to run and was tackled from the side. He fell to the ground, and his right leg twisted under him. The pain encompassed his entire body. He tried to get up and fell back down. He was in a daze.

Everything seemed to be moving in slow motion—even the voices from his coach and teammates. He was rushed to the emergency room. He was scared and lonely and kept asking what was wrong with his leg. He didn't receive an answer from the medical team. The only thing they told him was that they needed to wait for his father before they told him anything.

Jeff sat up and yelled, "This is my fucking leg—not my father's leg. I will not shut up until you tell me what is wrong."

The doctor tried to calm Jeff down.

Jeff yelled, "Just tell me what the fuck is wrong with my leg."

The doctor told Jeff that his leg was broken in two places. He needed surgery to repair the damage.

Everything went blank in Jeff's mind. He realized his dream of playing in the pros was over. Even if he fully recovered, no team would take a chance on him. He was damaged goods. He began to cry.

When William arrived, he said, "Stop acting like a baby. If you need to cry, then you should be crying for letting your team and the school down. If you're crying for yourself, then you must be weak and not much of a man."

Jeff asked where his mother was.

William said, "I ordered her to stay in the car. There is nothing she could do in here, and she would only be in the way."

Jeff was given an injection and taken away to surgery.

John Mudzyn

He woke up several hours later in his hospital room. His leg was in a cast from his thigh to his ankle. All alone in his room, he tried to comprehend what had happened and where he would go from here. He took inventory of his life. He didn't like what he saw. He thought of all the pain and hurt of losing Elliott, not by his choice, but by William's. He was forced to move to Washington; again, it was William's doing. Having to deny his true nature was another of William's demands. He made a promise to himself that going forward, he would take every dollar his father threw at him, but he would never again be William's political pawn. He didn't know how or when it would happen, but one day, he would get even with his father. It might take him a lifetime, but William, without a doubt, would know who his son really is.

Once again, he had no one to confide in. His dreams had all gone up in smoke. He thought he might be better off dead, but that would let his parents off too easy. They would turn his death into their moment. He wouldn't give them that satisfaction. It scared him to even think that way. He knew there was something more for him to accomplish. It was time to move in his own direction. Before he could move on, he would have to endure several months of intense physical therapy to regain the mobility of his injured leg.

Elliott woke up late on that Saturday. Coming from the kitchen was an aroma of fresh coffee brewing and bacon frying. He looked over to the other side of the bed and realized that Jim was already up and in the kitchen. The two of them had been seeing each other for several months. It was more comfortable and convenient for Elliott to stay over at Jim's apartment on weekends instead of Jim sleeping over in Elliott's dorm room.

Elliott got up, stood in the living room, and looked out at the lake. Jim came up behind him and gave him a hug and a kiss. Jim had the weekend off, and Elliott did not have any classes. They decided to make it a lazy Saturday and just hang around the apartment.

Elliott excused himself to take a shower. Jim joined him in the shower a few minutes later, and they started to make out.

Jim said, "This could happen every morning if you would make up your mind and move in."

Although Elliott enjoyed Jim, he still wasn't completely sure that Jim was the one. There seemed to always be something holding him back from making a full commitment. Elliott smiled and said, "No talking until we are finished."

Later that afternoon, Jim was bored with the show they were watching. He took the remote from Elliott's hand and began surfing the channels. He came across a football game and said, "Let's watch this. We can look at all the hot football players prancing around that field."

Elliott said, "I didn't know you liked football."

Jim answered, "I hate the game. I only like to watch the players. I'll change the channel if you want."

Elliott said halfheartedly, "No. Leave it on. We can watch it for a while." He noticed Jeff running onto the field and became fixated on the screen. He lit up with a smile when the quarterback was introduced. There was Jeff on national TV, and he looked so damn good. Elliott was amazed at how much sexier Jeff had become. He had matured and looked like a hot movie star.

Jim teased Elliott and asked why he was smiling. "It looks like you like watching football players as much as I do."

Elliott explained that he knew the quarterback a long time ago.

Jim said, "Is that Jeff?"

Elliott said, "How do you know about Jeff?"

Jim said that he had always felt like Elliott was keeping a secret about someone else in his life. Since Elliott wouldn't talk about it, he asked Darlene if she knew anything. Darlene explained the entire story.

Elliott said, "Yes, it was Jeff."

As the game went on, Jim asked Elliott to explain his relationship with Jeff.

Elliott answered, "I am sure Darlene has told you everything."

Jim persisted, which began to anger Elliott.

"Look," Elliott said, "I haven't asked who you were with before me, so drop this line of questioning. I feel as if I am on trial."

Jim laughed and said, "Seems like I hit a nerve. You have your reasons not to tell me, so, for now, I will leave it at that."

When Jeff was seriously injured, Elliott leaped off the couch and stared at the TV.

Jim made a smart-ass comment about Jeff, and Elliott told him to shut his mouth. He grabbed his coat and left without saying goodbye.

The minute he arrived at his dorm, he called Darlene. She had been watching the game with Heather. Elliott kept telling her that he needed to get in touch with Jeff.

Darlene said, "It would be foolish to try. William would certainly be there with him. He would never let you speak with Jeff. Remember William's threats? You need to get over this shit. You need to forget about Jeff. It's time to grow up. It's obvious that Jeff has forgotten all about you. Has he ever tried to contact you? From now on, if you want to talk about him, please find someone else to cry to. I am done talking about spoiled little Jeff."

Elliott was speechless. He wasn't expecting to hear anything like that from her. He said, "You are wrong. Jeff would never forget about me." He cut the call short and hung up the phone.

Later that evening, Jim called Elliott and gave him an ultimatum. Although he sympathized with what Elliott had gone through with Jeff, he would not play runner-up to Jeff or anyone else. "You need to decide who you wanted to be with: me or Jeff. I will not wait long for an answer."

Elliott told Jim that it would be better if they stopped seeing each other.

Jim said, "Go fuck yourself." He hung up, and that was the last time they spoke to each other.

Elliott felt empty and hollow that night. He was beginning to accept the fact that he would probably be alone for the rest of his life. No matter how hard he tried, he would always compare everyone to Jeff, and that was not a recipe for success.

The next morning, he called the hospital to ask how Jeff was. He was told that no information would be given over the phone. It would take several months before Elliott would find out the extent of Jeff's injury and his inability to continue playing football. Elliott knew that Jeff had built his entire life around playing that game. He remembered that first day of school when Jeff told the class how he wanted to play pro football one day.

Elliott realized Darlene was right. Jeff has never tried to contact him. It seemed like he had moved on with his life. It was easier for Elliott not to know the truth if Jeff had really forgotten about him. Not knowing, he felt, he always had some hope.

Acceptance and Change

The room was filled with balloons, and the entire staff applauded enthusiastically as Jeff walked in for his last day of physical therapy. It had been a grueling four months since that disastrous day on the football field. The therapy sessions helped Jeff regain motion in his leg and helped him accept the fact that football was no longer a major part of his life. It was time to move on and devote his energy and focus on his studies.

William continued pressuring Jeff to switch his major from broadcasting to political courses that would be beneficial for an easy transition into a political career.

Jeff said, "I intend to continue with broadcasting. You need to understand that I have no intention of ever going into politics." Jeff knew his father was an empty, bigoted politician. He suspected that William was a sad man who had made a pact with the devil years ago.

As Jeff left the clinic, he looked up at the sky and felt the warm sun on his face. He began to look forward to the journey that lay ahead for him.

Elliott, in a couple of months, would be graduating with an associate degree in business. He had doubled up on his classes to graduate earlier than expected. He had already been accepted to a law school near Cleveland and would be starting in the fall. It had been four months since he broke it off with Jim. He never regretted his decision. Other changes were happening in his life as well.

Becky and Luke were making plans to move to Los Angeles in July. Luke's parents lived there, and after he and Becky visited them on vacation, they fell in love with the area and decided to give California a try. Peg and Dan didn't relish the idea that they would be moving and taking little Mark with them. However, they would never stand in the way. Instead, they offered encouragement and help in any way they could.

Elliott told Becky that he was happy she was able to find her true love in Luke. Although he was sad they would be moving, he said, "Now I have a place to go on vacation." It seemed as if the sun was shining a little brighter, and for the most part, the darkness of the past was behind him. He was looking forward to the road ahead.

CHAPTER 6

Exploration and Ultimatums

Jeff got out of the cab and looked around to find the address of his destination. He was standing on an extremely dark side street in the part of the city that was farthest from campus. He noticed the numbers on a large old warehouse. The address was dimly lit by a small flickering light. He was beginning to second-guess his idea, but something inside kept telling him to go ahead. Cautiously opening the door, he was greeted by an extremely good-looking young man, wearing only a towel and standing behind a glass partition. The guy in the towel looked Jeff up and down and asked if he wanted a room or just a locker. Jeff was not sure how to answer.

The clerk then said, "Honey, with your looks, you will not have any problem. I'm sure you will end up in as many rooms as you want tonight. That will be ten dollars for a locker."

Jeff handed over the cash, the clerk pressed a button, and another door opened. Jeff was about to discover one of the darker sides of gay life. He had never been to a gay bar, and of course, never to a gay bathhouse.

As apprehensive as he was to enter, there was a weird feeling of adventure deep inside him. Walking through the maze of dimly lit halls and rooms, he passed a room where a movie was playing on a big screen.

Men of all shapes and sizes were watching. Some wore towels, and others wore nothing at all.

Several of them were engaged in different sexual acts. As he passed by, the men kept looking at him and smiling. Their looks and smiles made Jeff feel uncomfortable and adventurous at the same time. He found the lockers, opened his locker, and found a fresh towel inside. He wasn't shy about undressing. He had done it hundreds of times in the locker rooms.

As he took off his shirt, other men started to walk past him slowly, and a few of them exposed themselves, which caused Jeff to get extremely aroused. He knew he couldn't just stand there, and he wrapped his towel around his waist and looked for the steam room. His only concern was running into someone he knew. He tried to convince himself that he should be safe from that happening because it was extremely far from campus.

He passed several small rooms with doors cracked open to ensure anyone walking by could see who was in the room. In the steam room, Jeff found an open space between two of the men on the benches. He began feeling uncomfortable about how many men were staring at him. In the corner was a good-looking man who appeared to be a couple of years older than Jeff. That guy got up and motioned for Jeff to follow. He followed the man into a small room.

Their towels dropped to the floor, and the two of them became entangled in each other's arms. The guy started kissing Jeff's neck, which aroused him to the point that he pulled the guy on to the small bed where they engaged in wild, dirty sex. When they were finished, Jeff looked down at the floor and noticed a few empty condom wrappers. He started thinking that he might not have been the first one that guy was with that night. Jeff asked the guy about the wrappers on the floor. He was told there were a few guys before him—and hopefully a few more before the night was over.

Jeff noticed a wedding ring on his finger and said, "Are you married?"

The guy laughed and said, "Yes. This is my night out with the boys. I got married to please my parents and help me get a promotion. Half the men in this place are married. I hope I see you again next weekend."

Jeff left without saying anything and went back to his locker. He just wanted to get dressed and get out of there. While he was dressing, he kept thinking about that guy and his wife. *Why in hell would anyone want to live a life like that?* He thought about how that guy said he married to please his family. That was exactly what William seemed to be demanding of him. *I'll never end up like these pathetic men who refuse to live their lives true to who they really are.*

He was almost finished getting dressed when someone called out his name. One of the guys on the football team was standing in a towel and smiling. "I would never had guessed that I would see you here, Mr. College Jock, cruising the bathhouse." He had a sinister smile that Jeff took as a hint that he wanted to hook up with him.

Jeff said, "This was my first time here, and it will probably be my last time. It isn't my kind of place."

"Don't worry," Jason said. "I won't tell if you won't tell. Let me give you some advice, Jeff. It appears that you are extremely uncomfortable in here, and that is okay. It's not a place for everyone. Let me write down a few names of gay bars and addresses for you. You should check these out. I think you will feel more comfortable in those places."

Jeff took the piece of paper, thanked Jason, and left.

On his way back to campus, Jeff kept thinking about the gay bars and decided that he needed to check out a few of them. He wanted what he had with Elliott. *Hope is eternal,* he thought. *Perhaps one day I will find another true love. Better yet, maybe I will find Elliott—and we can start again.*

Over the next several weekends, Jeff went to the bars and became very comfortable around so many gay people. He even started making a few friends. He was not at the point of being completely out, and he took great strides to make sure no one knew where he went on or what he was doing. He didn't know if he would ever be completely out. Jeff spent his summer living two very different lives. Monday through Thursday, he was straight Jeff—constantly waiting for Friday night to become true Jeff. Juggling two worlds was an art that he became an expert at. He navigated it all alone.

The Cleveland Pride Center was a flurry of activity. The gay pride parade and celebration was scheduled for the last weekend of June. Elliott and Darlene were helping with all the last-minute details. The city had delayed in preparing the proper permits, causing concern that there might not be a place to hold the important celebration. When the permits arrived, as if they broke free from the grasp of some bigoted city employee who had no regard for any type of diversity.

For months, Elliott had been on a mission to learn as much as he could about gay culture and heritage. He was in awe of the drag queens who stood up and fought back during the Stonewall uprising in 1969. He was proud that 1969 was the same year that his parents met, as young teenagers, at the Woodstock festival, another group that gathered for what they believed in—just as the drag queens did. He hoped he would be that determined and committed to stand up and fight all the discrimination that was hurled toward the lesbian and gay community. He was proud to be gay, and he didn't care who knew it.

He and Darlene contacted several gay organizations across the country to better understand how they were celebrating Gay History Month. Darlene gave a presentation to the Gay Pride committee on their findings. It was a tremendous help in organizing their own celebration. Everything seemed to be falling into place. It was just a matter of who would show up—or if anyone would.

Elliott helped the group organize the order of the floats. The city blocked off the street, so they had ample room to arrange the spectacular floats.

Elliott was concerned that very few people were lining up along the street. Darlene kept assuring him that it was still early. "People will show up." Darlene's projection came true as both sides of the street soon became a sea of people of every color and background.

Elliott began to cry when he saw his mom and dad standing next to Becky and Luke. Mark was perched on Dan's shoulders, and they were all waving small rainbow flags. Heather drove up with Peg and Dan and gave Darlene a big kiss. They were celebrating what Elliott had tried to hide from them for so long. Elliott wished Jeff could have been there with him, both arm in arm in front of everyone and not ashamed of their love. He deeply missed Jeff.

Elliott spent this summer celebrating who he was with his family. He finally understood that he had a place in society.

Rocco

That first day of law school was a frenzied, feverish ball of confusion. This campus was drastically different from the community college. There were acres of crisp, detailed lawns and majestic century-old buildings.

Elliott grabbed a bagel and coffee and hurried to the bus stop. He was advised not to drive to school because parking spaces were few and expensive. Elliott relied on a map from the admissions office to navigate the campus. They had highlighted the buildings where his classes would be held. When that first day was over, Elliott's new boyfriend came to his dorm with a bottle of Cabernet to celebrate the first day of school.

Elliott had met Rocco that summer at a fund-raiser for the AIDS foundation. Rocco worked as a nurse at the Cleveland Clinic. He devoted much of his time to helping at the city's free clinic. Rocco, unlike Jeff, had no desire to play sports. His parents were both teachers who lived in a modest home in the suburbs. His parents always insisted that the family had dinner together at least once a week. They were extremely devoted to each other and embraced their son's homosexuality with open arms. He enjoyed going to movies and taking long walks in the parks. On weekends, Rocco spent hours helping patients at the free clinic navigate the world of HIV.

Elliott was first attracted to Rocco by his stunning good looks. Rocco's mother was a first-generation Egyptian. Rocco seemed to be the perfect partner for Elliott. He considered Elliott the sexiest man he had ever dated. Also, Elliott had direction in his life. He never made false impressions about who he was.

Darlene and Heather loved seeing the two of them together and considered Rocco a perfect match for Elliott. Dan and Peg welcomed him into their home.

As they relaxed on his bed, Rocco asked if there were any good-looking guys in his classes.

Elliott said, "Yes, there were several students who are extremely attractive. There was a good-looking professor in one of my classes too. If I ever need help with his class, perhaps he will do some private tutoring with me."

Rocco jumped off the bed and asked Elliott if he wanted to sleep with the guy.

Elliott said, "What are you talking about? It was a joke. Don't take everything so literally."

"You're right, Elliott. I am sorry. It's been a long day, and I guess I am tired." Rocco finished his drink and said that he would see him tomorrow.

Elliott began to realize he didn't like part of Rocco's personality. When they would go out, Rocco's demeanor would change whenever Elliott talked to someone else. Rocco would become quiet and demand that they go home because he was tired. Elliott always blamed himself since Rocco seemed to be perfect in every other way. Perhaps Rocco being so possessive was a good thing and Elliott just needed to get past this one flaw.

No matter how hard he tried, Elliott couldn't keep Jeff out of the equation. He didn't want to end it with Rocco. He considered getting professional help, thinking that someone not connected to his life would be able to help him sort out his thoughts and feelings about Jeff. He didn't want to hurt Rocco the same way he hurt Jim.

Rocco called Elliott and said, "Please forget how I acted and what I said. I was wrong, and I am sorry I accused you of wanting to sleep with your professor. I just want you all to myself."

A couple of days later, Elliott and Rocco went to dinner at a Mexican restaurant near campus. While they were placing their order, Elliott smiled at the server, and the server smiled back.

"Who is that?" Rocco demanded to know. "Is he someone you have slept with—or are you hoping to sleep with him?"

Elliott said, "No, he is our server, and I was being polite. Would you prefer we move over there and have that miserable-looking woman wait on us?"

Rocco said, "I was just checking to make sure that nothing was going on with the server."

Elliott looked at Rocco and said, "You have brought this subject up to me more than once, and I don't like it. If you don't trust me, then you need to say it. If not, then you need to back off. Let me ask you something, Rocco. Who do you sleep with when I am not around? Do any of the doctors at the clinic give you private anatomy lessons? Perhaps some of the male nurses suck your dick on your lunch hour. How does that sound to you? How does it make you feel? Do you like being questioned about things you haven't done. Or perhaps, you are doing them—and that's why you think I am sleeping with everyone. Anyway, suddenly, I am not hungry. I am tired. I am leaving. Maybe you can hook up with our server after I leave. After all, he is cute."

Rocco stood up and said, "If you leave, then we are through with each other."

Elliott laughed and said, "Honey, I think we were through when you implied that I was a whore. Have a good life."

Once again, another one didn't work out for Elliott. He began second-guessing himself. Should he have given Rocco the benefit of the doubt? There was one question that scared Elliott the most. Was he subconsciously sabotaging every relationship, hoping that Jeff would one day come back?

Concerns and Reflection

Peg called Elliott to see how his first week of law school was going. She invited him over the next weekend to celebrate Dan's birthday. She said, "Please bring Rocco."

Elliott explained that they were not seeing each other anymore.

She said, "I trust your judgment, but make sure you take a deep look to find out what motivated you to break it off with Rocco. Make sure it is something you won't regret later. Don't forget that we are here for you if you need us."

Elliott said, "What's wrong, Mom?"

"Dad has not been feeling well. I'm concerned. Please help me convince your father that he needs to see the doctor and get a thorough checkup."

Elliott said, "Don't worry. It probably is nothing serious. You and Dad are reaching the age when everything starts to hurt."

She laughed and said, "If you could look through the phone, you would see my middle finger."

Elliott knew he could always get his mom to laugh. He mentioned that they should consider getting more help with the pizza shop—so that she and Dan could relax more and not work so damn hard.

Peg reminded him that they come from an extensive line of hard workers who had to endure much more, and they made it. She told him that it would all work out.

After he hung up, Elliott thought about his grandparents working day and night at the pizza shop. They always found time to watch their grandchildren while Peg and Dan finished college in the evening. He never heard them complain. He was amazed at how devoted they were to each other. He thought about how good the house smelled when Grandma Estelle made her famous chocolate chip cookies. It seemed like every kid in the neighborhood stopped by on those days, and his grandmother loved every minute of it. He missed them deeply, but he was grateful that he had them for as long as he did.

Jeff's Routines

Jeff woke up on his first day of his third year of college and walked down the stairs to the dining room in the fraternity house. The cook had breakfast ready and coffee poured. There was no need to rush because after two years, Jeff knew the campus by heart. He had gone out the night before, enjoyed a few drinks, and hooked up with some guy. It was well after two o'clock in the morning when he arrived home. He really needed a couple of cups of coffee to get his day started.

That behavior had become Jeff's routine. He would go out by himself, never telling anyone where he was going. Whenever anyone would ask him where he was off to, he would reply, "I am seeing a girl who lives several miles away from the school." This seemed to keep the questions to a minimum.

Because of his striking good looks, he never had a problem hooking up with some stranger and engaging in anonymous sex. That was the way he planned it. He wanted encounters with no strings attached. He was extremely careful to make sure no one knew who he was. He always insisted on safe sex with very little, if any, conversation. It was as if he was going through a fog. He was hiding who he was from everyone around him, and he was looking for the one man who would make him feel the way Elliott made him feel. He was beginning to believe that it would never happen.

John Mudzyn

Patricia's Secrets

That year was also the beginning of his remaining two years of his father-funded college education. Patricia had left him an extremely large amount of money when she died, which angered William to no end. He thought Laura should have had the money, and he made sure Jeff knew it. Jeff could not touch the money until he finished college and was working in his chosen career. The money would be held in a trust until then. It was stipulated in the will that William would be the one to make the final decision and distribute the money when he felt Jeff was complying with Patricia's wishes. William never stopped reminding Jeff that he had his lawyers looking for ways to overturn the will and award the money to Jeff's mother.

Jeff always wondered why his grandmother left him anything. Patricia rarely displayed any type of affection toward him. Even thought she was never the cookie-baking, Sunday dinner-making grandmother, Jeff had always hoped she would be the one family member he could confide in. He always felt that Patricia held resentments or secrets deep in her heart. He knew his father held a tremendous amount of influence over her. Perhaps leaving him all that money was her way of slapping William in the face. She had to have known how angry he would be. Maybe she had a sense of humor after all.

As a child, Jeff would ask his mother and grandmother about his grandfather. They seemed to always skirt around most questions. There were never any pictures of his grandfather anywhere in the house. Jeff knew that his grandfather's name was Mathew and that he was a self-made business man, making a fortune in the shipping business. He was a four-term congressman from New York who abruptly quit politics, and after Patricia divorced him, he moved to Europe.

One weekend over the summer, while Jeff was at his parents' home in Washington, he went up to the attic to look for some of his things that were packed away. Going through the boxes, he came across one marked "Patricia." It was filled with photos of his grandparents. As he looked over the old photographs, he was taken aback by how much he resembled his grandfather. They had the same height and build. Mathew looked extremely athletic. Their hair and eyes were the same. There could be no doubt that he was related to this man. There were very few pictures of his grandparents together. There were, however, several pictures of his grandfather with the same extremely attractive man next to him. At the bottom of the box, there were several old newspaper clippings. One of the clippings had a picture of his grandfather with the man. The caption read: "Ex-congressman and millionaire leaves for Europe with his business partner."

Suddenly, all kinds of questions started running through Jeff's mind. Why did Mathew suddenly resign from Congress and move to Europe? Who was that other man? Why didn't his family ever talk about Mathew? Why did his grandparents divorce? Was the other man his grandfather's lover? Was that the reason he was never told anything about Mathew? Looking at his watch, Jeff realized that his parents would be home soon. He took a couple of photos and the newspaper clipping with him.

Jeff never told his parents what he found in the attic. He promised himself that he would take the time to find out the truth about his grandfather. For the time being, he needed to search for the truth about himself. He was trapped between two worlds: one where he knew he would never be accepted if he revealed his true nature and one where he was still ashamed to fully admit that it was where he belonged. He needed to go through more obstacles and learn more lessons before he would could totally accept himself.

I Know Who You Are

Sunrise was still a couple of hours away as Jeff looked around for his clothing. He wanted to get dressed quickly and head home to get a few hours of sleep before his first class. The owner of the apartment was in the bathroom, and Jeff thought he could leave without saying anything. The good-looking man in the bathroom was in his late thirties—and very much an expert at rough, wild sex. Jeff met him a few hours earlier at a gay bar he had never been to before.

Although their time together was an enjoyable experience, Jeff was only in it for the sex. In Jeff's mind, there was no need to exchange much conversation. The guy told Jeff that his name was Tom, and he pressed

Jeff for his name. In a moment of weakness, Jeff broke his own rule and told Tom his name.

Before Jeff could get out the door, Tom came out of the bathroom and stood naked between him and the front door. He seemed surprised that Jeff thought he could leave without saying anything.

Jeff said, "I called for a cab and need to get home."

Tom offered to drive him, suggesting it would be an enjoyable time for the two of them to talk and make plans to see each other again.

Always aware of his privacy, Jeff declined the offer. He said, "I can get home on my own. Perhaps we will run into each other again at the bar."

Tom walked over to his desk, wrote down his phone number, and said, "It is okay to call anytime. In fact, I expect you to call." He asked Jeff for his number, but Jeff refused to give it to him. He thanked Tom for the evening and hurriedly left the apartment.

The confrontation with Tom made Jeff feel extremely uncomfortable. Anyone Jeff picked up understood what it was about—and nothing more than that. This one was different. He felt somewhat vulnerable. He put it all in the back of his mind, knowing he must be careful to avoid running into Tom in the future. He felt relieved that Tom didn't know much about him and certainly didn't know where he lived.

Several days after the encounter with Tom, Jeff was walking on campus and thought he saw someone who resembled Tom. He turned and took another route to his destination. Jeff thought, *There is no way it could have been Tom. I need to stop being so paranoid.*

A couple of days later, a letter addressed to Jeff arrived at the fraternity house. The envelope contained a note: "Why haven't you called? I miss you and want to see you again. Here is my number in case you lost it. Tom."

Jeff freaked out. He couldn't understand how Tom knew who he was or where he lived. Jeff then realized that the man he saw on campus the other day must have been Tom. Jeff tore up the note and decided the best thing to do was ignore it, hoping that sooner or later, Tom would get the hint and give up.

A second letter arrived three days later. Jeff returned home from class when one of his fraternity brothers handed him a letter: "I am still waiting for your call. You may have been busy with school, so I will wait a few more days. I will not wait forever. If you don't call me, then I will come to you. Forever yours, Tom."

Jeff became upset and considered calling the police. However, going to the police would become public, especially if anyone connected him to his father. He decided the best thing to do was call Tom and confront him. They arranged a meeting at a restaurant not far from campus.

When Jeff arrived, Tom was already seated at a table near the back of the dining area. Jeff walked over to the table, and before Tom could say anything, Jeff said, "What the fuck are you doing? Can't you take a hint that I don't want anything to do with you? You need to leave me the fuck alone. Understand?"

Tom sat there, smiled at Jeff, and asked him to have seat. The next thing Tom did was give Jeff back his student ID. "I took this from your wallet that night you were at my apartment."

Jeff never realized it was missing.

Tom told Jeff that he was in love with him.

Jeff said, "You are crazy, and you need to stop this harassment."

Tom, still smiling, calmly said, "I knew I had seen you somewhere else—before we met at the bar. I came across a picture in the paper of you standing next to your father at some college function. I put it all together when I saw your name on the ID." Tom pulled out some pictures and handed them to Jeff. The pictures were of Jeff and Tom, both naked on Tom's bed. Tom had taken a few pictures of them in various positions when they were having sex. Jeff had a few too many drinks and smoked some weed, which made him not care about posing for the pictures. "I wonder how the senator will react if he sees these pictures? Better yet, maybe the papers would like a story about the upstanding senator and his all-American son. I wonder how your naked ass will look spread across the front page. Oh, by the way, isn't this an election year?"

Jeff knew exactly what he meant. He got up in his face and said, "Leave me alone. You are seriously mistaken if you think you know my father. Go ahead and fuck with his election. He will take you down. You won't know what hit you."

Tom said, "Think back to that night and how freaky and wild it was. Think about all the ways we did it that night. Don't you want more of that? Either we get together and fuck whenever I want—or I go public with all of this." Tom continued sipping on his drink. "Of course, cash is king in my world. I think you're smart enough to know what I mean by that."

Jeff said, "Go ahead and fuck with my father. I will enjoy watching you get what you deserve."

Tom said, "Let me know what direction I need to proceed in: your father or your money. Don't take too long to give me your answer." Tom got up, kissed Jeff on his forehead, and left.

Jeff was beside himself, not knowing what he needed to do. Should he call the police or give his father a heads-up in case Tom went to the papers? Perhaps the best thing to do would be to do nothing. Maybe Tom would just go away. Jeff decided the best thing to do was keep quiet.

After a week without hearing anything from Tom, he figured that Tom must have backed out and that it was over. A few days later, Jeff's father suddenly showed up at the fraternity house. Jeff was up in his room when William walked in without knocking. He grabbed Jeff by his shirt and slammed him up against the wall. He yelled, "You motherfucking fag! You are nothing more than a whore and an embarrassment to the family."

Tom had sent William the photos and was demanding money. William had his team find out where Tom lived, and he went to see him. He told Tom that he knew all about him and how he had tried the same thing in the past with other prominent people. He informed Tom that those others may have paid him well, but he had no intention of giving him one cent. He let Tom know that all it would take would be for him to call a few of his not-so-nice business associates.

Tom yelled, "Are you threating me, dude?"

William said, "No. I am making you a promise. You have fucked with the wrong man." William had Tom sign a confession that he made up the story and fabricated the photos.

William, still holding Jeff against the wall, shouted, "I got that other little fag out of your life—and now I had to do it again. If you know what's good for yourself, you will keep men's dicks out of your mouth and ass. I control the money, and if you continue with this disgusting lifestyle, I will hold up that money until you're too old to enjoy it."

Jeff shoved William across the room and said, "Don't you ever try to put your hands on me again. You never hugged me as a child, so don't think you have the right to touch me now. I am not one of your phony-assed supporters. I am your son. As much as I disgust you, I detest you even more. Believe me, after I graduate, I don't care if I end up living in one room and eating food out of a can. I will be done with you. Until then, we will have a strictly monetary relationship. You owe me that, and I will hold you to it. If not, I have plenty of ammo on you to go public with. I hope you understand me. One more thing—don't ever call Elliott a fag again. If you do, I will destroy you."

As soon as William left, Jeff collapsed onto his bed, shaking and trying to take stock of what had happened. He was a year away from graduating and didn't want to mess that up. He realized that he needed to stop having anonymous sex with strangers. No longer was he that naïve young boy who fell in love with his best friend on the first day of school. Those days were long gone. He needed to start acting like an adult. From now on, whatever he did in his life would be his own responsibility. He would always have to keep one eye on William. He still had a score to settle with his father for what he did to Elliott. However, for the time being, he needed to focus on graduating.

CHAPTER 7

Life Changes

Elliott breezed through his first year of law school. He knew it was the best choice he could have made. Even though he had often been preoccupied and concerned about his father's health, he ended the year at the top of his class.

Dan had been diagnosed with diabetes earlier in the year and was on a regiment of insulin and a strict diet. Peg took over more of the duties at the restaurant, which allowed Dan more rest and relaxation. Elliott spent as much time as he could helping his mom on weekends. Darlene stepped up and would stop by on her days off to help serve customers and give Peg a break.

Darlene said, "These kids today were just babies when I started hanging out here with Elliott. It's is amazing to witness the circle of life and how things change and stay the same both at the same time."

Elliott scaled back his time volunteering with Gay Pride. School and family took top priority. He also didn't have time to go out as much, and he decided that, for the time being, he wouldn't get involved with anyone. He didn't need—and certainly didn't have time for—all the drama a boyfriend would bring. He was tired of not finding the right guy and considered that he might never find him. That routine went on well into his third year of law school.

Dan's health was rapidly declining. He was admitted to the hospital, and the doctors discovered a mass growing on one of his lungs. It was cancerous and needed to be removed.

Elliott said, "I will take off the last semester of school and take over working at the restaurant. Mom, this will allow you to take care of Dad at home."

Dan said, "We will close the pizza shop before we allow you to quit school. I hope you understand that this is no longer open for discussion."

Peg cried the day Darlene announced that she had taken a leave of absence from the post office. She and Heather would devote all their time to keeping the restaurant open. Darlene's mother also stepped up and offered to help in any way she could.

Elliott kept Becky and Luke informed about what was happing with Dan. They would talk to each other every day on the phone. Peg wanted to keep everything as normal as possible.

One morning, Becky called and said, "Mom, Luke and I have discussed this, and we want to move back and help you through all of this."

Peg said, "I don't want you to do that. You and Luke have your lives all set in California. Your father would also tell you no. Hang tight. Let's just see what happens with your father's surgery."

Surgery

On the morning of Dan's surgery, Peg Elliott, Darlene, and Heather were all in the hospital waiting room. Another woman was waiting while her husband had cancer surgery. Her son had gone to school with Elliott and Darlene.

At first, Peg exchanged small talk with her.

After a few minutes, the woman said, "I hope you realize your husband is sick because of your son and his disgusting lifestyle. God is punishing your husband because of Elliott's sins."

Everyone heard the woman, including the nurses. Elliott couldn't believe what he heard coming out of the woman's mouth. Darlene started to get in her face, but Peg stopped her. Peg said, "I don't know what kind of God you pray to. My God is the one who created my son, and he loves my son. I have a question to ask you. Who in your family is gay? If what you just said is true, then it seems to me that your husband is being punished for the same reason. Please sit here and think about what you just said while your husband is in that operating room being cut wide open. Perhaps he is being punished for your sins."

A nurse came over and gave Peg a hug. She turned to the woman and said, "I suggest you go and wait in the other waiting room. I just looked, and it is empty. There is no one there for you to insult. I am sure you will be more comfortable in there."

The woman got up, but before she left, Peg said, "I am praying for your husband. I wish him well. Try sharing some love and a little less hate."

The woman left without saying anything else.

Peg looked over at Elliott and said, "Are you okay?"

Elliott smiled. "Mom, I am good. I hear this crap all the time. She is the one who has some serious issues and is extremely unhappy. Don't worry about me."

During surgery, it was discovered that Dan's cancer had spread and was inoperable.

When Elliott heard the news, he broke down in tears.

Peg took hold of him and explained that she needed him to stay strong and continue with school. "Your father and I have made peace with all of this. It is out of our control. Quitting school won't make this go away." She smiled and told him it would be all right.

Elliott called Becky and said that she needed to come home. Becky, Luke, and Mark needed to be there for Peg.

Dad, I Love You

Dan refused to go into hospice. He wanted to be in his home for whatever time he had left. Elliott decided to drive home every day after class and spend nights there. It was only a thirty-minute drive, so commuting was not a problem.

Becky and Luke helped Darlene and Heather at the restaurant, and Peg stayed home taking care of Dan and Mark.

Sister Mary Therese would stop by every day or so to check up on everyone. One afternoon, she brought a bag of get-well cards that the students at the school made for Dan. Peg taped them on the walls of Dan's room. The cards brought a little sunshine in the room and smiles from everyone who came to visit.

One evening, Dan asked Elliott to close the door and sit next to his bed. "I have something to talk to you about. Don't ever forget how proud I am that you are my son. Wherever your life leads you, don't forget to stop occasionally and think back to all the love we have in our family. Your mother is a strong woman, but she is going to need your help. She may object, but you need to convince her that she needs to sell the pizza shop. She will be okay financially. You and your sister need to make sure she is not lonely. If selling the house and moving somewhere else will help, you need to be the one to encourage her. I know you won't let me down."

Elliott hugged his father and said, "Dad, I have always been so damn proud that you are my father. You have taught me so much, and I will never forget that. I love you."

Dan passed away two weeks before Elliott's graduation. Peg, Elliott, and Becky were in the room when he died.

Darlene and Heather were getting ready to open the pizza shop for the day when Elliott called and told them the news. The girls hugged each other and cried. Darlene said, "This place will never be the same."

Heather printed a sign on the computer: "Closed due to a death in the family." She took a picture of Dan off the wall and taped it along with the note on the front door. "Let's go. We don't need to be here today."

The morning of Dan's funeral was sunny and warm. As they were walking into the church behind Dan's casket, Elliott was amazed at how many people showed up. As they continued walking to the front, Elliott looked at who was filling all the pews. He noticed many of his former classmates—the same classmates who pointed fingers at Jeff and him. The ones who whispered all the hate and avoided him after they learned about Jeff and him.

Many of them had their own little children with them. Would these young children be taught the same hate their parents learned from their mothers and fathers? Would any of them have to endure the same hate he and Jeff had to endure? As he held his mother's hand, he held his head up high, proud of who his parents were—and proud of who he was.

Sister Mary Therese was waiting for them near the alter. Elliott gave her a hug and invited her to sit with the family.

After the service, Dan was buried in the small village cemetery next to his parents. As Peg was thanking everyone who came, Elliott looked at all the flowers and read all the sympathy cards. When he got to a small bouquet of red roses, the attached card said one word: "Jeff." He took the card with him and held it close for the rest of the afternoon. He said goodbye to his dad, and it was over. He had to be the man of the family. Even though she didn't show it publicly, Peg was deeply hurt and lost in this new world she now had to face. He understood why his father asked him to take care of her.

During the reception, so many people came up to him with kind words of sympathy. He couldn't help but wonder if they meant it or if it was all for show.

Kathy took full charge of the reception, and Peg did not have to worry about any detail.

How Are You Doing, Kid?

At one point, Elliott stepped outside to get some fresh air and get away from the crowd. Heather joined him and brought two glasses of wine. "How are you doing, kid?"

He said, "It's a tough day, but I will get through it."

She said, "Darlene and I looked over all the cards at the cemetery. We noticed that Jeff sent one. Darlene wanted to take the card to keep it away from you. She didn't want you to see it. I told her to leave it alone. It belongs to Elliott. She was just trying to protect you."

Elliott took the card out of his pocket and showed it to Heather. "I need to ask you something. Why can't I get this guy out of my head? It takes everything in me, and I try, but I just can't. He is always there in my mind and heart. I always hoped he would try to reach out to me. After all this time, I decided he didn't want to. I began believing that Darlene was right. Jeff only looks out for himself. I know he hasn't forgotten me. I have his card from those beautiful flowers. He didn't need to send those flowers, but he did for a reason. Is this all there will ever be for us?"

Heather took hold of his hands. "There is nothing wrong with keeping Jeff on your mind and in your heart. What you two had at such an early age is something most people look for all their lives. Sometimes we only get one chance at it, so cherish those memories. You have a long road ahead of you and so much promise. Never forget him—and never give up hope."

Becky came out and said that people were beginning to leave.

Elliot needed to go inside and thank them for coming. He hugged Heather and thanked her for being his friend.

That evening, there wasn't much conversation at home. Peg sat in the living room and stared at the wall. Becky and Luke sat outside on the double-wide swing Dan had put up years before. Elliott stayed in his old room, looked at family photos, and remembered all the happy times they all had together. He was angry at how life always seemed to go off track, bringing change, sadness, and pain. He looked at a picture of the family taken on the Christmas when Kathy and Darlene were there. All his family and friends were sitting around the tree and smiling. He thought, *This is how I want to remember my dad.*

Diploma in Hand

Elliott graduated from law school two weeks after his father's funeral. Becky and Luke remained in Ohio to attend his graduation. The ceremony included long speeches from several dignitaries and faculty members. While waiting in line to receive his diploma, Elliott thought back to when he graduated from high school. Darlene told him to grab the diploma and get the hell out of there. He was in no hurry to leave now. Once it was over, he would be on his own—looking for a job and beginning the next chapter of his life.

Every facet of his life was about to change. He hoped he was ready to handle what was ahead for him. Standing on the stage, he looked out and smiled at his mom, Becky, Luke, Darlene, and Heather. They had been his security blanket through all his tough times. He wished his father could have been there to share the joy. His face lit up with a huge grin when he noticed Peg wearing a red rose in her hair.

Soon his name was called, and the diploma was the reward for all his challenging work. The remainder of the day was a sea of hugs and congratulations—along with plenty of food and drinks. He would begin to study for the bar exam the next day. By the end of the summer, he would be a lawyer.

The Same Old William

Jeff had been packing for a week prior to his graduation. He couldn't wait to get out of there and focus on his new career. The hopes and dreams he had on that first day of college to be a pro football player were only memories now. He had his sights set on working for a major television network as a sports or news reporter.

He had reached out to several network affiliates around the country and had gone out on a few interviews prior to graduating. He knew he had the sports knowledge along with a strong confidence in his ability to look at a camera and speak with conviction. During his senior year, he had taken part in several workshops that were designed to develop his on-air skills. He was thrilled when he received a phone call to arrange a second interview with a network affiliate in Los Angeles. He decided to fly out to the West Coast the day after graduating.

Jeff's parents attended the graduation ceremony, no doubt in Jeff's mind, because it would provide a perfect family photo opportunity and plenty of press coverage. They hosted a formal dinner party at a country club, but they didn't invite any of Jeff's friends—only political donors and several of William's colleagues from the Senate.

In public, William bragged about Jeff and his future in television. William made an announcement that he had arranged for Jeff to join a news outlet in Washington.

Jeff stood up and said, "My father must be talking about another son of his who I don't know about. I am planning on moving to California and working out there. You must be confused, Dad. Don't worry—it happens to the best of us."

William was pissed that Jeff would belittle him in front of others, but he kept his cool and laughed it off.

When Jeff and his father were alone after dinner, William said, "First of all, don't you ever try a stunt like that in public. How dare you try to embarrass me. I forbid you to move to Los Angeles."

Jeff started laughing. "What? You forbid me? Who the hell do you think you are? This is not your choice, Father. It never was, and it never will be. You were never part of this decision. And for your information, I spoke the truth out there about you being confused. Now if speaking the truth is what embarrasses you, then I guess I did that."

William said, "If you persist with this stupid idea of moving to California, the only way I will disperse Patricia's money will be in extremely small monthly installments. You will be too old to ever enjoy it."

Jeff looked at him and laughed as loud as he could. "This has nothing to do with the money. If you think it does, then you are even more foolish than I thought. Why couldn't you just say congratulations and good luck? That's what a normal father would have done. I guess I just answered my own question. You have never been normal." Jeff walked to the bar, ordered a vodka tonic, and handed it to his mother. "This is for you. Thanks for coming."

The next morning, he was on a plane headed to Los Angeles.

A New Adventure

Los Angeles was a totally new world for Jeff. The weather, the people, and the traffic were completely different from what he was accustomed to. His interview went extremely well. He was called back the next day with a request for second interview. During the interview, he met with executives who were in higher positions. They watched his demo tapes and had him test on camera with other reporters to see if there was any chemistry.

Thinking that the interview was over, Jeff started to leave. One of the executives stopped him and began asking questions about his father. They wanted to know how his relationship was with William. They also wanted to know if he would be able to separate family loyalty and fairly report the news.

Jeff said, "There is no loyalty in my family. In fact, I find that question hilarious. We are connected in name only, nothing else. I have never agreed with my father's misguided conservative policies. However, that would never be a factor in my reporting. If it comes down to reporting less-than-desirable news about my father, I would hold myself as a professional reporter. If you are looking for a different answer, one that showed a perfect family with love and respect, then you are interviewing the wrong guy. I have a gut feeling that my father has spoken to one or all of you prior to this meeting. Let me make myself perfectly clear. My father will have no part in my life going forward. If these answers lower my chances of landing this job, then so be it. This will be the last time that I will discuss my family with you." He shook their hands and thanked them for their time.

He was asked to wait in the next room for a few minutes. When he was called back in, a man introduced himself as the chief executive of the network. He had flown out from New York to take part in the interview.

Their Los Angeles weekend news show was taking a beating in the ratings. The entire show was being revamped, and they were looking for the right person who could take the show to the top of the ratings.

The CEO told Jeff that he was watching him from the other room as he was being interviewed. "I like the way you looked directly at these guys and didn't hesitate to tell them exactly what you were thinking. Yes, you were correct to believe that your father called me this morning. He was trying to derail your chances of landing this job. I told him that the last person in the world I would ever take any advice from would be a Washington politician. I told him the conversation was over, and I hung up. I believe we have found the right guy in you. I am offering you the job. I hope you accept it."

Jeff accepted and was told that the contracts would be ready in a couple of days. He was free to have his attorney look them over before he signed them.

On his way back to his hotel, he decided to call his mother to tell her the good news. He knew she would tell William as soon as she got off the phone. Laura told him not to do anything that would embarrass them. She offered no congratulations or words of encouragement. He hung up the phone, sat on the hotel bed, and he thought about Elliott. He wished he could call him and tell him the news. Since Elliott had never made any attempt to reach out to him, he was most likely a distant memory for Elliott. He should have been happy and celebrating. Instead, he was lonely, sad, and thinking of what could have been.

There were a million things that Jeff needed to get done now that he was going to live in Los Angeles. After he signed the contracts, he met with Liz, his new co-anchor. The two of them went out to lunch to get better acquainted.

During lunch, Liz asked, "Are you married—or do you have a steady girlfriend?"

Jeff took a long sip of his drink and decided it was now or never. He needed to say those three little words—the words he had never said to anyone since Elliott. Three small words would be the biggest words he would ever have to say: "I am gay."

He waited for the sky to part and the world to crumble around him. Instead, Liz didn't bat an eye. "Well, you must have a boyfriend or a husband. I would like to meet him."

He said, "No, I don't. I am alone."

"Well then, we need to find you one. Don't forget where you are now going to live. Several of the employees at the network are gay or lesbian. I will introduce you to them." She gave him advice for where to look for an apartment or condo. She offered to help him find his way around the city and show him where the gay establishments were located.

When lunch was over, Jeff had a tremendous feeling of accomplishment. He laughed when he thought about how great it would have been if his parents were at that table when he told Liz one of the family secrets. He didn't think there would be enough vodka in the place for his mother. For the first time in his life, he could be himself.

Moving On, More Changes

With his heart beating loudly in his chest, Elliott slowly opened the letter that would change his life. In a moment, he would learn if he had passed the bar exam. As if the weight of the world fell off his shoulders, he saw the word: Passed. He let out a yell, hugged his mom, and let out another yell.

Peg was smiling from ear to ear.

When Elliott said that he wished his dad could have been there for the big day, Peg said, "He *is* here."

During law school, Elliott had been working as a paralegal at a small law firm in Cleveland. The two partners had promised Elliott a position as an attorney when he passed the bar. He happily accepted. He was now an attorney who walked to the office every morning, brief case and coffee in hand.

Peg lost all interest in the pizza shop after Dan passed away and offered to sell it to Darlene and Heather. They explained that ever since they took a vacation to Los Angeles last summer, they wanted to move out there. Darlene could transfer with the post office. Luke would be able to get Heather hired where he worked. Becky and Luke were there to help them find their way around. They would be moving in a few weeks.

Peg's sister lived in San Diego and had been also been recently widowed. She convinced Peg to sell everything and move in with her. Elliott and Becky agreed that it would be the best move for her. The weather would be perfect, and Elliott teased her that she could get the good Mexican weed easier there than in Ohio.

Peg sold the restaurant to a national pizza chain. She would have preferred to sell it to someone locally, but the chain made her an unbelievable offer that she couldn't turn down.

One afternoon, her real estate agent called and asked if she could bring a young couple to look at the house.

Peg said, "I need time to get ready and leave before you arrive."

The agent said, "You don't have to leave. It will be okay if you are there."

Soon, a young couple with a girl around ten and a boy around eight arrived with the agent. As they walked through the house, Peg couldn't help but notice how this family resembled her own family when they moved there. The parents said the children would be attending the Catholic school. The house was in the perfect location to walk to school.

Peg told them everything about the school and promised to call Sister Mary Therese and arrange a meeting for them. After they left, Peg accepted their offer.

Elliott took Darlene and Heather out for a beautiful dinner the night before they left for California. He told Darlene that he probably would not have made it out of high school if it hadn't been for her help and friendship. They laughed, reminiscing about the good old days, and remembering how they first met. They talked about the fun they had in the school plays and at the pizza shop.

Darlene told Elliott that he and his family were the biggest part of her life. Without them, she didn't know where she would have ended up. "I know you are still in love with Jeff. I hope you never forget him. What you had was something special. I never liked him that much. I always thought he was just a spoiled, rich, good-looking football jock who was out for himself. I have come to realize that I never gave him a chance. I want to apologize to you for the way I would always bad-mouth him."

After dinner, the three of them hugged, cried, and said goodbye.

As they walked away, Elliott shouted, "Hey, girls, don't think for a minute that I won't be out there for a vacation. You can't get rid of me this easy."

One Last Look

Elliott helped his mom pack and said that he would take care of the final arrangements on the sale of the properties. Peg shipped everything to San Diego, and then she was on her way west. Elliott had to hand over the keys to his parents' pizza shop. That place was more like a home to him than a restaurant. He had spent most of his life in that place. He wanted to take one last look through the house before he handed over the keys to the new owner.

As he walked through the house for the last time, he looked at the empty kitchen where he and his mother had many of their deepest talks. In the dining room, he thought about that horrible night when William and Laura took Jeff away from him. He hoped the new family would never have to go through anything like that.

As he was driving away, he decided to take one last look at the town. He drove by the high school, got out of the car, and walked over to the fence that overlooked the football field. It was the same fence he stood by when Jeff was practicing. In his mind, he could see Jeff and the team on the field. He looked over at the bleachers and remembered all the Friday nights watching Jeff play. He looked at the school and remembered how he and Darlene would walk the halls between classes, catching up on all the gossip. He remembered all the times he would pass Jeff in the hallway. He also thought about the hate—and everything that went along with it. He got back into the car and drove away.

There was a stop sign at the end of the street. He had to turn either left or right. In front of him was the Catholic grade school. He parked and noticed two young boys sitting on the same curb that he and Jeff sat on at the end of that first day of school. The difference now was that these two boys weren't talking. Instead, they were looking down at their phones.

He thought it was sad how things had changed. He kept thinking about that first day of school and how that day ended up being the one that would take Jeff and him on a journey that neither one could have imagined. He turned left and drove away for what he thought would be the last time.

CHAPTER 8

It's a Small World

Jeff said, "This feels like the first day of school—and I'm the new kid."

Liz hugged him and assured him that he would do great. He felt nervous and excited at the same time. The opening story was about a local high school football player who had been injured during a game the night before. That made Jeff feel more confident since he knew how that kid felt and what he was going through.

In an instant, the opening music was over, and he was looking at the red light on the camera as Liz introduced him to Los Angeles. Jeff started the segment, and within a few minutes, he felt like he had been doing it his entire life. When the first show was over, calls started coming into the station. The viewers were voicing their approval of Jeff and his performance.

The station manager told Jeff that he knew he was a winner during their first interview.

Jeff beamed with pride, and his beautiful eyes were shining brightly again.

That night, Jeff poured a glass of wine, went out to the patio, and began to process what had happened since he moved to Los Angeles. For the first time in his life, he was his own person. He did not have to hide in the shadows anymore. Nobody cared if he was gay—something he wished for all those years prior. He was comfortable going out to gay bars and restaurants and not having to make excuses to anyone.

He had started making a new circle of gay friends and was even dating a few different guys—not just for anonymous sex in some dark area of town but out in the open. They wanted to know all about him, and he told them about himself. He accepted that his relationship with his parents was more like a business transaction than a loving family. Even though he was three thousand miles away, he still needed to be careful of William. That fear did not take top priority. He was always jealous that Elliott had such a loving family, and now he had to make his own family with new friends and a boyfriend or more.

After his second glass of wine, he began thinking of Elliott. No matter what was happening in his life, it always came back to wanting to share it with Elliott. So many things had changed since they were together. They were no longer the same two people. They were grown adults and living their own lives.

William could not hold any more threats over Elliott or his family. Jeff could care less if anyone disclosed his relationship with Elliott. He even thought that Elliott would welcome it. So much time had passed, and Jeff knew that Elliott had moved on with his life—and probably never gave him a thought anymore.

Jeff was finding his new life, but he was sad that Elliott would not be a part of it. The doorbell rang, and five of Jeff's new friends walked in with gifts of wine and beer, ready to celebrate his success on his first day on the air.

OMG—It's Him!

Darlene and Heather were eating dinner when the evening news came on. Darlene was clearing the table as Jeff was being introduced. When she heard his name, she let out a scream and ran to the living room to verify what she thought she heard.

Heather didn't know what was going on.

Darlene said, "Oh my God. It's him. It's Jeff. I can't believe it. He is here in fucking Los Angeles."

Heather said, "Wow, he's hot—no wonder Elliott hooked up with him."

Darlene grabbed the phone and called Becky.

"I see it. I'm watching the news. I can't believe it. He is here in Los Angeles. I need to call Elliott and tell him."

Darlene yelled, "Absolutely not. We can never tell him. Your brother has never completely gotten over Jeff, and this will set him back years. Promise me you won't tell him."

They made a commitment to keep it a secret.

Heather said, "Darlene, what will happen when Elliott comes to LA on vacation, isn't he bound to see him?"

Darlene said, "I didn't know. This all too sudden."

They watched the entire show.

Heather said, "You know, Jeff is very good-looking, and so is Elliott. Can you imagine how hot they were together—naked and sweating?"

Darlene made a face and said, "That's disgusting. That's so wrong, but it's true."

In Plain Sight, Yet No One Cares

Jeff was completing his third weekend on the show when a news story came across his desk by accident. The story was about a student at a local high school who had committed suicide. Liz had a nephew, Christopher, in the class and he left a detailed message for his aunt.

The studio receptionist mistakenly left the message on Jeff's desk. Jeff read the message and apologized to Liz for reading her message.

She said, "Why don't you investigate the story and make it yours? It may end up being nothing. You know how high school kids react to everything. Then again, it may end up being an extremely important story."

Liz called her nephew and arranged for him to meet with Jeff at her home that evening.

Christopher said, "The student who killed himself was not openly out as gay. Some students found out he had been seeing a boy from another school. They saw him holding hands with this boy at the movie theater one weekend. Everyone assumed that because it was dark in that theater, these two guys felt that no one would see them and felt safe enough to hold hands.

"The next day at school, the bullying began. David was ridiculed in homeroom. As the weeks went on, the insults kept coming his way. Gay slurs were written on his locker, and he was thrown into the showers fully clothed. Before the bullying started, David was on the basketball team. He was considered one of the team's best players. After a couple of weeks, he quit the team. One by one, he lost his friends. He became withdrawn and eventually stopped coming to school.

"The story going around was that David went through his parents' medicine cabinet and took a handful of his mother's antidepressants. He was found in their basement holding his basketball jersey. His note said he couldn't live anymore being ashamed about who he was. He felt that it would be better for everyone if he was dead.

"This type of bullying has been going on for a long time at the school. If anyone is even suspected of being gay, they become a target. The school will do nothing about it."

Jeff asked Christopher to explain the school's response.

Christopher said, "Gay bashing was a low priority for the school, and complaining never seems to help. It is better to just keep quiet."

Jeff thanked Christopher for his candidness and assured him that he would investigate. "I will keep your name out of it."

Christopher said, "You don't have to do that. There are so many students who want this to end, and I am not ashamed to be the one who reported it to you."

That night, Jeff couldn't stop thinking about Christopher's story. In a way, he had listened to his own story. Of course, his story didn't end in suicide, but it could have. He wondered how many kids were going through the same thing at that very moment. He knew firsthand about everything they had to endure. The hatred needed to stop, and he needed to find a way to help get it stopped.

Jeff spent the next day developing a plan to effectively handle the story. He understood that he couldn't walk into that school angry. He needed to act as a professional reporter and find out the facts. He kept comparing what Christopher told him to what he and Elliott had gone through. He started to focus on how he handled his own guilt and shame—and how he always felt like the victim. A new realization started to stare him in his face.

He began to reason why he felt that way. He knew his father was the cause of most of his pain. He began to accept the fact that he could possibly be responsible for more than he ever dared to admit. That may be the reason why he had been so unhappy. Even though he had become comfortable with being gay, he never reconciled the path he took to get there. Why couldn't he stand up to William? Was it easier to play the sad victim? He could have found a way to get back to Elliott, but it was easier to fall prey to his father's threats.

Jeff realized that he wasn't a victim; instead, he was a coward. A coward always blames others, and that was exactly what he had done all his life. That was the reason he lost Elliott. It was easier for him to hide in the cracks of bigotry and believe their hate was right and he was wrong. *That was exactly what these students are going through every day. David killed himself because it was easier than trying to stand up and fight.*

Jeff arranged a meeting with the school superintendent, the principal, and a few teachers. He explained in detail what he had been told about David and the gay bashing and bullying. He asked, "Do any of you think there is any truth to all of this?"

None of them answered.

Jeff said, "If you don't want to comment, it's okay. I will write the story using the student's perceptions. Either way, this story is going to be told on the air. If it's not true, then you have nothing to worry about. If it is true, you must be the ones to fix it."

The superintendent abruptly ended the meeting.

Several hours later, Jeff received a call from one of the teachers. "Yes, it's true—and everyone knows it's true."

Several other teachers and students contacted him too. Through his investigation, Jeff found out there had been two other student suicides from gay bashing.

For weeks, Jeff devoted almost all his time to the story.

David's parents were grateful that he wanted to tell David's story.

David's father said, "We never suspected there was something wrong going on with our son. He loved sports. He had so many friends. He also had a gentle side to him that everyone loved. His mother and I can't get past what he did. We never thought he would be afraid to talk to us. We would have understood and continued to love him. We failed him."

David's mother said, "I am angry at all of his so-called friends. They used to hang out here in our home with David. When they found out that he was gay, they turned their backs on him—and that's when he needed their friendship the most. I will never forgive them."

When Jeff showed the finished product to his boss, he was told that it needed to be the lead story on the news. He warned Jeff that there would be some backlash, but the facts would speak for themselves.

After the story aired, a sort of revolution happened at the high school. Parents demanded change in the school's administration, which eventually happened. Guidance counselors at the school were instructed to take any complaint from a student seriously and report it immediately to the school board.

Jeff received a few threatening phone calls and emails that accused him of "trying to make heroes out of faggots." None of that mattered to him. He did what he felt he needed to do.

The story was picked up nationally, and Jeff received a congratulatory call from the network president in New York. He said, "We need to get you here to work in New York someday. This is where you belong."

The Education Secretary

Jeff decided to cash in on some of his father's political capital. He used William's name to get directly in contact with the secretary of education. She was a woman of great wealth, and she had no educational background. Many people considered her not qualified for her position.

He flew back to Washington and arranged a meeting in her office. He brought a camera crew to record the meeting. At first, all she wanted to talk about was his father and how proud she was that he was a strong champion for the Republican platform.

He cut her off and said, "I am not here to talk about William. I am here to talk about something important. There is a major epidemic in our nation's school system concerning gay bashing." He showed her all the data he had compiled and statements from students and parents from across the country.

She laughed and said, "You're crazy. I saw your fake news story on television. All I will tell you is that if there are one or two gay kids complaining that they are being bullied, they need to change their lifestyle and grow up. It's a tough world out there."

The camera crew looked at each other in disbelief.

Jeff had to hold back his emotions. When he caught his breath, he said, "Great. I am not surprised by your answer. I figured you would hold the line and not stray from the administration's religious, anti-gay platform. However, I also thought you might have some compassion. I guess I was wrong. So that I am perfectly clear, Madam Secretary, I intend to report the answer you just gave me on national news. I believe that every student and parent—and more importantly, every voter—needs to hear your views on this."

She immediately picked up the phone and called William. She smiled and said, "Your father will stop this bullshit. He is on his way over here as we speak."

Jeff laughed. He said, "Well, perhaps he can take you out to lunch when he gets here."

William walked in and said, "What the hell are you doing here?"

Jeff smiled and said, "That's none of your business, Father—unless you are here to persuade the secretary to form a committee to investigate school bullying. This will go one of two ways. You can do nothing and take the heat from my story—along with all the damage control both of you and the administration will have to do—or you both can be heroes and form a task force to investigate and stop all kinds of school bullying. I must tell you, Dad, watching you in action all these years has taught me quite a bit. It's your call."

The secretary suddenly changed course and apologized to Jeff for her rude answers. She assured him that she would investigate immediately. She asked him to sit on his story until she could give him some answers.

He agreed but warned her that he would not wait long for an answer. As he was leaving, Jeff looked at his father and said, "You see, there is always more than one way to solve a problem. Present the facts, offer more than one solution, and presto, things get done and no one gets hurt. You should try that sometime, Dad. It's not always about you. Oh, before I forget, tell Mom I said hi."

As soon as he was out of the office, Jeff headed to the nearest bar. It took a couple of drinks to get his hands to stop shaking. He couldn't believe what he had just done. He felt relieved that something might change to help these students. He felt empowered. For the first time in his life, he knew he had accomplished something important—for the students and for himself. In a strange way, it helped him put together some of the pieces of his own life. The most important part of his life was still missing, and it was the one piece he didn't know how to fix.

Nigel

It was strange for Elliott not to be able to drive back home to see his mom and Darlene on weekends. It had been almost a year since they moved to California. Although they talked often on the phone, he deeply missed the personal contact.

He had settled comfortably into his new job. He was working long hours, helping clients negotiate contracts, and dealing with other issues. The partners looked at Elliott as a future partner. Clients began sending the firm referrals because of their interactions with Elliott. That was something that did not go unnoticed by the partners.

For relaxation, Elliott joined the Gay Pride bowling team. The team bowled every Sunday at a bowling alley across the street from Elliott's apartment. Living so close made his home the logical choice for the team to meet on Sunday mornings. Elliott served the team Bloody Mary's before they headed down to the main floor for brunch and then across the street to bowl. After bowling was done for the day, they would head over to one of the bars that always had a spread of food for the bowling league. Sundays began to be referred to as "Brunch, Bowling, and Bar Sundays."

One Sunday, they bowled against a team that was new to the league. One of the members of the new team was an attractive young man whose name was Nigel. Elliott was intrigued by his beautiful accent and asked where he was from.

Nigel said, "I moved here from Spain with my parents when I was eleven."

Their conversation lasted for most of that afternoon. At times, the other team members had to remind them that it was their turn to bowl.

Nigel explained that he was not out to his family. Being devout Catholics, he felt they would never accept him if they found out.

Elliott said, "I understand where you are coming from and how you feel. Trust me, I was there once in my life, and that was not fun. It got better after I told my family. My mom told me that she had already known I was gay, and guess what? I still had my loving family after I came out."

Nigel said, "That's you and your family. It isn't my family. I know it will not end up in a happy situation if I come out to my them."

At the end of the day, they made plans to meet up on Friday for dinner. After they exchanged phone numbers, Nigel gave Elliott a warm kiss. Elliott kissed him back and said, "I am looking forward to Friday."

All week long, Elliott kept thinking about Nigel. He kept telling himself not to overthink anything. Friday was going to be for dinner and a few drinks—nothing more.

The first date went extremely well, and they made plans for a second date the following weekend.

Elliott and Nigel started seeing each other every weekend. Nigel would always stay overnight at Elliott's apartment. He was worried that his parents would stop by unannounced at his apartment. Even though Elliott understood Nigel's reluctance about coming out to his family, he couldn't help but compare it to how he and Jeff had to always hide from Jeff's parents and the public. He didn't want to get himself into the same dilemma. Elliott was proud of who he was.

All his attempts to persuade Nigel to come out fell on deaf ears. Elliott worried that their relationship didn't have much of a chance of succeeding with the wall between them, but they saw each other for the better part of a year.

One evening in bed, Nigel said, "I love you."

Elliott was caught off guard. He did not feel the same way about Nigel. Whenever a relationship got to that point, he would start thinking about Jeff. It was time to explain a few things about his relationship with Jeff, and he knew Nigel would be the one getting hurt. After telling Nigel all about Jeff, he added, "I cannot continue living in the shadows of your fear of coming out. If this means I will be alone, at least I will be alone but proud and true to who I am."

Nigel accused Elliott of leading him on for sex and nothing more. "Elliott, you are living in a fantasy world, waiting for some imaginary long-lost lover to ride up on a white horse and take you away. How can you be so coldhearted? I just opened my heart to you, and instead of doing the same, you spit in my face. You are a lonely, lost man, and you will probably be that way for the rest of your life." Nigel got dressed, and Elliott tried to give him a hug. Nigel pushed him away and said, "Go to hell. I never want to see you again."

Elliott opened a bottle of wine, sat on his couch, and thought about how he always took a couple of steps forward and then a step backward. Jeff was the reason he was always going backward. He felt like a coward for not dealing with his feelings about Jeff. It was time to make some changes in his life, but he was unsure about what those changes should be.

The Fork in the Road

Peg once said, "In your life, there will be times that you come to a fork in the road. It happens to everyone. At first, you won't know why it's there or which way you should go. You may be stuck there for a moment. Then, when you least expect it, the answers will come to you—usually in the form of new opportunities. You need to be smart enough to recognize when these opportunities appear and then make the best decision you can."

He did not know when or what answers would come to him. He trusted his mom, and Peg was seldom wrong. He was brokenhearted that he had hurt someone again. He knew he could not go on doing that.

Several months after his fallout with Nigel, Elliott was approached by a partner of his law firm. They were planning to open an office in Phoenix, but the plans were put on hold after the other partner died in an automobile accident. Elliott was asked if he had any interest in moving to Phoenix to open the office and run it. If he wanted it, the partnership would be his.

Elliott started laughing. He apologized and said, "I was thinking about something my mom told me a long time ago about a fork in the road and opportunities."

The partner said, "Take a day or two to decide. After all, this is a major move for you."

That evening, Elliott thought about the offer. He would have to pack up and leave his entire life behind in Ohio. In reality, a great deal of his life had moved away when Becky, Peg, Darlene, and Heather moved to California. It would result in a substantial monetary increase for him, and Phoenix was only a six-hour drive from California. He would be able to visit everyone more often.

There was nothing keeping him in Cleveland. He called the partner and accepted the offer. Elliott called his mom and shared the news. Peg told him how proud she was of him and how the move could be the step forward he was looking for.

He called Becky and then Darlene. Becky reminded him on how hot it was in Phoenix. He reminded her how warm it was there during the winter.

Darlene was elated and offered to help with his move in any way they could. "Fantastic. Heather and I have been to Phoenix several times, and we have become good friends with a few lesbian couples who live there."

Elliott said, "I will be flying out to Phoenix in about ten days to look for a place to live. I also need to make sure the Phoenix office is on schedule to open."

Heather grabbed the phone from Darlene and said, "We will drive to Phoenix to help you find your way around and help you find a place to live. It will be the perfect time to introduce you to our friends."

Elliott spent most of the flight going over the plans for the office. Before he checked into the hotel, he drove around to check out the city. It all looked strange to him, but he had a deep feeling that it was where he belonged.

Old Friends Together Again

As he was checking into the hotel, Darlene and Heather quietly walked up behind him and yelled, "Guess who?" They hugged while looking each other up and down. It had been quite a while since they had seen each other.

Elliott smiled and said, "Darlene, I love your new haircut. It makes you look much younger. I don't think I have ever seen you without that damn baseball cap."

Heather replied, "That haircut makes her look so butch."

Elliott laughed and said, "Thank you. That's what I was thinking, but I still like it."

Not a word was mentioned about Jeff living and working in Los Angeles. The three of them spent two days looking for an apartment. Elliott finally decided he would buy a condo. Owning a home would be an investment in his future and the first steps in putting down roots for his new life.

He found the perfect place. It was located within a couple miles of his new office. It also had easy access to the light rail. He would be able to ride the train to work every day instead of dealing with all the traffic. He made an offer and was delighted that it was accepted. The wheels were in motion. In a few short weeks, he would be living in Arizona.

The night before flying back to Cleveland, he took the girls out for dinner. While eating, Darlene cautiously brought up Jeff. "Remember how we used to hang out at your parents' pizza shop with Jeff?" Elliott smiled and said, "Yeah. Those where good times. I can't believe some of the stupid things the three of us used to talk about. Remember all the plans we made for our future? Funny how things really end up. Never once did we imagine celebrating my new job and my new home in a restaurant in Phoenix."

He called the server over and ordered another round of drinks. "I always wished Jeff had been there with me on my life's journey, but that was not in the cards for us. It has taken me a long time to accept that fact. Even though it has been a long time, I still think of him often. I know, in a way, I will always love him." Elliott turned to Heather and said, "Have you ever met Jeff? I am sure you have seen him on television. I understand he is quite the celebrity around LA."

The girls looked at each other, not saying a word.

"Come on," Elliott said. "Did you think I didn't know anything about him? The internet makes for a small world. I always knew he would become successful. I am extremely happy for him. Jeff and I will most likely never see each other again. I don't think I even want to see him again. He never reached out to me, but I never reached out to him either. It is what it is—and nothing more. Oh, by the way, thanks for trying to protect me."

Darlene changed the subject by suggesting they explore some of the gay bars that were located not far from his new condo.

The next morning, Elliott left for the airport.

As Darlene and Heather were driving back home, Heather said, "Even though Elliott said he doesn't want to see Jeff again, something in the way he sounded and looked told a different story."

Darlene said, "I saw the same thing. He can't fool me. He has never stopped wanting to be with Jeff."

Elliott spent the next several days getting everything packed and ready for his move. He decided to sell his car and buy a new one once he was settled in Phoenix. Going through everything in his apartment, he came across a picture with Jeff from the night of the homecoming dance. *Damn. We did look good together. Oh well, that was then. Now it's time to look forward and not backward.*

He threw the picture in a box and continued packing.

CHAPTER 9

It's Sunday—Must Be Time for Brunch

Because of his father's phone call, Jeff was late to the station party being held in his honor. After a year on the air, the weekend news—with Jeff as co-anchor—was number one in the local ratings. The network bosses in LA and New York knew that Jeff was responsible for getting the show to number one. He was the star of the weekend news, and they wanted to show him their appreciation.

William had called to demand that Jeff find a girl and get married. "My colleagues in the Senate are beginning to ask questions about why someone as good-looking as you, and as successful, is not yet married. A wedding with plenty of publicity would help strengthen my commitment to fight for morality and the conservative issues we need for the next national elections."

Jeff's attempt to stay calm during the call ended when his father announced that he was considering running for the presidency, and any rumors connecting Jeff to an immoral lifestyle needed to be stopped now.

William said, "It wouldn't even matter if you didn't love the girl—you just need to get married. I will release all of Patricia's money to you as a wedding gift."

"You are a fucking idiot," Jeff said. "Do you mean a marriage like yours and Mom's? A marriage with absolutely no love or affection. Perhaps Mom could teach my wife how to drink and keep her mouth shut. Is that what you mean? Listen to me very carefully, Dad. I have no intention of ever helping you become president. I only worry because I know there are many idiot voters who have bought into all your lies, and they could get you elected. Won't that be a great photo family for your collection when your gay son joins you on the inaugural stage? I wouldn't miss that for the world.

"And since you brought it up, I have my attorneys looking at Patricia's will. They assure me that you won't have to worry about her money much longer. When I get it, I may even donate all of it to the Democratic candidate." He laughed. "I have better things to do than sit there and listen to this bullshit. Trust me, I will certainly let you, Mom, and the world know when, who, and if I get married. By the way, it will be a fabulous wedding—you can count on that."

William said, "Think twice before you throw any threats at me again. I can ruin your life. Do you think that because you managed to get that fucking education secretary to go along with you that you can talk to me like this? Watch your back."

"Go to hell" Jeff said. "Leave me alone, and I will leave you alone. If you want a war, it won't be difficult to find things against you. A word to the wise, Father, watch your back!"

A few days later, Jeff was getting ready to go on the air when he was told that he had a visitor waiting for him in the lobby. When he got downstairs, he was shocked to see his mother. Laura told him she had been meeting with governors' wives and Republican officials on the West Coast to help William's chances at the nomination.

Jeff said, "My show is about to start. You can wait here until it is over."

"I think it's disrespectful that the studio doesn't have a VIP lounge I can wait in."

Jeff rolled his eyes and said, "There is a bar across the street. You can wait there."

After the show, Jeff asked what she thought about seeing him on TV.

She said, "It was okay."

He invited her to come over to his condo.

She said, "No. I don't think it is appropriate for me to be seen there. An upscale Beverly Hills restaurant would be a better place to be seen."

He said, "You must have misunderstood me. I meant to say I have plenty of vodka at home—so you wouldn't be lonely."

She motioned for her driver to pick them up.

At the restaurant, she said, "I understand you need to live your life as you see fit. I don't understand that type of lifestyle, but I hope you are happy."

Jeff was at a loss for words. He had never seen this side of his mother and wondered where it was coming from.

She said, "Your father doesn't know about this visit. You don't owe me anything. I know that. I haven't been the perfect mother to you, far from it, but please keep your lifestyle as low-key as you can. Please don't let it interfere with your father's ambitions. Don't do it for him. Please do it for me." She motioned to her driver to escort her out. "I'm sure you can find your own way home."

For the first time in his life, he realized that she could think on her own. Perhaps there was some feeling in her as a mother. *Why didn't she ever show me that when I needed it the most?*

He didn't have any further conversation with his parents for several months after Laura's visit. Jeff tried to avoid reporting on his father during the news. He always asked Liz to do those segments. He felt it was best to keep William's career as far away as possible.

Their ratings continued to stay at number one, and the station offered Jeff the coveted anchor spot on the popular morning show. "Morning in LA" was considered a major stepping-stone for a career with the national network. It allowed Jeff to work Monday through Friday and have weekends off.

As expected, he was a hit on the new show. That popularity also made him somewhat of a celebrity around the city. Whenever he went out, everyone wanted to be his friend. He loved all the attention. It made him feel like he was back in high school and the star of the football team. He was extremely careful about who he became friends with. He understood from past experiences that who he hung out with could have a negative impact on him. The experience with Tom left him with serious trust issues.

William challenged every move Jeff's lawyer made to secure his rightful inheritance. Finally, through persistent work from Jeff's lawyers, a judge ruled that William had no right to withhold the money. He issued a court order to release it to Jeff immediately. His father's attorney advised William that a long fight with the courts would be harmful to his presidential campaign. The only thing the public would see was a father fighting with his successful son.

Laura convinced her husband to drop the fight and give Jeff what was his in the first place. Jeff became an extremely wealthy man. He had absolutely no ties to William except in name. He would not speak one word to help his father. He still had so many unresolved issues and scars caused by William. He knew his parents would someday realize what they did to him. He didn't understand yet, but he would find a way to make things right and get even with them.

Brunch

On Sunday mornings in West Hollywood, friends get together for brunch. It's a day of catching up with friends, being seen, and networking. Most restaurants are extremely crowded, and the wait time is usually around forty-five minutes. Often, Jeff would be recognized by the host, and he and his friends would get priority seating. That made him uncomfortable, and he soon declined all those offers, preferring to wait like everyone else.

One Sunday morning, he noticed a familiar face sitting with three women. They were drinking mimosas, eating, and laughing. He was surprised to realize it was Darlene. He turned away, not sure if he wanted her to see him. After all, it was another place and time when they were friends. It was possible that she would not even recognize him. Perhaps she wouldn't want to see him—let alone have some sort of conversation with him.

As he was being seated, he had to pass by her table.

Darlene looked up and said, "Jeff? It's me, Darlene. Do you remember me?"

He said, "Of course I do. How are you?" They hugged and made some small talk. Two of the women at the table excused themselves, and Darlene introduced Heather to him as her soon-to-be wife and asked if he would like to join them.

Jeff apologized to his friends, explaining that she was an old high school friend from Ohio. They hugged Jeff, said hello to Darlene and Heather, and told him to enjoy his brunch. They would catch up with him later.

There was so much to talk about, and it was awkward to begin. Heather told Jeff that they watched him every morning while getting ready for work. "We have been in LA for quite a while now, and you're the first celebrity we have met."

Jeff smiled and thanked her for the compliment. "I'm just Jeff who reports the news. I'm not a celebrity." With the introductions and small talk out of the way, he ordered breakfast for himself and a round of drinks for the three of them.

They talked about everything. After an hour, Jeff finally asked about Elliott.

Heather said, "Thank God. It's about time someone asked about him. I was ready to bring his name up if one of you didn't. If Darlene won't tell you anything, don't worry because I will tell you everything."

Darlene said, "Elliott is a successful lawyer and is a partner in his law firm."

Jeff asked, "Is he involved with someone or married?"

Heather said, "Hell, no. He's not with anyone—none of them ever worked out. He won't admit it, but he's been secretly waiting for you. Oh, by the way, he lives in Phoenix."

Darlene gave Heather a look that could kill.

Heather said, "Darlene, you know as well as I do that Jeff needs to know. This game has been going on too long for anyone's good."

Jeff was smiling with tears in his eyes. "I miss him very much. I always have. As much as I have tried to get him out of my mind, I just can't."

She Says What's on Her Mind

Darlene said, "Are you involved with anyone?"

Jeff answered, "Yeah, right. They also never seem to work out for me. I am not with anyone."

Darlene said, "Elliott is my dear friend, and I won't stand by and let you or anyone else interfere with his life to further hurt him. All the hell your father put him through, along with all your shit, has left deep scars. It's taken him a lifetime, and he still is not fully healed. Don't you dare try to hurt him again."

Jeff stood up and said, "Who do you think you are? Suggesting that I would try to hurt him? I know you never liked me—and never passed up an opportunity to tell that to Elliott. Did you ever give any thought to what I had to go through? Really? At least he had you and his family to help him pick up the pieces. Do you want to know who I had? I had shit, yeah, you heard me, shit to help me. An evil father and a drunk, cold mother. I had to do it all myself. And guess what? I don't think I ever picked up all the pieces of my life. I understand that you are his dear friend, but don't you dare go there with me.

"I was so embarrassed and hurt about what my father did to both of us and to Elliott's family. Time after time, I wanted to run away and go back to him. I was so afraid of what my father would do. If you believe William would not have done more damage, then you're sadly mistaken. I hoped that when I sent flowers to Dan's funeral, Elliott would have found it in his heart to get in touch with me. He never did, so I assumed that he had moved on with his life—and wanted me to stay away. I will tell you and anyone else that I have never gotten over him. It looks to me like you never understood what we had and how much we loved each other."

Heather said, "Elliott held the card you sent to the funeral throughout that day and keeps it on a shelf in his living room. I can't tell you if you should or shouldn't try to see him. All I can say is that he has a good life, but he has never been completely happy."

Jeff got up and said, "I think I better leave before I say something I will regret. I knew it was a mistake to stop and talk to you. Darlene, you haven't changed at all."

Darlene started crying and said, "Jeff, please sit down and stay. I didn't mean to say those things. I was just thinking about Elliott. I assure you that I don't believe that you would hurt him. We all just assumed that when you moved to Washington—the rich, spoiled kid of a politician, living the life of private schools and parties—that you erased all of us out of your life."

Jeff said, "That is so far from the truth."

Heather got up, went to the bar, and returned with three shots of the best whiskey the restaurant sold. "Here. Drink up. Please, both of you, calm down."

Darlene asked for Jeff's cell number and sent him a text with both of their numbers. "Please call us anytime. We need to get together again very soon."

Jeff said, "Please do not tell Elliott anything about meeting me today. I need to process all of this in my own space and time."

Darlene assured him that they would not say anything to Elliott or Becky. "Please take my word on that."

Jeff got up, drove to the beach, and stared at the water for hours.

Decisions

That night, Jeff replayed everything he heard from Darlene and Heather. He realized that he had to make a decision that would change his life. He had two choices. He could get in the car, drive to Phoenix, and hope that Elliott would at least talk to him—or he could just forget it and leave everything as it was.

Years ago, it would have been a no-brainer. He would have dropped everything to get to Elliott. Now, after all this time, perhaps Darlene was right. He could end up hurting Elliott and himself in the process.

A couple of days later, an idea came to him that he had never considered before. He decided that it was the one he needed to pursue.

On Saturday morning, he set out on his mission. The sun was shining, and there wasn't a cloud in the sky as Jeff pulled out of his garage. He headed to the Starbucks on Santa Monica Boulevard to meet Heather for coffee. He asked her to come alone.

He ordered a hot green tea with honey and sat down. As he began to think that Heather was not going to show up, she walked in, ordered a chocolate latte, and sat down with him.

She apologized for being late. "I needed to wait until Darlene left for work before I could leave the house. I am beginning to like you. I like the mystery you bring. So, why are we meeting in secret?"

Jeff smiled and said, "Even though we only met one time, we have some sort of connection. I like that. Darlene, understandably, is too close to Elliott to have an open mind. She is Elliott's faithful protector, and I am now the outsider asking too many questions. I need an address. Can you give it to me? I believe you will understand why I need it."

Heather started laughing and said, "You're a smart son of a bitch, and I mean that in the best of ways. I really like you, and I will help you." She sent Jeff a text with the address and assured him that it was their secret. She promised never to disclose it to anyone, especially Darlene. They hugged, and she said, "Good luck—and let me know how it worked out when you get home."

Am I Making a Mistake?

Jeff programmed the address into his BMW's GPS, and in a few minutes, he was finding his way to Interstate 5. As he was driving, he kept asking himself if he was doing the right thing. It could all blow up in his face, but he kept driving.

Before he knew it, the GPS signaled him to take the second San Diego exit. The street took him alongside the ocean with beautiful homes lining both sides. Finally, the GPS said, "You will arrive at your destination at the next right." He took a deep breath and pulled into the driveway. With his heart beating loud and hard, he rang the doorbell. As the door opened, he recognized the white flower in that beautiful long hair and that long colorful dress.

Peg said, "I've been waiting for you for a long time. I'm glad you're finally here." She invited him in and led him to a patio that overlooked the ocean. She introduced him to her sister and opened a bottle of red wine.

Jeff explained how sorry he was about Dan's passing. "And I want to apologize to you for all those nasty things my father said that night to you, Dan, and Elliott. I remember how you tried to hug me and how my father told you to keep your hands off his son. I want you to know that you are the mother I always wished I had. I want to thank you for allowing me to be part of your family—even though it was only for a brief time."

Peg went over and hugged him like he was her son. "You never have to apologize for what your father did. I hope he apologized to you. You will always be a part of this family. Elliott has never forgotten you. He has tried so hard to get past it, but he can't completely do it. I suspect that you feel the same, and that's the reason you are here."

"You're so right," he said. "It should never had ended the way it did. I need to make it right. I'm afraid Elliott will not want anything to do with me—or even want to listen to me. My family and I have hurt him so much, and the last thing I want is to hurt him anymore. I am a successful person at the top of my game at work. I figured out how to navigate around my parents, but I can't figure this out. I'm asking for your help."

Peg said, "Do you remember when Elliott had the lead in *Our Town*? I saw you sitting all the way in the back, trying not to be seen. I knew then, beyond a shadow of a doubt, how you felt about my son. I just couldn't say anything. It was not my place to interfere. That was for you and Elliott to figure out. I can't tell you what to do. All I can say is to follow what's in your heart. I know Elliott better than anyone. Trust me—he won't hate you. As it was then, this is for you and Elliott to work out for yourselves.

"Out of respect for Elliott, I won't give you his address or phone number. He will give it to you if he wants you to have it. I will tell you this. He loves living in Phoenix. He has an illustrious career and some good friends. I talked to him yesterday, and he told me that next Friday evening, he is meeting friends at one of the bars on Seventh Avenue. There is some sort of retro disco party going on that night, and he told me I should go because it was my kind of music back in the day." She gave him a wink and a smile. Jeff understood what she meant.

They said their goodbyes, and she hugged him and kissed him on his cheek. "Don't be a stranger," she said with another wink.

On his drive back to Los Angeles, Jeff found one of the answers he was looking for. He understood what he needed to do to get on with his life. Whatever the outcome would be, it was long overdue.

CHAPTER 10

An Emotional Revelation

Elliott dropped his beer, and it sprayed all over him and his friends. One of them grabbed his shoulder, and Elliott pushed him away. "Stop it. Leave me alone."

His friend said, "What the hell is wrong with you?"

Without taking his eyes off the door, Elliott said, "My whole life—my whole fucking life—that's what's wrong with me." His friends noticed Elliott staring at an extremely good-looking man standing at the front door.

Jeff was wearing a tight, bright white tank top and he was staring directly at Elliott.

One of Elliott's friends said, "Wow, that guy is hot—no wonder you're staring at him."

Elliott shoved his friend and yelled, "Shut your fucking mouth. You don't know a damn thing. I know who he is. His name is Jeff."

Jeff made his way through the crowd and stood directly in front of Elliott.

The light from the overhead strobe was bouncing off everyone, and Donna Summer's "I Feel Love" was blaring from the speakers, with every beat pulsating through Elliott's head.

Elliott looked Jeff directly in the eye, and without saying a word, he pushed Jeff away, fought through the crowd, and walked out to the parking lot.

Elliott's three friends looked at Jeff, and one of them said, "I don't know who you are, or what just happened, but we have never seen Elliott act this way. What the fuck is going on?"

Jeff pushed his way toward the door and looked around for Elliott.

Elliott's friends followed him outside.

Jeff turned to them and said, "Don't get involved. This has nothing to do with you."

Elliott was leaning against the side of the building, and tears were streaming down his face.

Jeff tried to say something—,

Elliott shouted, "No! You don't get to say anything—not one fucking word—until I say what I need to say. Why the hell are you here? Do you have any idea what you being here is doing to me? I am so goddamn mad at you. I am mad at your fucking father and all those motherfuckers who thought they knew what was best for us. Most of all, I am so fucking angry at myself for not having the balls to stand up to you. I have wasted all these years trying to get you out of my mind and out of my heart. Just when I was beginning to think that possibly I have put the past behind me, here you are, and it brings it all back to the front of the line.

"Do you think I didn't know where you live or where you work? I saw your national news report on high school bullying. As I watched it, I couldn't help noticing how happy you looked. I was so proud that you had found your place—and angry that I couldn't be there to tell you that. Oh, yes, everyone, especially Darlene, tried to keep everything about you from me. I always knew you would become successful. I wish you knew how many times I wanted to drive to LA and go up to you and tell you how much I still loved you. Reality is that I am a coward, afraid that you would tell me that you had forgotten all about me and that there was no room in your life for me. That would have made it final, and I don't think I could have survived that. All these years I have wasted, all for nothing. You know something? At first, when you left, I began to believe what everyone was saying about us. It was just a passing phase, or the one fucking one I hated the most, we were just kids experimenting. Trust me, Jeff, it wasn't an experiment for me. The older I got, and the more I grew up, the more I knew what it was for me and how I felt for you. You can't tell me that you didn't feel the same because I felt it in you, and I saw it in your eyes every time we kissed.

"All those boyfriends I hurt along the fucking way, for a long time, I blamed that on you. It was all my fault for not dealing with you when I should have. Always waiting for you to come back—and so afraid you never would. Hotshot, rich, spoiled Jeff, the star of the team who could do no wrong. That is what Darlene kept telling me all these years. I refused to listen to her or believe it. I just kept waiting. So, for whatever fucking reason you're here, if you're just visiting Phoenix and happened to come into this bar, and by chance, you saw me. If that made you feel awkward, and you thought you needed to come over and say hi, well, you did, and I hope you're fucking happy about it." Elliott pushed Jeff backward, crying and yelling, "Why didn't you come back for me? I hate you for letting me fall in love with you." With every push, he kept yelling louder. "I hate you. I hate you. I hate you." With one last push, Jeff fell back on to the hood of a car.

Elliott froze, unable to move or say anything. It was done. All the emotions he had held so deep inside for so many years suddenly surfaced. He felt as if he was stuck inside a tunnel all those years, not being able to get out. He could see the end, but it always felt like a dream, trying to run and not moving, just running in place, over and over again. Now he was moving, running for his life. Every word he shouted at Jeff moved him closer to the end of that dark tunnel. When he caught his breath, he realized that he was out. He had crossed over the line. For the first time in his life, he didn't care where he would land. The important thing was that he finally did what he needed to do. He exposed himself as honestly and passionately as he could. Totally exhausted, he sat down on the curb.

Jeff was pacing back and forth like an expectant father. He was in tears. "I didn't just happen to be here tonight. I came here looking for you. What you just said is exactly what I have been feeling for all these years. I also hate my father for what he did, and I hate that school for how they treated you afterward. Every fucking step I took in my life, you were always there beside me—in my mind and in my heart. The day I broke my leg, as I was lying in the hospital, I wanted to call you and tell you I needed you. You have been in my heart since that first day of school when we first met. I also wasted all these years. I kept blaming my father for all of this. Yes, he started it all, but I was also a coward for not standing up to him when I should have. I am angry that my parents never understood how I felt. It was only when I realized that I control my own destiny, and that it doesn't matter what anyone thinks, that I knew that I needed to come for you. I was also afraid that you would not feel the same anymore. It was easier for me to keep the dream alive in memories and not face the reality that you had moved on with your life. I knew instantly when I saw you tonight how much I still love you. I am so sorry for everything we both went through. I just want to hold you again and hear you tell me everything will be all right. Please don't hate me. I need you to look me in the eye and tell me that I was wrong for coming here tonight. If you believe it was a mistake, I will get in the car—and you will never see me again. I am fucking in love with you. Do I need to stand on this car and shout it to everyone? I am so sorry I caught you off guard like this. I just didn't know what else to do. I'm waiting—so tell me your answer. Tell me, damn it, tell me."

Elliott stood up and grabbed Jeff's head and kissed him like their first kiss in the ravine.

They stood there for a few minutes, not saying anything and just looking at each other.

When Elliott caught his breath, he said, "You did not make a mistake by coming here. I need you, and I have never stopped loving you."

One of Elliott's friends walked over and handed them a few napkins to wipe their eyes and suggested that they go inside and have a drink. By then, half of the bar was outside and had heard everything they had said to each other.

The security guard and the bar owner were outside to make sure it would not escalate. The owner was a friend of Elliott, and he asked if they wanted to go inside and have a drink.

Jeff assured him that there was no trouble and thanked him for being concerned.

Elliott didn't want to go inside. "It's too crowded and loud. I just need to go home."

Jeff said, "I need to go back to the hotel. I have caused enough commotion here tonight. I think we both need some alone time with our thoughts to digest all of this. I will walk you to your car."

Elliott said, "I didn't drive tonight. I need to order an Uber."

Jeff said, "I will drive you home. Come on. My rental car is over there."

Totally exhausted, they left the bar and headed to Elliott's condo.

A Bit Awkward

Elliott opened the garage door with an app on his phone, and Jeff parked beside Elliott's new BMW.

Jeff said, "Nice, you have a new Beemer. Being a lawyer must be lucrative."

Elliott laughed and said, "It pays the bills. What kind of car do you have?"

Jeff said, "I also have a BMW. Great minds think alike."

As soon as Elliott opened the door, they were met by Elliott's Jack Russell terrier.

Elliott said, "Jake rarely warms up to strangers, so don't take it personally if he ignores you and growls at you."

Jeff fell in love with Elliott's home. Everything was first class and in its place. He told Elliott how comfortable it felt. He studied all the photos of Peg, Dan, Becky, and Luke. "Who is this little guy?"

Elliott beamed with pride and said, "That's my nephew, Mark, Becky and Luke's son."

Jeff paused at a picture of Peg and Dan at the pizza shop. "This really brings back memories for me. I always loved going to your parents' restaurant. They always made me feel like I belonged there. I envied you for having such great parents. I'm sorry about your father. He was an outstanding man and a great friend." Jeff noticed the small florist card tucked in the corner of that picture. "I almost didn't send those flowers. I wasn't sure if it was appropriate for me to do that."

Elliott said, "Those flowers were the best thing anyone sent to the funeral. They meant a great deal to me and my mom. I wanted you there with me so badly during that time. My father talked about you just before he died. He told me how sorry he was about what happened to us. He told me to never give up hope. Looks like he was right."

Elliott suggested having some wine. "Jeff, tell me something about your life as a television star."

Jeff said, "This career was my second choice. I always wanted to play pro football. When I broke my leg, I was glad that I had this to fall back on. It's all working out for me now. I couldn't ask for a better working relationship with everyone at the studio."

When the first bottle of wine was finished and the second one was opened, Elliott said, "I am curious about how you knew I would be at that bar tonight?"

Jeff explained about how he ran into Darlene and Heather. He said, "Darlene is so protective of you and didn't offer many details, but Heather, who thinks somewhat differently, told me everything—much to Darlene's objections. Please don't fault Darlene. She is your loyal friend, I always knew that, even when we were in high school. Don't ever lose her. Heather and I really hit it off. We have the same type of connection that you and Darlene have. I asked her for your mom's address. I needed Peg's approval to pursue finding you. After all this time, a phone call would not be the proper way to reach out.

"I was so nervous. I was afraid she would slam the door in my face. I almost turned around and went back home. I am glad I didn't. As soon as she saw me, she made me feel welcome. Your mom is a first-class lady. While protecting you, she found a way to let me know where I should look for you. Her smile and wink told me I had her approval."

Jake jumped up onto the couch and put his head on Jeff's lap. Elliott moved Jake over and put his head on Jeff's lap. They had said everything they needed to say that night. They fell asleep on the couch and did not wake up until Elliott's phone went off at seven. Darlene was texting to see if he was okay. Elliott's friends had sent her a few texts to let her know some deep shit was going down with Jeff. Elliott replied with a text: "It's all good."

Jake let Elliott know that he needed to go outside for a walk. Jeff asked if he could take a shower, and Elliott showed him where everything was in the bathroom.

When Elliott got back with Jake, he went into the bathroom to shave. Jeff had just started his shower. When he noticed Elliott, he opened the shower door and pulled him in. They both stared at each other without saying a word.

As the water showered down on them, and the steam rose around them like fog coming in from the ocean, they started kissing. Elliott started applying soap all over Jeff's body. He kissed Jeff's chest and nipples, and Jeff started to lose control. He grabbed Elliott, pushed him against the wall, and began sliding his tongue down from Elliott's lips to his hot, wet body. Giving him every inch he had to offer, he didn't stop until he was deep inside Elliott. When they both exploded into a sensation that neither one had experienced since the last time they were together, they looked at each other and said, "I love you."

Let's Talk

Elliott and Jeff spent that first weekend by themselves, talking about their lives. Everything was on the table for discussion. Elliott told Jeff about all the boyfriends he had over the years and how he was the one who would always break things off. He took Jeff on a tour of the city, stopping by his office to show him where he worked.

Jeff asked about the several awards behind the desk, many of them from gay pride associations.

Elliott said, "I have worked with the gay community in Cleveland and here in Phoenix. I find comfort in helping gay students with their legal situations. If I can, I do not charge these clients very much—if anything. Many of them have very few resources, and several have been thrown out of the homes by their parents. I guess it is my way of giving back to a community that was there for me when I needed them the most."

Jeff hugged Elliott and said, "While you were helping, I was hiding. I wasted so much time."

Elliott reminded Jeff about the news story about the high school gay bashing. "It was remarkable. You helped so many people with that story. Don't ever say you were hiding."

Jeff talked about how devastated he was when he broke his leg and had to give up football. He had so much difficulty accepting, exploring, and adjusting to a gay lifestyle. He laughed, telling about how he would discreetly leave the fraternity house and sneak away to a gay bar.

Elliott said, "You are not alone in this type of behavior. There are so many in our community who fear being found out. They hide almost every aspect of who they really are. Think about it, Jeff. You had resources, yet you still had a tough time accepting all of this. What if you didn't have everything you had. How would you have handled it then?"

Jeff said, "In college, that was my problem. I never thought about anyone but myself. I lived in a fantasy world, thinking I was the only one who had problems. It certainly wasn't the perfect college experience I planned on having."

Jeff said "One time, I was drunk and brought this girl I didn't know over to the fraternity house. If that wasn't stupid enough, I took her up to my room. I thought that if I had sex with her, that would be proof that I was not gay. The good thing that came out of that was that I never questioned myself again about whether I was straight or gay."

Elliott laughed and said, "Is there video of that encounter? I would love to see it."

Jeff smiled. "Thank God, no!"

"Jeff, what's going on with your parents?"

"Well, they are still alive. Not much more to say except they haven't changed. My dad will probably run for president. If he wins, he will try to destroy our community. Trust me on that. I don't have much contact with them. They only come around when it pertains to some political thing. I want to keep it that way. They never gave me what I needed growing up, and I will never give them what they want now. It's too late to repair the damage, and I don't have the desire to even start."

They took Jake for a walk in the park, stopped for lunch, and did some shopping. While eating lunch, they ran into two of Elliott's friends from the bar.

Elliott said, "I am sorry for leaving without saying anything." He introduced Jeff, and Jeff also apologized for the night before.

They suggested getting together for dinner.

Jeff looked at Elliott and said, "That's up to him—if he invites me back. We still have many issues to resolve."

Elliott hugged Jeff and said, "I might not let you leave."

All or Nothing for Me

Driving around the city, Jeff put his hand on Elliott's knee. When they realized it, they both smiled. That evening, they stayed home and talked. They were no longer children, and only they could determine how they should, or even *if* they should, navigate going forward together.

"Jeff, most people thought there was something mentally wrong with me because I kept talking about you. I was even starting to believe them and considered getting professional help. I was lucky to realize that I wasn't wrong then, and I know I am not wrong now. Last week, I could never have imagined that we would be here having this conversation. I want you to know that I am ready to be in this 100 percent—I always have—but only if that's what you truly want. This can't be, and I won't allow it to be, a casual friendship with benefits. It's all or nothing for me, babe. I know Darlene will have some opinions, but I will handle her in my own way."

"Really?" Jeff said. "Darlene has opinions?"

Elliott laughed. "Some things never change. You thought she was opinionated back in high school? Well, you haven't seen anything yet. As she gets older, she tells it like she sees it even more than before. I ignore half of what she says—so please don't take everything she says to heart. She is a good kid down deep inside."

Jeff sat up and asked Elliott to look at him. "I want you to understand something. I have been fucked up in my head for a long time—ever since I had to move away from you. Whenever something went wrong for me, or even when things went well, I always thought of you, and that would always help me. I am not perfect, far from it, but I will do my best to never fail you again. I can see a long road ahead for us with rewards, challenges, and obstacles. The biggest obstacle is my parents. I will never allow my father to threaten you or harm you again. I want this relationship and a life with you. This is not a game for me. I love you and want both of us, together, to discover all the future holds for us. For me, it's also all or nothing. The stakes are too high, and the damage would be too severe if we fuck this up a second time. Let's catch our breath and take this one day at a time. To answer your question, yes, this is truly what I want."

Elliott cooked breakfast on Sunday morning, and Jeff mentioned how impressed he was.

"Honey, I didn't grow up in a restaurant for no reason. My parents ensured that I would know my way around a stove."

Jeff started laughing. "I doubt my mother even knows where the stove is, but she taught me how to fix a mean drink."

Jeff needed to return the car and head to the airport. As they hugged and kissed goodbye, Jeff made Elliott promise that he and Jake would come to LA the next weekend. The weekend that started out with so much raw emotion was ending with a sense of peace and great promise for the future.

That night, Elliott's only thoughts were about what had occurred over the past two days. For the first time in years, he was at peace with his feelings. He didn't have the desire to call his mom or Darlene to tell them all about it. What transpired over the weekend belonged only to the two of them. He didn't need anyone's approval, and he didn't want their opinions. There would be time for all of that in the days and weeks ahead.

Jeff was relieved and happy that he took the chance to go to Phoenix. He understood it could have ended in a disaster. He knew he made the right decision. He was so deep in thought during the flight back to Los Angeles that he didn't notice they had landed. For the first time in his life, he was at peace.

CHAPTER 11

Making the Pieces Fit

The drive between Phoenix and Los Angeles became routine for Elliott. He would not schedule any clients or court hearings for Friday afternoons. That way, he could be on the road by one o'clock. On the weekends that Jeff came to Phoenix, he would head to the airport as soon as his morning show was over. It usually took longer to get to the airport than for the flight to Arizona.

During the week, they would call each other often and make plans for upcoming weekends. They visited Sedona, spent a romantic weekend at Big Bear, and went swimming in the ocean. They spent time with Becky, Luke, and Mark. They visited Disney Land with Darlene and Heather. One weekend, they drove to San Diego and spent time with Peg. She could not have been happier for the two of them. They also enjoyed the weekends when they just stayed home together. They were getting to know each other again and beginning to heal the damage. They understood they still had unsettled issues that needed to be dealt with.

Jeff still had to deal with his parents. He knew that they would never approve of Elliott, but he didn't care about what they thought. He wasn't going to tell them anything, but he wasn't going to hide Elliott from them or anyone else. They would have to find a way to get over it. Elliott had to deal with Darlene and her views. She was not convinced that the relationship was a good thing for him. She said, "Dude, you need to be careful. Jeff could end up hurting you again." Her attitude around Jeff bothered him tremendously.

Elliott and Jeff invited Darlene and Heather out for lunch, and Jeff tried his best to have a conversation with Darlene. She would only respond vaguely—or not at all. Elliott could see how frustrated Jeff was getting.

As they walked back to the car, Heather noticed a drugstore. She said, "I need to stop in there and buy something for the house."

Jeff said, "I'll go with you."

As soon as they were in the store, Elliott said, "What the fuck is wrong with you? How dare you treat Jeff that way? He is trying everything to be friends with you. You treat him like shit, and I am sick of it."

She looked surprised and said, "I will try to act better around him. I promise I will try harder—just for you."

When Jeff and Elliott arrived home, Jeff said, "I don't want hang around Darlene if she is going to act like she hates me. I am really trying to give her the benefit of the doubt, but she needs to meet me halfway."

Elliott told Jeff about their conversation. "She promised me she would try, but I have my doubts. There is something bothering her that I can't figure out."

Jeff said, "Well, she needs to figure it out soon. I am not going to take this shit from her much longer."

The next weekend, after Elliott arrived at Jeff's condo, Jeff said, "I have invited the girls here for dinner tonight. I need to confront Darlene. She needs to understand that I am not going anywhere. If she can't deal with this, then it's going to be her loss."

When dinner was over, Jeff opened another bottle of wine and asked all of them to have a seat in the living room. He said, "Darlene, I need you to tell me the truth. What is it about me that bothers you? It is evident that there is a wall between us. It's been there ever since we were in high school. This must end, and the wall needs to come down."

Darlene said, "I don't trust you, Jeff. I never have. I have always considered you to be exactly like your father. I know that if he demanded you to stop seeing Elliott again, you would be out the door as fast as you could. You are a spoiled rich kid who looks out for only yourself, just like your father. What will you do with Elliott if your father runs for president? Bring him with you to the Republican National Convention and parade him out on the stage? I don't think so. You would be out of here so damn fast. You're afraid to go against your father. I know it's wrong for me to think this way, but I can't help it. It's on my mind all the time."

Elliott jumped up off the couch, almost knocking over the bottle of wine. "Shut your mouth, Darlene. You don't have a right to say these terrible things."

Jeff said, "Darlene, please continue."

Heather stood up and said, "Darlene, what you just said is not the real problem. You and I both know what the real issue is. Since you won't talk about it, I will. I don't care if you get mad. This needs to end now. Darlene, you are jealous of Jeff. You always have been. Every time Jeff is in Elliott's life, or Elliott talks about him, you begin to feel second best. I have seen that in you all these years. You resent that Jeff is taking all of Elliott's time, and you are afraid that Elliott won't need you as a friend. This has nothing to do with Jeff's parents. That is just a smoke screen. The issue you have is not with Jeff. It's with Elliott. If both of you don't find a way to figure this out, it will grow like cancer and destroy all of us. Elliott, have you ever had a heart-to-heart conversation with Darlene about your own friendship?"

He replied, "No. I just assumed that she knew that no one could come between us. I love you, Darlene, and you will always be in my life—just as you have always been there in the past. Jeff and I are working on a commitment to each other the same way you and Heather have. I need you to understand that you will be there with us all the way. Jeff cannot, and will not, ever attempt to take your place. In a strange way, we are all in this together."

Jeff walked over to Darlene and gave her a big hug and a kiss. He said that she was part of their family and that he loved her.

Crying, she hugged him back and then hugged Elliott. "I am sorry I didn't understand." She sat down next to Heather and said, "Thank you."

Heather's Story

Jeff and Heather took Jake out for a walk, leaving Darlene and Elliott to talk by themselves.

Jeff said, "Thank you. Now I get to say, 'You're one smart son of a bitch, and I really like you.'"

Heather laughed and told him that it took one to know one. "Trust me. You and I will never come between those two. Don't forget that we are the stepchildren in that relationship. Elliott and Darlene will find their way through this. I am not worried. How long does it take this dog to pee? I could use another glass of wine."

"Before we go back, Heather, I want to ask you something. You can tell me that it's none of my business, and I will accept that. You never talk about your family. Why is that?"

Heather stopped and sat on a wall in front of a house. "Well, my dear friend, it seems that we have a few things in common. My family is as miserable as yours, possibly even more so. My father is an alcoholic who never showed any of us any love. My mother is a religious fanatic. I think she belongs to a religious cult. My brother is in prison for armed robbery, and my sister is just a miserable bitch with a motherfucker of a husband. My parents threw me out of the house during my senior year of high school. They told me that I would burn in hell for being a lesbian—and they had no plans of going there with me. My sister's husband tried to rape me on their wedding day. He held me down and told me all I needed was a real man. I kicked him in the balls and ran out of the room. When I tried to tell my sister about it, she accused me of lying. Both have forbidden me to ever see their two children.

"I never told the school that I was living in a rented room and waiting tables at a greasy spoon for most of my senior year. Shall I go on? Jeff, I understand what it's like to grow up in a dysfunctional family. That's why I believe you and I have this connection. Elliott has what most consider a perfect family, and Darlene, even though her parents are divorced, still grew up with a loving mother. As much as they love us, they could never fully understand what it's like to never get any type of acceptance from their parents. You and I know how that feels. I never want to hear from my family or see them again. I found my way out of that mess. That's my story, and I'm sticking to it. Any more questions, lover boy?"

Jeff said, "Nope. You're a remarkable young woman, and I'm glad you are in my life. Thank you for sharing your story with me. Let's get back before they drink all the wine or kill each other."

Heather said, "The hell with the wine. I want one of those delicious-looking cannoli I noticed in your kitchen."

CHAPTER 12

The Night Belonged to Elliott

Darlene tossed around the idea for several weeks. She had been contacted by a friend from high school concerning a class reunion that was coming up. The school was looking for former classmates to speak during the event about what they had accomplished since graduating. Immediately, she thought of Elliott and his work with the LGBT community. She was proud of how he donated his time and advice to those who could not afford attorneys. Over the years, she had witnessed the positive impacts of this.

Although she had not forgotten how cruel the students were during those final two years, she thought it would be a way for him to show them how successful he had become. She submitted Elliott's name, address, and reasons why she thought Elliott should be selected. Knowing he would probably not even consider going, she felt that being selected would help heal some of his open wounds. She decided not to tell him.

A few days later, Elliott received an invitation to the event. He laughed at the thought of being invited to the reunion—let alone as a speaker. He tossed the letter on his kitchen table and didn't give it another thought.

Darlene called to ask if he had received an invitation to the reunion.

He said, "Yes. I can't believe the school would even think I would spend time and money to sit with them like we have been best friends forever. You go if you want but count me out." It was Friday, and he needed to pick up Jeff at the airport. He cut the phone call short, putting the conversation out of his mind.

Elliott ordered pizza and wings for dinner. He and Jeff wanted to hit a few bars later, so ordering out was easier. While Elliott was taking a shower, Jeff cleaned up the kitchen and noticed the envelope from the high school. As tempted as he was to read what was inside, he resisted. As soon as Elliott was out of the shower, Jeff said, "I noticed you have a letter from high school on your kitchen table."

Elliott said, "Can you believe it? They want me to speak at their stupid reunion. What a joke."

Jeff said, "Why don't you go? Show those bastards that you made it despite their bigoted minds. I'll go with you if you want. That will for sure make some of them shit themselves."

Elliott said, "I am most angry about how they forgot about you as soon as you left the school and the team. You were the champ and made the school shine with all those wins on the field. You gave the school a name. Then, overnight, you were nothing to them. Did anyone ever get in touch with you to see how you were handling all that shit?"

"Nope—not one call or letter. I think we should both go and laugh about how fat everyone is and how good we look. Let's give them something more to talk about."

Elliott said, "You're right, Jeff. I want them to know all about my career. I think this is what I need. In fact, the more I think about it, the more I want to go. I want all of them to see us together! I need to call Darlene and tell her that we are going."

Jeff arranged for one of the writers at the station to help Elliott craft a speech, ensuring that all his successes thus far would be represented. Elliott wanted to make sure the main topics would be about his work with the LGBT community. Everything else would fall into place as soon as they saw them together.

Back to Ohio

On the flight back to Ohio, while sitting in first-class seats, Jeff said, "This will be my first visit since William took me to Washington. We both need to be prepared for the good and bad memories that will surface. I am a lucky guy because the best memory I have of that town and that school is you—and you are sitting next to me. That's all that matters."

Elliott smiled and said, "Same for me."

Darlene and Heather were staying at the same hotel in Cleveland. They made plans to meet for dinner and drinks. In the morning, they would leave early and drive to their hometown to see if anything had changed.

Heather was impressed at the Cadillac Escalade the guys rented.

Jeff said, "Honey, we are going to arrive in style."

In the morning, Elliott wanted to stop by a florist to purchase some flowers for his dad's grave. He bought four white roses, one for each of them, and a red rose for his mom.

As they placed the flowers on the headstone, Darlene said, "I can still see Dan making pizza after pizza in that kitchen. He always took the time to explain how to make the best pizza."

Heather said, "And don't forget about that sauce. It was his pride and joy. He kept that recipe secret."

Elliott laughed and added, "Even from my mom. He never told her the recipe. I don't think he knew Grandma Estelle gave my mom the recipe years ago. Mom just played along." He reached into his pocket and pulled out two shiny stones he brought from Arizona. "I read that putting a stone on a grave was a sign of respect. The stone will last after the flowers wilt away."

The three of them left Elliott alone at Dan's grave for a few minutes.

As soon as he was back in the car, they headed to see the pizza shop. It was sad to see that it wasn't there anymore. In its place, there was an Olive Garden and a chain drugstore.

Darlene said, "Where do the kids hang out on weekends?"

Jeff said, "Right there. Look at your phone—that's how they hang out now."

They headed to the street Jeff used to live on. His parents had sold the place and bought a condo in Columbus. Two young boys were playing in the front yard. Jeff asked Elliott to stop for a minute. "I hope that whoever lives there now has more love and compassion for each other than my family had. Elliott, do you remember that afternoon we spent in my parents' bedroom?"

Elliott smiled and said, "I will never forget it. I also remember when we were walking down the steps and realized your grandmother had come home early. I almost peed my pants when I saw her."

Darlene asked, "What the fuck were you doing in Jeff's parents' bedroom?"

Heather laughed and said, "Think about it, Darlene. What the hell do you think they were doing—playing cards?"

Jeff and Elliott looked at each other and smiled.

Elliott did not want to drive past his old home. "Becky told me that the new owners painted the house an unusual color. I want to remember how it looked when I grew up there."

On the way back to the city, Jeff said, "Pull into the next driveway. It's our old grade school. Come on. Let's get out. Follow me."

Even though it was Saturday, the school doors were open. They walked in and looked around.

Elliott said, "Wasn't it much bigger then?"

The cafeteria looked the same as when Elliott sat next to Jeff on the first day of school.

A woman asked if they needed help finding something. To their surprise, it was Sister Mary Therese. She was the principal. When Elliott hugged her, she said, "Take your time looking around."

Jeff asked everyone to go out to the front of the school. "Elliott, it's the curb where we waited for my mom. Remember?"

Elliot said, "I could never forget that day."

Jeff handed Darlene his phone, took Elliott's hand, and sat down on the curb while Darlene took pictures.

Jeff smiled and said, "This was worth the whole trip." He turned and kissed Elliott.

Darlene said, "We need to start heading back to the hotel to get ready for tonight."

Getting Ready

For the reunion, everything had to be perfect. Jeff and Elliott had facials and manicures at the hotel spa. Next came the haircuts and shaves. With eyebrows trimmed, haircuts, and perfectly radiant skin, they headed up to get dressed. They had purchased new suits earlier in the week in Beverly Hills. The suits were tailored to perfectly fit their extremely tight bodies. Each of them would wear new Rolex watches, which Jeff received from the network for all the success on his shows. To finish off the look, they had purchased Italian shoes.

Elliott remarked on how good Jeff's suit made his crotch look, leaving nothing to the imagination. "Should I be jealous? For sure, others will notice."

Jeff looked Elliott up and down and said, "No. Everyone will be looking at how hot you look. Make sure you take that jacket off sometime during the evening. Let everyone see how your pants fit your ass perfectly."

They headed down to meet the girls in the bar. Heather looked stunning in a short sequined black dress and heels. She had her long red hair done up just right. Darlene shined in a black almost tuxedo-looking suit with a pair of red sneakers and a red tie. The four of them looked like a million bucks.

Elliott suggested getting the valet to bring up the car.

Jeff said, "I will take care of it." When he got back to the bar, he said, "Okay, we are all set to go."

In front of the hotel, a black limousine was waiting for them.

Heather asked, "Where is the rental car?"

Jeff smiled and said, "I told you earlier that we are going to arrive in style. Get in before the champagne loses its fizz."

It's Now or Never

The reunion was being held in the brand-new gymnasium. The reunion would be the first event there. Pulling up to the school, the valet motioned the driver to the front, opened the doors, and helped them out. They looked each other up and down and said, "It's now or never. Let's go in." Darlene took Heather's hand, and Jeff held Elliott's hand as they walked into the building.

They walked past all the glass cases with the trophies the school had won over the years. Jeff looked at the trophies for a moment and smiled.

Elliott stopped and looked down the main hallway. When he saw the restroom, he started reliving all the fear from the day after Jeff left.

Darlene said, "Did you ever tell Jeff what happened to you in that bathroom?"

Elliott replied, "No. I tried to forget all about it. Looking at it brings it all back." Elliott explained to Jeff how he had been assaulted by his classmates because he was gay.

Jeff said. "Let's get out of here. I may hurt someone tonight if we stay."

Elliott smiled and said, "No, I don't want to leave. I need to be here tonight. Don't worry about me. I will say what I have to—in my own way—tonight."

Jeff gave Elliott a kiss and said, "Do what you need to do. I am here for you."

A few people stopped, stared at Jeff and Elliott, and whispered to each other.

Jeff stared at them and said, "What the hell are you looking at?"

Darlene said "Come on. Let's go in and find our table."

Before they checked in, Darlene turned to Elliott and said, "Knock it out of the ballpark. Show them who you really are."

As they walked into the gymnasium, all heads turned to their direction. Elliott noticed more whispers, but it didn't matter. He was there as his own man and could care less what anyone thought.

The dinner reminded Jeff of all the dry tasteless dinners he had to endure as a kid in Washington and Florida. Because it was a private party, the school could serve wine and beer.

Heather told the server to pour the wine—and mentioned that it would be a good idea to bring another bottle over to the table. "I think we might need it tonight."

After dinner and the faculty speeches, Elliott was called up to the stage. He took a long sip of wine, looked at Jeff, and said, "Here I go. Wish me luck."

John Mudzyn

Standing on the stage with his speech in hand, Elliott looked like he belonged on the cover of a magazine. For several moments, he didn't say a word. He just looked at everyone, slowly folded his speech, and put it back into his pocket. He didn't need a written speech—he knew what he was going to say. "Good evening. My name is Elliott. I am sure that most of you remember me as the gay guy in your class. Sitting over there at my table is Darlene. She was the gay girl in our class. I am here to tell you that we weren't the only ones. If you think we were, then you are sadly mistaken.

"I was supposed to talk tonight about what I have been doing professionally since graduation. Before I can do that, I need to talk about something else. As I said, I am that gay guy—the guy who many of you picked out of the crowd to make an example of. I'm the one who several of you in this room pointed fingers at and whispered about as I walked by. I am also the guy who a few of you in this room assaulted—just because I was gay.

"Please don't misunderstand me. I'm not here to complain; I'm here to thank you. You tried to bring me down, but that only made me stronger. You threw stones at me with your actions to make me bleed. That only made me more determined. You helped me realize that this was a battle I needed to win. It was not a win for anyone but me. Guess what? I won. If I had lost this battle, then I would have lost myself.

"Because of you, I understood that no one could ever allow me to deny who I was or who I was going to become. I was lucky. I figured it all out. I want to ask all of you a question. I certainly don't expect an answer, but I am going to ask it anyway. Why was I the one who had to figure it out? Why didn't all of you have to figure it out too? Why couldn't we have met each other halfway? None of you had to figure it out when you realized that you were straight. You knew, without shame, who you were supposed to be. I'm sure I am correct about that.

"I don't believe any of you had any idea what any gay student in this school had to go through to come to terms with themselves. So why is there a double standard? This has bothered me for as long as I can remember. I was friends with many of you until the day you heard something about me that you didn't like. To your loss, and mine, none of you ever came up to me to ask how I was doing. No one asked if I wanted to talk or just hang out? Of course, you didn't do that. You had a fear that if you were seen talking to me, you would be perceived as being gay. I was never perceived as being straight when I talked to you. So why the difference?

One person here tonight was my friend from the time we started grade school. You know who you are. When you found out about Jeff and me, you picked up your chair in English class and moved it to the other side of the room—away from me. The week before that, you were sitting with me in my parents' restaurant, laughing and having a good time—and you didn't refuse the free pizza. When it all came out in the open, you didn't want to figure it out. It was easier for you to walk away. I thank you for giving me the opportunity to figure it out. I hope you have the same opportunity someday.

"However, there is something I cannot thank you for—and will never forgive you for. I will never be able to understand why you did what you did to Jeff. Oh, by the way, in case some of you didn't notice, he is sitting there at my table. He is that hot guy who I have the pleasure of waking up with every morning. For two and a half years, Jeff was your hero. Many of you pushed your way to be seen with him. He took this school to two national championships. That is an accomplishment that has never happened again. If you forgot that, then I suggest you go out to the hallway and look at all those awards with his name on them.

"Think about this for a minute. A gay boy won those awards for you. If this school had known that he was gay on his first day here, he would never had been allowed to be on the team. I have looked at pictures in our yearbooks. Many of you here tonight are in those pictures with your arms around Jeff, in the hallways and on the football field, with smiles on your faces. You appear to be having an enjoyable time. If you only knew then what you know now, most of those good times would not have happened. Think about that.

"Perception was all it was. The media always portrayed a homosexual as looking a particular way. With blinders on, you never considered that Jeff could be gay. It's time to take your blinders off and look around at your own family and friends. Encourage conversation occasionally. You may be surprised at what you find out. Your actions helped separate Jeff and me for a long time. Even though you tore us apart physically, we never left each other's hearts. We are the lucky ones. We found each other again. As I look out at you, I can't help but think that most of you have children who are at or nearing the same age we were when we attended this school. I hope, for their sake, that some of your bigoted, hateful perceptions have mellowed.

Please think about what you did to Jeff and me when one of your children tells you what you don't want to hear. It will happen—trust me on that. Perhaps they will have better memories of their years in this school. For their sake, you need to figure it out.

"My life is complete now. I have beside me the only one I have ever loved. I wish that same kind of love for all of you. I have a wonderful career that allows me to help underprivileged people navigate through hate and bigotry. I also have a beautiful home, and my dog, Jake, who never judges me. I also have something extremely important to me. I have lifelong friends in Darlene and her soon-to-be wife, Heather. Without them, I don't know if I would have made it. I have a family that has always been there for me. And Jeff. Without Jeff nothing else matters.

"I have one other request for you. The next time you walk into your place of worship, take a moment to think about why you are there. Did you go there because someone told you, early in your life, that you needed to be there, and it looks good to others that you go to church? Or are you there to try to find out the true meaning of humanity, compassion, and respect for all people? Only you can answer that. I thank you for allowing me to speak this evening. I wish peace for all of you, but most of all, I wish you love. Thank you."

As Elliott stepped off the stage, there was complete silence. Some people turned their heads away as Elliott walked to his table. A few got up and left the room. Others stood up and gave him a resounding ovation. Many of them had tears in their eyes. Some look ashamed.

Darlene and Heather were both crying.

Jeff stood up, gave him a long kiss, and said, "Do you want to leave?"

"No way," Elliott said with a smile. "I want to sit here and enjoy another glass of wine."

Many open wounds were healed for Elliott that night, but Jeff still had some issues with his parents. The night belonged to Elliott, and Jeff knew that—with Elliott at his side—he could get through anything William threw at him.

Back at the hotel, the two of them had no boundaries.

Jeff gently helped Elliott out of his suit, and Elliott helped Jeff get undressed. Elliott melted under Jeff's touch, and he kissed and licked Jeff from head to toe. They ended up in positions that someone half their age would have had difficulty getting into. They stared in each other's eyes until the final explosions made them collapse on the massive bed.

They were still in each other's arms when they woke up to the bright sunlight shining in through the windows.

CHAPTER 13

Who is That Man in This Picture?

Several weeks after the class reunion, some water damage occurred in Jeff's condo. It had rained hard and steady for four days, which caused water to run down the wall in one of his closets. The contractor was scheduled to arrive on Monday morning.

On Sunday, Elliott helped Jeff take everything out of the closet and sort it all out in one of the spare bedrooms. Elliott said, "Why are you keeping all this stuff?"

Jeff said, "You're right. I don't know why I'm keeping some of this. Most of it has to go."

They started opening boxes to see what could be thrown out.

Elliott opened a small box full of old photographs and couldn't resist looking at them.

Jeff sat down beside him, and they started a journey back in time. There was Jeff's high school senior picture, which Elliott had never seen. "This one is a keeper."

There were various pictures of the two of them in junior high.

Jeff mentioned how mad he was when that girl went around and snapped the pictures of everyone in the class. Looking at them now, after so much time, he saw how handsome Elliott was even at that early age.

Elliott messed up Jeff's hair and said, "You were a damn good-looking football player."

Near the bottom of the box, Elliott came across an old photo of two men standing extremely close to one another. "Who is that man in this picture? My God, you look just like him!"

Jeff said, "You remember my grandmother? That was her husband and my mother's father. I never met him. He moved to Europe a long time ago. Nobody would ever tell me anything about him. What I know is only what I got from the photo and from this old newspaper article. His name was Mathew, and the other man's name was Calvin. After searching the internet, the only thing I found out was that he settled in Paris. It seemed to me that someone or something totally deleted everything else from the internet. Calvin could have been my grandfather's lover. I regret that I was never told anything about his life, and I wish I could have met them. Family secrets seem to be the glue that holds my family together. If they don't talk about it, then it never happened."

"Jeff, did you just hear yourself? Did you just say that you think your grandfather was gay? That's intense. If it's true, it may answer some questions about why your parents are so antigay."

Jeff said, "I know, but I have this deep feeling that I am right. If I find out more, it will lead to many more questions. I think I am afraid to know the answers, but I know I need to find out more. Let's get this stuff picked up and go for brunch."

The Perfect Gift

Jeff's birthday was coming up in a couple of weeks, and Elliott was having trouble thinking of the best gift for him. He kept thinking about Jeff's grandfather and how sad Jeff sounded when he talked about him. Elliott asked Becky if she would arrange a surprise party at her house for Jeff. Mark was in school, and she was now a part-time event planner for a Beverly Hills hotel.

She said, "Leave everything to me. It will be a grand gay affair."

On the night of the party, Elliott told Jeff that he was taking him out to dinner and then Becky had invited them over for cake. They walked into Becky and Luke's house, and no one was there. Elliott took Jeff's hand and led him out to the pool.

"Surprise!" everyone yelled.

Peg was there with her sister, and so were several of Jeff's coworkers. Champagne, appetizers, and an awesome cake were on a table that was decorated with huge vases of flowers.

Jeff said, "I have never had a birthday party. I guess that there isn't any political value in a birthday party."

Elliott held his gift back until Jeff had opened all the others.

Jeff said, "This is almost too perfect to open."

Inside were two round-trip tickets and hotel reservations for Paris.

"This is something you need to do" Elliott said. "I want to be there at your side to help you find some of those answers you are looking for."

Several of the guest started asking about the trip and what Jeff hoped to find in Paris.

Jeff explained that he didn't know what he would discover, but he wanted to find something that could answer his questions.

Peg said, "I remembered hearing about how your grandfather helped so many people with his generosity."

Jeff kissed Elliott and said, "I am the luckiest man in the world to have this man by my side."

On their way home, Jeff said, "I don't have much information about my grandfather, and it is possible that we will not find out anything."

"Then we will relax and have a great vacation. I think we have earned that. I have a good feeling that we will find out something interesting about your grandfather."

Elliott dropped Jake off at his mother's house and said, "Don't get too attached. He comes back when I get home."

She winked and said, "We'll see."

Jeff's station manager told him it was about time he used up some of his vacation time.

Heather and Darlene insisted on driving them to the airport, and Heather said, "Don't you guys dare fall in love with Paris and never come back."

Jeff and Elliott waved as they disappeared into the airport.

Paris

They spent the first three days exploring Paris. They visited as many museums as they could, ate at outdoor cafés, and had their pictures taken on top of the Eiffel Tower. The afternoon of the third day, they went to Jeff's network affiliate in Paris. Jeff had contacted them from LA. He asked if they could locate any information pertaining to his grandfather. Mathew had been extremely wealthy, and there had to be a trail to his life in Paris.

The station manager explained that Matthew lived an extremely private and quiet life in Paris and had died several years ago. He was buried in a cemetery next to the nursing home where he lived.

Elliott said, "Is Calvin buried in the same place?"

The manager told them there was no record of Calvin passing away, and he gave them the name and location of the nursing home and wished them luck.

Jeff couldn't sleep at all that night. Seeing his grandfather's grave and touching his headstone would mean so much to him. He woke up Elliott and said, "What if Calvin is alive and still there in that home? Should I try to talk to him?"

Elliott told him to relax and try to get some sleep. "Whatever happens tomorrow, you will at least have some answers. It will all be good. Just be careful. You might find out something you won't like. You're the son of a possible presidential candidate, and news of you searching around for some information on your family could piss your father off."

"I don't give a fuck about that. Let the asshole get mad. He will certainly come up with some sort of lie to cover it up. Who the fuck cares?" Jeff got out of bed and started pacing. "What is more troubling to me is my mother. Mathew was her father, and she never talked about him. There were no pictures of him in the house. It was as if he never existed. She must be the coldest, most uncaring person who ever lived. Well, next to Patricia anyway. It makes me sick that I came from these miserable people. They better hope I don't find out they had anything to do with my grandfather's downfall. They won't know what hit them if I find out they did."

As they were getting dressed in the morning, Elliott said, "Whatever happens today, I will be there with you—and we will face the news together."

They went down to the lobby, had coffee, and waited for their ride.

Jeff was too nervous to eat breakfast.

Elliott smiled and said, "Relax. I have a feeling that this will end up being a good day."

Calvin

The taxi driver pulled onto a long, wide driveway lined with perfectly manicured poplar trees and shrubs. The building looked two hundred years old, but it was in pristine shape.

Jeff held Elliott's hand as they got out of the car and paid the driver. "Let's check this place out," Elliott said with a smile. "I'll bet nobody poor has ever lived here. Look at it. It's magnificent. Look over there—it's a cemetery. The station manager was right."

They opened a massive oak door and located a nurse. Jeff tried to speak the little French he knew, but the nurse smiled and said she spoke English. Jeff handed her a piece of paper with Matthew and Calvin's names. "Did you know these men?" he asked.

She told them that she had worked there for many years and had forgotten most of the people who had passed away. She began to smile. "Oh, Mathew? Yes, I took care of him. I will never forget him. He was the life of the party and had such a beautiful soul. You must be related because you look so much like him. I always thought it was strange that no relative ever came to visit him, and he never talked about his family. His only companion was Calvin."

"Yes, I am his grandson. I never knew him, and I want to find out as much as I can about his life."

The nurse said, "Would you like to meet Calvin? He is quite old and mostly confined to a wheelchair, but his mind is as sharp as a tack. I would be happy to take you to his room."

Elliott grabbed Jeff's hand and said, "Yes! We would like to meet him!"

"Oh my God," Jeff said. "I have waited so long for this, but I don't know if I should do it. I don't want to disturb him or upset him."

The nurse said, "Trust me—you will not upset him. I know he will be happy to meet you. Come on. Follow me."

As they walked down the hallway, she told them that Mathew made sure Calvin would be looked after and would never have to worry about anything. She also mentioned that Calvin never seemed to be very happy after Mathew died. "You two look very happy, and it's time that Calvin meets you."

She took them to a beautiful room filled with eighteenth-century furniture. The walls were covered with paintings of numerous sizes and colors. She said, "Calvin is an artist. He loves to paint, and he has had several pieces displayed in galleries throughout Europe. His eyesight is beginning to fade, but that doesn't stop him from putting the pictures in his mind onto paper and canvas."

By the window, a man in a wheelchair was drawing at an easel.

The nurse said, "Calvin, you have some visitors."

Calvin turned around and began to cry. "Mathew? You look just like my Mathew."

Jeff walked up to him, shook his hand, apologized for the intrusion, and explained that he was Mathew's grandson.

Calvin said, "Then your mother is the daughter of that bitch Patricia?"

Elliott burst out laughing, and the nurse said, "I told you he is as sharp as ever."

Calvin was smiling and invited them to sit down. He shouted at the nurse to bring some wine and cheese and never took his eyes off Jeff. "We heard about you, but after what your parents did to us, Mathew was forbidden to have any contact with the family. As time went by, he seemed to forget about it. He told me it was best not to interfere. You see, that was a different time, and we weren't considered proper, moral people."

Calvin glanced over to Elliott. "Who is this handsome young man with that beautiful smile?"

Jeff introduced Elliott as his partner.

Elliott extended his hand, but Calvin said, "The hell with shaking hands! Come over here and give me a kiss. I may be old, but I'm not dead yet. Please forgive me. I need to gather my thoughts. Seeing you standing here, looking so much like your grandfather, is something I never anticipated. I am happy you are here. Please sit down. I believe that you are here looking for answers about your family. Am I correct?"

Jeff said, "Yes, you are correct. I have many questions about my grandfather and my family. I don't want to intrude on your privacy. I will totally understand if you don't want to talk about it. I have never been told anything about my grandfather. It was as if he never existed."

Calvin replied, "It's been a long time. I will be happy to explain it to you the best I can. But first, please eat and drink some wine. I think you will like this wine. It's made next door at that winery. They have been producing wine for more than two hundred years."

The Story

"Let me start. Your grandfather was an extremely wealthy man. He had several businesses all over the country. Your father began working for him while he was still in college. As time went on, William rose through the ranks and became the most powerful man in the organization next to Mathew. That was when your father married your mother, much to Mathew's objections.

"Mathew had already been elected to Congress as a Democrat. He was extremely popular and fought for the working class as hard as he could. He anonymously donated substantial amounts of money to charities every year. He never portrayed himself as wealthy, and he never thought he was above anyone else. That wasn't true for Patricia or your father. They took full advantage of all assets after Mathew began devoting most of his time to Congress.

"That was why he didn't want his only child, your mother, to marry William. He wanted her to live a normal life. Mathew knew that William would never settle for a quiet life. He liked the finer things in life too much. He was worried that William would turn Laura into a miserable bitch—just like Patricia.

"Mathew noticed that your parents were living way above their means. He didn't like how close William and Patricia had become. Your grandfather flew to California and had a secret meeting with an accountant who was not affiliated with his business empire. He wanted a full and complete audit of every aspect of his businesses, especially the ones Patricia had interests in. The audit took several months. When completed, it was evident that Patricia and William had embezzled millions of dollars from the company.

"They were smart. They hid the money quite well. When your father found out Mathew had done the audit, he knew they would be exposed. Patricia already knew about Mathew and me. She didn't care about us because she didn't love her husband. She only cared about his money and the social status it brought her.

"Your father went into damage control. He decided that Mathew needed to be exposed publicly as being homosexual—and that he had a lover. He knew Mathew would be destroyed. It was a different time. Patricia and William hired a private detective to follow us around. He took pictures of us kissing in private and holding hands over dinner.

"As soon as Mathew found out about the detective, he arranged a meeting, in his office, with your parents and Patricia. He scheduled the meeting on a Sunday, knowing that no one else would be in the building. They would be all alone, but he wanted me there as a witness. He hoped they would admit what they did. He wasn't looking for them to give back the money. He wanted an apology and your father's resignation from the company.

"If William resigned, Mathew would not press charges against them. Your father stood up, laughed in Mathew's face, and told him to go to hell. He would not resign; instead, he showed Mathew the pictures from the private detective. He warned Mathew that the pictures would be made public if he persisted.

"The argument escalated. As they were arguing, your mother started to walk out. She was crying, and she told Mathew that she was sorry, but she would not go against her husband or her mother. She walked out of the office, got in the elevator, and left the building.

"Your grandfather started to call the police, but Patricia reached over and pulled the phone cord out of the wall. She told Mathew that if he knew what was good for him, he would forget all about the audit and leave things as they were. If he didn't, she would fabricate a story that he had molested their daughter. She laughed in his face and said, 'Who do you think everyone will believe? Me, the scorned wife, or you, the queer?'

"I had never seen Mathew so angry. He grabbed Patricia's neck and pushed her against that sixteenth-floor window. He called her a motherfucking bitch and told her he could snap her neck with one twist. He screamed, 'I will laugh as I push you out the window and watch as you hit the street. I don't care what happens to me after that. Seeing you dead on the street will be good enough for me.'

"William grabbed Mathew, pulled him off of Patricia, and punched him. Your grandfather hit him back. Patricia regained her composure. She was concerned that her pearl necklace had broken when Mathew grabbed her and screamed that he was going to pay for it. Mathew laughed and told her to take it out of the money she embezzled. Patricia told him that she and Willman had paid off the account. He would swear that if there was any money missing, it would look like Mathew had embezzled it from his own company to avoid paying taxes. Your father and Patricia got up and walked out.

"I hugged Mathew and told him that none of it was worth what would certainly happen if they both followed through on their threats. I offered to go away until it all blew over. Mathew didn't say anything for a few minutes. He went over and poured both of us a drink. He gently explained something I had never realized before. He told me why he worked so damn hard building his company and getting involved with politics.

"In the beginning, it was fun and a challenge. As the company grew along with his fortune, it slowly started not to be fun anymore. He needed to find something more to do with his life. He began working with charities and donating money to causes, which gave him a new outlook on life. He knew politics would also give him more opportunities to help those in need. The one thing he strove for the most was to leave his only child a legacy that she could be proud of. He wanted her to continue his work with helping others.

"When he saw that look in her eyes and she walked out of the room, he understood that none of it mattered to her. He knew he had failed as a father—and there was nothing more he could do. I could see how defeated he was. That afternoon, we decided it was time to sell the company and start our lives in a different place—far from away from there.

"A strange series of events happened in the weeks after that meeting. The accountant was killed in a suspicious car accident. A few days later, there was a fire in his office building—and all his files were destroyed. They never determined the cause of the accident or the fire. About a month later, Mathew was contacted by the private detective. He was demanding money in exchange for the negatives. I had nothing to lose, so I went to Patricia and demanded that she figure out how to get the negatives from that detective. If she failed, I would convince Mathew to press charges against her and William. I asked her to think about how much it would cost her to fight the charges and not to forget what it would do to her social standing.

"Almost overnight, William had the negatives. The only way he would hand them over was if Mathew would sign over the company to him. William believed that Patricia owned a greater share of the business than she actually did. If it didn't happen, he would expose him as a gay congressman. He knew that would destroy Mathew. William wanted every dollar he could get out of the business.

"Mathew told him that would never happen and told him to keep the damn pictures and to do what he wanted with them. He was tired of hiding. We both knew William and Patricia would make good on their threat. Sure enough, your father and grandmother sold the pictures to some magazine. Our lives became front-page news. In the press, Patricia played the victim to perfection. She never stopped talking about how her husband left her for another man. We had no choice. We had to leave. There was no other option. We moved to France.

"Before we left, Mathew sold his company for an extremely large amount of money—but nowhere near what it was worth. Patricia had signed a premarital agreement that allowed Mathew to keep all but a few million. William tried for years to have that agreement overturned, without any luck. They were extremely wealthy from the money they embezzled, but Mathew never had them prosecuted because he didn't want to put Laura through that." Calvin took a sip of wine. "You must be tired of hearing an old man talking so much, but I hope it helps you understand things about your life more clearly."

Jeff said, "Mathew should have pushed them both out of that window. Everyone would have been better off."

Calvin said, "You look very happy together. Mathew would have been proud of you. Even though I am an old man, I can still think for myself. When William discovered you were gay, he probably was afraid that someone could connect it to Mathew and to what happened all those years ago. If this old story resurfaced, there would always be questions about his part in it. He would never be elected."

Elliott told Jeff to relax and not let any of it eat away at him. "At least you know the truth."

Calvin said, "Yes. Elliott is right. You can live your life proud and happier than your parents. That's all that matters."

The Story of the Drawing

Elliott called Jeff over to a drawing on the wall. It was a simple pencil drawing of two young men sitting on what appeared to be a curb. They were looking out at a beautiful body of water. Calvin explained that the drawing was of Mathew and him. It was how he remembered the day they first met on the boardwalk in Atlantic City.

Calvin said, "Do you want to hear that story? I know I have been talking too much, but I don't get to do that often. Once I am gone, you will never have the opportunity to hear our story."

Jeff hugged him and said, "I would be proud to know how you and my grandfather met."

Calvin asked the nurse to pour him another glass of wine, and he asked Jeff and Elliott to move in closer. He was getting tired, and his voice was beginning to fail. "Don't worry. I will be okay. The wine helps.

"Mathew was already married to Patricia and had a young daughter— your mother. Patricia and Mathew were vacationing and had gotten into a huge argument. She went home, leaving Mathew alone. I was a young, struggling artist looking to make some cash by drawing portraits for vacationers. As Mathew walked by, I noticed the deep hurt in his eyes. We talked for hours, but we didn't realize it was the beginning of a lifelong love affair.

"He would come by every day after that. We would sit and talk or sit in silence. Mathew would always put his hand on my knee while I painted. I loved when he did that. Some people find it hard to believe, but we knew on that first day that we would be together for a long time. I can't explain it better than that. We just knew."

Elliott said, "You don't need to explain it. We know exactly what you mean."

Jeff and Elliott told Calvin about their lives and struggles.

Elliott told Calvin that he couldn't imagine how much more difficult it must have been for them.

Calvin smiled and said, "Things are slowly changing, but it's much faster in Europe than the United States." He asked Jeff to take a box from under the bed. It contained several photos of Mathew. "Take the ones you want. Mathew would have wanted you to have them."

Jeff took a picture of his grandfather and one with Mathew and Calvin on a beach in Italy. He called the nurse in, handed her his phone, and asked her to take pictures of the three of them.

Elliott said that Jeff and Calvin should be alone in the pictures.

Calvin yelled, "Elliott, bring that nice ass over here and get in the picture. You are part of this family."

The nurse couldn't stop laughing.

Goodbye

Calvin asked the nurse to get his jacket. He wanted to take the boys out to the cemetery.

Jeff asked the nurse if he could push the wheelchair, and Calvin asked Elliott to bring the walker. "When we get close, I will walk. I always do."

Mathew's headstone was simple. His name and dates were engraved along with Calvin's name and date of birth. Jeff knelt and placed a small stone he had brought from California.

Calvin asked the nurse to take him back to his room so Jeff and Elliott could have a few moments alone with Mathew.

Jeff started to cry as they were standing at the grave. "I hate them more now than ever. I hope my parents rot in hell."

Back in Calvin's room, they said their goodbyes.

Calvin thanked them for making an old man extremely happy. "Do me a favor. Go back to the hotel and fuck. Keep it fresh while you are young," he said with a wink.

On the flight back home, Jeff said that he felt a deep sense of relief. "In a way, I think we met my grandfather through Calvin. I never thought I could hate my parents more, but I don't think I can ever look at them again. The thought of what they did makes me sick. I will never forgive them."

Elliott mentioned that the money Patricia left him in her will could possibly be the money she and William stole from Mathew's company. "Do you think that was your grandmother's way of apologizing for what she did? Jeff, think about it. Your father fought very hard to get her will overturned. She had to have known he would be extremely angry when he found out about the will. Maybe, after all this time, her conscience got the best of her. That could have been her way of spitting in William's face. Don't forget the way your mother went against your father. She didn't want him to challenge the will and told him to give you what was always yours. Your mother has never gone against your father except for this. I might be grabbing at straws, but I think Laura played a part in convincing Patricia to leave it all to you."

Jeff said, "You may be right, but that doesn't make up for what they did to Mathew and Calvin. And one other thing, the will and the money don't make up for the lack of love and the way they have treated me all my life. I will never forgive them."

Calvin's Gift

A few days later, Elliott pulled into Jeff's garage. He had left Phoenix earlier than usual and was glad the drive was over. Darlene and Heather had driven down to San Diego to pick up Jake. He couldn't wait to see Jake again.

Elliott was concerned that Jeff hadn't been the same since the trip. He was quiet, and he seemed to be miles away.

Jeff had asked Elliott to be patient while he processed what he learned about Mathew and Calvin and how he would deal with his parents. "They need to know what we found out. This must stop now. I will make them understand that they can never hurt us again."

Before Elliott could close the garage, a delivery man came with a package that was postmarked from Paris. Elliott called Jeff at the station and said, "I hope it's a gift for me."

Jeff said he wasn't expecting anything.

Elliott replied, "Okay. We can open it when you get home."

Elliott called Darlene and made plans to go out to dinner. He and Jeff had gifts for the girls, and he would pick up Jake.

Jeff came home early to see what was in the package. He found two envelopes and a wrapped package. The first letter was from the nurse. She explained how happy Calvin was to have met them. "He seemed to have a new lease on life for a few days. Unfortunately, Calvin passed away. Do not to mourn his passing. Instead, celebrate his and Mathew's life. As he told you when you left, you made an old man very happy. Before he passed, he handed me a letter and a package and asked me to make sure you got them."

Jeff opened the letter and began to read. He couldn't continue and asked Elliott to read it to him.

Dearest Jeff,

The days since your beautiful visit have been filled with warmth and sunshine. Although those few hours we spent together were not nearly long enough, they were enough to remind me that, in many ways, Mathew lives on in you. Your grandfather and I dedicated our lives to each other. However, I always knew there was something missing in his life. I now know that it was you that was missing. Jeff, I want you to know that your grandfather would have held you up for the world to see. He would have given you everything you didn't receive from your parents. Most importantly, he would have given you love and understanding. Some may have called us cowards for leaving instead of fighting the hate that was thrown at us, especially from your grandmother and your parents. I want you to understand that we were living in a time that was much different from today. Mathew always told me that, even if we stayed and even if the hate faded away, the damage was already done. It wasn't for us to love in the shadows. I know what you have experienced in your life—all the hatred, shame, and fear of being who you are. I find comfort in believing you have found your own way. Always remember that for as much love as you two have for each other, there will be storms that blow through your lives. That is inevitable. When those storms appear, think back to today and remember all the joy and love you give each other. Don't allow the storms to destroy you. Instead, let them make you stronger and bring you closer together. I consider you my grandson and wish you—and my other grandson, Elliott—a life of love that will last forever. The other package contains the drawing you and Elliott kept looking at. For a long time, it was what Mathew and I would look at to remind us of how we became one. It is time for it to hang in your home. Allow the sunlight to shine on it. Look at it every now and then. Never forget how you and Elliott met—and never forget us. I am ready to be with Mathew again. I can't wait to see his smile when he hears that you and I had those few hours together.

Calvin

Jeff and Elliott hugged each other and cried.

Jeff looked at Elliott and said, "I think I will be okay now. I have the answers I needed."

Elliott sensed that there was still something on Jeff's mind, but he also realized it was not the time to push. He reminded Jeff that they needed to get ready to meet Darlene and Heather at the restaurant.

Jeff's Outrage

Jeff asked Elliott if he would go by himself because he needed some time to be alone. "I will catch up with you in a while."

Elliott told the girls everything about what had happened in Paris. "Damn it! I should never have left him alone—"

Jeff walked in to the restaurant in a pair of old jeans and a sweatshirt. He had his backpack with him. "I need to do something, and I need to do it alone. You have to trust me on this. All I need right now is a ride to the airport."

Elliott said "Of course. I trust you. Come on. My car is outside."

On the way to the airport, Jeff was deep in thought, and Elliott was afraid of angering Jeff by asking any questions.

As Jeff got out of the car. Elliott cried and told him he loved him.

Jeff replied, "I love you. I will be back by Sunday morning."

Jeff waited at the airport all night. On Saturday morning, he managed to secure a ticket for a flight. As soon as he was on the plane, he collapsed in his seat. After a stop in Atlanta, he ordered a couple drinks. For the remainder of the trip, he was lost in his thoughts.

The pilot announced, "Welcome to Reagan International Airport. We hope you enjoy your stay in our nation's capital."

Jeff flagged a cab and gave the driver an address. When they pulled up to the house, he handed the cab driver two hundred dollars and asked him to wait. He knew it would not take long.

He walked into the house without knocking or ringing the doorbell. In the dining room, he saw Laura and two senators with their wives. The table was set with Laura's prized china. William was standing at the head of the table with a glass of champagne. He looked ready to make a toast.

Jeff walked up to his father, took the glass from his hand, and threw it against the wall. He grabbed William by his collar and shoved him up against the table. He yelled, "How could you have done this, you motherfucker? How could you have been so damn cruel? Why didn't you ever tell me about Mathew and Calvin? You goddamn motherfucker. Did you think I would never find out about them or what you did to them, you fucking asshole? You are evil. How can you sleep at night?" He shoved William against the wall and turned to his mother. "He was your father for God's sake. Don't you have any feelings of love inside you? Are you totally numb from the vodka? When did the drinking start, Mother? Was it when you found out you had a gay father? Then along came your gay son. Is that when the double shots started? Perhaps your husband was sleeping with your mother. Did you ever give that a thought? Wouldn't that be the icing on the cake? You let that son of a bitch husband of yours send your father away knowing what he and your mother did. You just sat by and let it happen. You are nothing but a cold, miserable bitch. You did all this for fucking money. You are both immoral thieves. No wonder you fit in so damn well in your fucking Republican Party!" He then knocked all the dishes onto the floor. "Look at it. It's all in pieces. You showed that ugly china more love than you ever showed me. Go to hell, all of you."

William grabbed him, but Jeff pushed his father to the floor. "Did I hit a nerve about the sleeping with Patricia comment? Or should I have said the embezzler husband? Go ahead and have me arrested. I dare you. You're a goddamn piece of shit. If you do, by tomorrow morning, I will be on every news show in the country. I'll be telling the world all about you. I will find a way to make this right for what you did. That's a promise."

As he walked out, he looked at the other people in the room. "Don't be so goddammed shocked. This is just a normal conversation in this fucking family. If that is who you want to be president, then you are as fucked up as he is." He turned to look at William. "We are done. You destroyed Mathew and Calvin's life here, but I will never let you destroy Elliott or me. Surprise, you both thought you tore us apart way back then. Trying as hard as you did to fuck that up only made us more determined. For some reason, I think you already know that he and I are back together. I don't give a fuck anymore. So, whatever threats or schemes you are thinking of doing to us, take them and shove them up your ass. You will never touch us again!"

He walked out the door, got in the cab, and went back to the airport. He had done what he needed to do. What should have been done years earlier was now complete. There would be no doubt in anyone's mind that he was his own man and that he meant business. He had a feeling that Mathew and Calvin had guided him to do what he did. He didn't only do it for Elliott and himself—he did it for his grandfathers.

Jeff arrived home on Sunday morning.

Elliott had fallen asleep on the couch with Jake. He jumped up when he heard the door open and grabbed Jeff and kissed him. "I was so worried about you. I put the pieces together and figured out that you were going to see your parents. I hope you did what you had to do. Please tell me that you didn't kill them."

Jeff held Elliott's hand and said, "No. I didn't kill them. I thought about it. That would have made them martyrs instead of the evil people they are. We are free of them. They won't interfere with us anymore."

CHAPTER 14

Fast Changes

The travel back and forth every weekend was time-consuming and expensive. Elliott considered selling his condo and moving to Los Angeles. He had already talked with the other partner about selling his shares and leaving. His partner advised him to take a leave of absence from the firm. It would be much easier to secure a position with another firm if he was still employed. He assured Elliott that he would help in any way with references.

Elliott asked a gay friend who was a real estate agent to start putting out feelers about his condo. Phil told him that he had a client who was from out of state and wanted a place in Phoenix near the gay bars as a winter home. "Great, please tell him about my place. You can show it to him anytime you want. Just let me know when he is in Phoenix. I'll make sure Jake and I are not home when you show it."

A few days later, Phil called Elliott to tell him that his client didn't need to see the condo. He liked what he saw in the pictures that were emailed to him. Phil presented Elliott an offer for the condo, which was more than he anticipated selling it for. It was a cash offer without any contingencies. Elliott explained to Phil that it was moving faster than he thought it would. He would have to discuss all of it with Jeff and would let him know his answer on Monday.

While driving to LA on Friday, he kept thinking about his conversation with Jeff the previous day. He had detected something different in Jeff's tone. Jeff assured him that everything was okay and that he couldn't wait to see him on Friday.

Jeff said, "What's going on with you? I can sense that you want to tell me something."

Elliott assured Jeff that everything was good. Although neither was convinced by the other's answers, they tried to get it out of their minds and sort it all out on Friday.

Jeff met Elliott in front of the garage, and Jake needed to go for a walk after the long ride. As they walked around the block, Jeff said, "I have something I need to talk to you about. Can we go back to the house? I really need to talk." He put his arm around Elliott and told him that he was so happy that he was there.

Jeff poured some wine, and they settled down in the living room. "Something has transpired, and I need your help with making a major decision that will affect both of us."

"Oh my God. You found someone else—and you're breaking up with me."

Jeff said, "You're crazy. Where do you come up with this stuff?"

"Jeff, please go on. You're scaring me. Tell me what's going on."

Jeff said, "I have been offered a major promotion by the network. This is something I had not expected so early in my career. I have been offered the position as one of the morning co-anchors on the number one-rated national morning news/entertainment show on the network. It would come with a substantial pay increase—and national exposure. On the other hand, I could never think of leaving you in Phoenix while I move to New York. I know you have your job and life there. I am so afraid that a cross-country relationship would end in disaster. It's hard enough on both of us now commuting back and forth every weekend. I love you and won't do anything to keep us apart. All you have to say is no, and I will turn it down."

Elliott stared at Jeff in disbelief. "You're the crazy one. This is the opportunity of a lifetime. You should be so damn proud that they want you. Isn't this what you have been working so damn hard for? I am sure there are countless numbers of reporters who would kill for this opportunity, and it's being handed to you." Elliott started laughing.

Jeff said, "Do you think this is a joke? This in not funny, and you are pissing me off with your laughing. Stop it. If you don't want to move to New York, then tell me that."

Elliott said, "This is hilarious. Look at this. Elliott took the offer for his condo out of his backpack. "Please read it, and then tell me this isn't funny."

Jeff looked it over and said, "This is an offer to sell your condo. When did all of this happen?"

"That's right," Elliott said. "It happened this week. This is what I wanted to talk to you about this weekend. I want to move here to be with you. If New York is where we need to move too, then I am all in. If you were transferred to bum-fuck Arkansas, I would be there with you."

Jeff started laughing too. "You could have told me this over the phone. I worried all week about telling you about my offer and how I would ask you to move to New York."

"What?" Elliott said. "Then we would have missed all of this fun. I'll call Phil and tell him to accept the offer, but there is one stipulation: Jake comes with us."

"Of course," Jeff said with a smile. "I can't wait for us to walk him in Central Park on weekends. You know he us going to be pissed at us during the winter."

"Yes!"

"Jeff, what are you going to do with this condo? Are you going to sell it or keep it?"

Jeff said, "I have an idea. I'll explain it to you later. I want to call Darlene and Heather and ask them to come over, so we can tell them the news."

"Great!" Elliott said. "I'll run to the store and get a couple of bottles of wine and some guacamole and chips."

When the girls arrived, Heather said, "What do you guys have to tell us? You are always so mysterious."

Jeff said, "We'll tell you in a minute. First, I want to ask you something. You guys have been looking for a new place to live, right?"

Darlene said, "Yes, but have you seen the prices out there? I don't think we can afford to buy anything yet. I think we will be retired before can buy a house."

"Well, I think I have found you the perfect place—and the price is right."

Heather almost choked on her wine. "Where is it? When can we look at it?"

Jeff said, "How about right now? Come on. Follow me." He took them into the kitchen and then through all three bedrooms. In the dining room, he said, "Well, what do you think?"

"You're nuts!" Heather said with a cautious smile.

"I probably am," Jeff said as he smiled back at her. "Elliott and I are moving. If you want to live here, it's yours. I will have contracts drawn up to state that the rent will be only what the condo association fee is every month. If we ever decide to sell it, you will have first choice—and I will carry the mortgage."

Darlene jumped up and gave Jeff a huge kiss and hug. "Why would you do this for us?"

Jeff said, "I know we started out on a rocky road, but I realize that was because we both wanted what was best for that guy sitting over there. We could never fully repay you for your lasting friendship all these years. So, what do you say? Do we have a deal? Make a spoiled rich boy happy and say yes."

"Yes!" both girls shouted.

Elliott stood up and said, "Don't you even want to know where we are moving?"

Heather said, "Oh my God. Yes! We are just so excited. Please tell us! I hope you aren't moving to one of those huge homes in Beverly Hills to become snotty old queens."

Elliott grinned and said, "Honey, we are not old and are definitely not queens. We are moving to New York."

Darlene said, "New York? Why the hell would you want to live in New York? Do you know how fucking cold and crowded it is in that city? And when will we ever see each other?"

Elliott replied, "Just tune in every morning at seven. You will see Jeffie's cute face on TV trying to be serious. Don't ever think we will stop seeing each other. We didn't all come this far to just throw it all away."

After the girls left, Elliott hugged Jeff and said, "You are a remarkable man. That is such a great gift you have given those girls."

"It's not just from me," Jeff said. "I had your name put on the deed months ago. I didn't want you to have to deal with my parents if anything happened to me. It's half yours. Follow me. I want to show you something in the bedroom."

Elliott replied, "No need to go in there Jeffie. I can see what you want to show me from right here. I also have something to show you. Why waste time going into the bedroom?"

Jeff responded, "Please don't ever call me Jeffie again! That is what that girl I took up to my fraternity room called me.

Jeff grabbed him and threw him onto the couch. "Let me show you how a national news reporter does it." Elliott said," Ok, but I need to say it one more time. I promise I will never say it again. Come on Jeffie, show me how it's done."

It was the perfect ending to the evening.

Planning

The next morning, they began planning their move.

Jeff said, "My first day will be on the first Monday of next month. There are a million things we need to do before that happens. We need to get in touch with someone in New York about an apartment. Do we rent or buy?"

Elliott said, "My condo was paid for a long time ago. All the money from the sale can go for the new place."

Jeff said, "I still have the money from Patricia. I think we will be okay to buy a place.

"Do you realize we are talking about millions of dollars."

Jeff smiled and said, "Perhaps Patricia wasn't such a bitch after all. Don't worry. It's all good."

They made reservations to fly to New York the following week.

"I will have Phil contact an agent there to get the ball rolling. He is making a nice commission on my place, so he owes it to me."

Jeff said, "I hate having to talk about this, but I have been contacted by the Republican National Committee to inform me that my fucking father is going to make an announcement to formally start his presidential run. I refuse to have any contact with him or my mother. They get around that by sending these Republican asshole puppets with information. Like I care. He has scheduled to make his grand announcement on the day before my first show."

Elliott said, "That son of a bitch! He always tries to upstage you. When will this shit stop? Why can't they understand that we want nothing to do with them? It is not going to be easy for us to ignore them or the media."

Jeff agreed. "The media has a way of getting whatever answers they want. So, our plan will be that we will do this our way. We will disclose only what we want them to know. I promise you that I will never stand beside him on any stage. If they ask, I won't hesitate to voice my true feelings. They may come after you. I can't tell you how to react or what to say. You need to do what you feel is right. Anything you do or say will be okay with me.

"My father is not a stupid man. I believe he wants as little conversation about us as possible. He is a vindictive man, and that may be exactly what we need to cause his downfall. The network has promised to do their best to keep his campaign away from me. I am having that put into my contract. That's all I can ask of them. Let's not spend time worrying about my dysfunctional so-called parents. We have a new life ahead of us, and that's all that matters."

Elliott said. "Am I missing something here? Why the hell would he even try to talk to you? Something doesn't seem right."

Jeff said, "You are correct, Elliott. This is really fucked up. When it pertains to politics, my father will do and say anything to get elected. If that means that he must put on his fake smile and try to convince me and the country that everything is good between us, that is exactly what he will do. My father is a master at deception, and he never forgets anything. He hasn't forgotten what I said to him that day, especially because I said it in front of those other senators. Because I know this, it puts us on an even playing field with him. Let's focus on us for the time being."

Visiting Peg

Jeff suggested that they needed to tell Peg about their move. "She deserves to hear it personally and not over the phone."

On the drive down to San Diego, Jeff put the top down on the car. "This will probably be the last time we can enjoy the warm weather and this beautiful drive."

Peg greeted them with open arms. She had prepared a beautiful lunch, and they ate on the patio.

Jeff said, "Peg—"

Peg said, "From now on, you call me Mom. Please don't forget it."

They told her about Jeff's new job, and she said, "Both of you deserve so much happiness together. Please don't ever forget the road that brought you to this point. Look back at it occasionally to remind you that light always comes out of the darkness. So now, when can I visit? I hope sooner than later."

Elliott said, "I left my phone in the car. I'll be right back."

As soon as Elliott was in the house, Jeff said, "Perfect. I need to talk to you about a plan I have. I would like you and the family to be in New York for my first show. I want to surprise Elliott with something special. I am asking so damn much from him to pick up and move on my account. He hasn't complained at all, so I want to do this for him."

"Of course I will be there. I am sure everyone else will also want to go too."

Jeff smiled and said, "Great. I will make all of the plans. All you have to do is get on the plane. Everything else will be taken care of—and not a word to Elliott!"

Later that afternoon, Peg said, "Is it true that William is planning to run for president?"

"Yes, Mom," Elliott said. "He is going to make his announcement the day before Jeff's first show. I think it is his way of getting even with Jeff for the fight they had."

Peg said, "I pray that he doesn't win. That would be a disaster for our country. Please be careful. William and his party are not your friends. I have a funny feeling that he will try to get in touch with you. He wants to tell the country what a fantastic job he did raising you. Don't put it past him to try to convince everyone that he is the reason you are a success on television."

Jeff started laughing. "If he knows what's good for him, he will keep his distance from us. I have already sent a formal request to the Justice Department to decline any type of protection from the Secret Service after he makes his announcement."

While they were driving back to LA, Darlene called to invite them to brunch. She told him they had something important to discuss.

Elliott said, "What is so important that you have to wait until morning to tell us?"

She said, "We will see you in the morning."

Darlene, Heather, and a Trip to New York

Jeff and Elliott arrived late to brunch. They had slept in and took Jake for a long walk on the trails in the hills. When they got to the top of the hill, they stood, arms around each other, and looked down at the Hollywood sign. Jeff asked two young guys, who were also walking a dog, if they would take their picture.

At the restaurant, Darlene got right down to business as soon as they sat down. "Heather and I are getting married in a few days. We wanted to do it before you guys left. We want you to be our witnesses."

Elliott stood up and gave them a hug.

Jeff said, "It's about time. Of course we will be honored to be in your wedding!"

The wedding would take place at city hall, and then Becky and Luke would have a small reception at their home.

Darlene said, "You guys need to wear casual clothes. No fancy suits. I know that won't be easy for you, but you better not upstage us."

Elliott traveled back to Phoenix for a day to clean out his office and say goodbye to his coworkers. His partner assured him that he had many connections in New York and would help him find a position at another law firm. He scheduled the movers to have everything shipped to Los Angeles. All of Jeff's furniture would be loaded on the truck and sent to New York.

They flew to New York to secure an apartment. They wanted to adjust to their new lifestyle and take their time finding exactly where they wanted to buy. The found a beautiful new two-bedroom, two-bath apartment in Tribeca with an option to purchase after six months. It was near the parks, which made it perfect for Jake.

In New York, Jeff met everyone at the network and was shown his way around the studio. They took photos and videos to start the on-air campaign to promote his first day. In a matter of days, Jeff's picture would be flashing on billboards and electronic signs in front of the studio, and above Times Square.

Jeff and Elliott talked about what Elliott would do with his career. Jeff suggested that Elliott take a few months off to get comfortable with the new city and get the apartment in order. Jeff would be busy with the show and would have very little free time.

Elliott said, "Once we're settled, I want to work for a law firm that allows me to work closely with the LGBT community."

Jeff suggested starting his own private practice. That way, Elliott could pick and choose who he wanted as clients.

Here We Go

When they arrived back in LA, they looked around and asked each other if it was really happening. Everything was moving extremely fast—perhaps too fast—but they hoped the best was yet to come.

For a few days, they lived out of boxes and slept on the floor, and they had a going-away party at Jeff's studio.

Elliott persuaded Jeff to go to Rodeo Drive to buy some appropriate clothes for the wedding.

Jeff said, "Darlene will kill us if we upstage them."

"No, she won't, "Elliott said. "She knows me, and I think she will be expecting it."

Peg and her sister drove up from San Diego the night before the wedding and stayed with Becky and Luke. Kathy flew in early to help get everything ready. Darlene's father was a no-show. Even though she said it was what she had expected, Heather knew it hurt her deeply.

The night before the wedding, Elliott and Jeff took everyone out for a beautiful dinner in Beverly Hills.

Jeff said, "Who could have ever dreamed that, after all these years, we would all be here together celebrating this wedding? I am so grateful to be able to call all of you family."

Elliott said, "You have all helped us both more than you realize. Jeff and I would not be together if it weren't for all of you. We will never be able to repay you for everything you have done for us."

When Elliott and Jeff arrived at the wedding, Darlene said, "Yeah right! That's what you call casual?"

Elliott smiled and said, "Of course, honey! It's casual chic."

The judge was extremely accommodating and spoke of the strong bond they had for each other. Kathy held Peg's arm and cried during the vows.

At the reception, Jeff and Elliott gave the girls a two-week honeymoon in Hawaii. Darlene and Heather both broke down when they opened the gift. Darlene said, "Thank you for this great gift. You guys being here was enough for us."

Heather said, "Yes. Thank you so much. Just because you guys are moving across the country, don't ever think you are rid of us. We are with you forever."

When it was time to say goodbye, Becky and Luke announced that she would be having another baby in the spring. She hoped they all would be there for the baptism.

Elliott hugged his mom, and she told him that she and Dan were always so proud of him. Peg took Jeff aside and asked him to take care of her son. Jeff said his goodbyes to Darlene and Heather.

Elliott hugged Darlene and said that she was the reason he never gave up when everything looked so dark. "You are my rock. Never forget that."

Darlene said, "You also are my rock. I love you."

Elliott hugged her and said, "Take care of yourself, kid. I'll be keeping tabs on you from New York."

Darlene said, "Elliott, remember how you interrupted me on that first day of drama class—and how you wanted to take control? You had balls, dude, and I'm glad you did. I would not have wanted it any other way."

Elliott said, "The way I remember it, you were the one who wanted to take control. I also would not have wanted it any other way. I love you."

It was over. All the goodbyes were said. That chapter in their lives was closing. What lay ahead was still a mystery. Each of them knew, no matter what was ahead, they would be able to handle it because of the bonds they had with each other.

The final 3 days before Jeff started on the show were busier than anyone could have expected. Not only did the moving van arrive, Jeff had many details at the studio to go over. He was busy working with the entire morning on air team taping a new opening for the show. Jeff made them re tape it several times before he agreed to the final product. Elliott took charge of the new apartment and arranging the furniture and unpacking. The one thing that was the hardest to get used to for Elliott was walking Jake. He joked that New York must have the busiest sidewalks in the world.

The day before Jeff's first day, William was planning to make his announcement that he was running for president. He sent word to Jeff that he needed to be in Washington standing next to Laura during the announcement. Jeff told the messenger to tell William to go to hell and to leave him alone. Elliott and Jeff were at home when the live news conference began.

William began by saying, "My son is extremely heartbroken that he could not be here with his mother and me this morning. He sent his mother a dozen roses with a card that said that he missed her and wished he could be there. My son is a true American and I am sure he will be at my side throughout this historic campaign." William continued, "I pledge to the American people that I will do everything possible to overturn the Supreme Court's ruling on Marriage Equality. I will bring our country back to what our founders envisioned, a moral and Christian country. I won't settle for anything less and neither should you."

Elliott said, "Are you fucking kidding me? He has serious mental issues!". Jeff just flashed his middle finger at the television screen.

CHAPTER 15

A Very Special Day

"Wake up, my love," Elliott whispered into Jeff's ear. "It's three o'clock, and the car will be here in an hour to pick you up. You need to get ready for your big day."

Jeff muttered, "Can't we both just run away and pretend none of this ever happened?"

Elliott climbed on top of him and reminded him of how hard he worked to get there.

Jeff said, "I know it's time to get up. Wow! I see something else that's hard and needs to be worked on."

"Well, we do have some time before they pick you up."

Jeff rose to the occasion, and they became engrossed in each other as if they were high school boys full of energy and vitality.

Jeff shaved, showered, and put on a pair of sweats and a T-shirt. His suit was waiting for him at the studio.

Elliott handed Jeff a cup of coffee and told him to hurry since it was almost four.

A few minutes later, the call came that the car was waiting downstairs. They kissed each other, but before he was out the door, Jeff made sure

Elliott would be at the studio before the show started. He told him that he needed him there for the first day and made Elliott promise to get there on time. "I'm sending a car. Don't be late—and wear a suit." He walked out the door and got into the waiting car.

As soon as he arrived at the studio, Jeff made sure everything was ready for his guests. He talked with the director about what he would say and who would be on camera with him.

The crew and staff were extremely excited about his opening segment. In the green room, the caterer was setting up the food and coffee. The florist brought in the two dozen red roses Jeff had ordered. There were hundreds of balloons directly above the anchor desk. The producer told him that it was their way of welcoming him to the show.

The Same Old William

With everything set to go, Jeff took a deep breath. He could relax and focus on getting dressed.

The director and producer told Jeff about a change in the guest schedule that had just occurred. His parents would be there to join him on his first day. William was fresh off his announcement that he was running for president. His father's campaign director got in touch with the president of the network to arrange for William and Laura to be scheduled as Jeff's first guests. The network president, realizing it this would be a gigantic win in the ratings, quickly instructed the director to make the new schedule work.

Jeff kicked a trash can across the stage as if it was a football and threatened to walk out and quit if they didn't cancel his father's appearance.

"It's too late. William holds a lot of power, and the name of the game is ratings."

Jeff said, "I will bring in great fucking ratings by myself. If you think I can't, then why the hell did you hire me? I am telling you all right now that I will not be in the same room with that son of a bitch! You figure this fucking mess out now! I am not kidding." Jeff walked back to his dressing room and slammed the door so hard that the overhead lights shook. He sat there for a few minutes and thought about what he should do. He started to call Elliott but stopped. He didn't want to worry him and was afraid Elliott would not show up if he knew what was happening.

The producers, director, and crew started rearranging the order of the guests. They had to hurry because it was nearing the start time of the show. They all agreed that Jeff would be introduced by his cohost and have the first segment all to himself. After the first commercial, William and Laura would come out and speak. The only question that remained was if Jeff would join his parents on camera.

The network president was eating breakfast in the lobby. Jeff called and informed him that there was no way he would be on camera with his parents. If the network didn't like that, then he would walk out and go back to California.

The call became heated. Angry words were exchanged.

The network president told Jeff that he didn't have—and would never have—final approval about guests.

Jeff informed him that the network didn't have final approval about anything pertaining to his family. Jeff also reminded him that his contract stipulated that he would never have to report anything concerning his father. "I will never share another stage or photo with that bastard!" Jeff hung up without saying goodbye.

The network president called the director to make sure Jeff and his parents were kept as far apart as possible and to not have them on camera at the same time. Everyone held their breath and prayed it would all work out.

The Shit Hits the Fan

The car arrived outside of Jeff and Elliott's apartment, and the driver opened the door.

Peg, Becky, Luke, Darlene, and Heather yelled, "Surprise!"

Elliott said, "What are you doing here?"

Peg said, "Jeff wanted to surprise you."

When they arrived at the studio, they were greeted by the Secret Service. They all had to go through scanners and have their bags searched.

Elliott said, "You're looking at us as if we are some sort of criminals, and I don't like it."

They told him he had to leave if he refused to be searched. Reluctantly he gave in.

Jeff was going over notes with his staff and couldn't greet them. They all settled in the green room, and a staff member brought in an easy chair and put it down in front of one of the monitors. They were told it was for a special guest.

Darlene laughed and said, "It must be for me. I am special."

The staff member looked at her, rolled his eyes, and said, "I don't think it is for you."

Becky asked who the guest was, but the crew member said he didn't know.

The door flung open, and William and Laura walked with a couple of other senators and their wives. Everyone stared at each other, and William demanded that they move these people to another room.

He was informed that there was no other room available because of extensive remodeling in the studio.

Becky took out her phone and started to record.

Darlene laughed and said, "I am not leaving. If you people don't like it, then you leave."

William grabbed Peg's arm, and Elliott stepped between them. "Take your fucking filthy hands off my mother. You did that once, and you will never do it again. Now take your fucking hand off her. If you don't, trust me, I will help you remove it. Get away from her—and stay away from her."

Becky said, "Don't worry, Elliott. I am recording all of this, and I can't wait to post it. Just think about all the hits it will get on Facebook."

The Secret Service agents grabbed Elliott.

Elliott pushed them away and said, "We are guests of this show—just like that son of a bitch senator you are protecting. He is the one who started all this shit. You need to shut him up—not me. If you don't keep him away from my mother, I will call the police. Now leave us alone!"

The crew came into the room to ease the tension, and William told the Secret Service agents to leave them alone. "You're still the little fag you always were."

Elliott laughed in his face. "You are absolutely correct about that. I am still the fag, but I'm not like I always was. I now have your son all to myself.

We fuck just like we did in high school, and we sleep together every night.
I see that you have not changed. Still trying to upstage your son for your
advantage. Now shut your mouth, Mr. Senator, and by the way, go to hell."

One of the other senators grabbed Becky's hand and tried to take her
phone.

Luke pushed the guy and said, "Who do you think you are, you son of
a bitch? You touch my wife again, and I will push you through that wall."

William told all of them to shut their fucking mouths for the remainder
of the show. The tension could have been cut with a knife.

Laura sat down and had the producer bring her a vodka tonic. She
never said a word.

Jeff put on his new suit, and the makeup crew put the finishing
touches on his face and hair.

The director told Jeff what had transpired in the green room, and
Jeff just smiled. He knew Elliott could take care of himself. He told the
director not to worry. He was going to make his parents proud. "This will
be a special day for my family—a day they will never forget."

The director replied, "Trust me. No one is going to forget this day."

Five minutes before showtime, Jeff and his cohost gave each other high
fives and found their seats at the studio desk. Jeff asked the director to
make sure Elliott would be standing just out of the camera's view.

When Elliott was summoned to come to the set, William said that he
was supposed to be the one on the set.

The crew member said that he was just doing what the director asked
him to do. "They asked for Elliott, not you."

William demanded to talk to the network president.

The producer ran in and explained that they had arranged a longer
segment for him after the first commercial, which seemed to appease him.

William said, "See? I carry a lot of weight around here. They are going
to give me more airtime than I expected. And it's all for free. Cha-ching!"

Something Special and Personal

After the director yelled, "On the air in three, two, one," Jeff's cohost recited her monologue and introduced Jeff. He was beaming from ear to ear.

William was prancing around the green room and looking at the monitors. He kept bragging about how it was perfect timing for all the free publicity. He couldn't have planned it better if he tried.

Darlene laughed and rolled her eyes. "I have a feeling it's going to be the best press coverage your son will ever be able to give you."

Jeff looked directly at the camera and talked about who he was and how happy he was to be part of such a great show. He told the audience that he felt like it was the first day of school—and he was the new kid in class. He stood up and said, "Because this is my first day, I want to start it off with something personal and special."

He looked toward the back of the set and motioned for Elliott to join him.

Elliott was confused about whether it would be proper to get in front of the camera, but the director told him it was okay because Jeff had arranged it in advance.

Darlene, Heather, Becky, and Luke clapped as loud as they could.

Peg took Darlene's hand and said, "Wait! I know what's going to happen. Jeff already told me."

With Elliott standing next to him, Jeff introduced him as the love of his life. "Elliott and I have gone through so much to get to this point. I am a lucky man to have him in my life." He turned and asked Elliott if he would do him the honor of marrying him.

With tears coming down his cheeks, Elliott said, "Yes! I will marry you! I love you!"

Jeff took hold of Elliott and gave him a kiss that could almost be felt by everyone watching. The studio became a sea of rainbow-colored balloons and confetti.

William yelled, "Get that goddamn faggot off the air!"

Heather laughed and said, "Which one—Elliott or Jeff?"

William threw his coffee cup against the wall and yelled about how no one was paying any attention to him.

Darlene, Heather, Becky, Peg and Luke were yelling congratulations and hugging each other.

William told them to shut up, which only made them celebrate louder.

Laura who was still sitting and nursing her drink said, "William, just shut your mouth. Please just shut the fuck up!" Without taking her eyes off the television monitor, she slammed her drink down on the table, stood up, and said, "It's about fucking time. Do you hear me, William? It's about fucking time that our son is finally happy!" She walked over to Peg, gave her a hug, and walked out of the room.

William stormed out of the studio without going on the air or talking to Jeff.

Peg's phone rang. It was Sister Mary Therese. She was watching the show with her students. She told Peg to never stop believing in the power of prayer. She had prayed that these two young men would someday find the courage and love they deserved. She had known there was something special between them since she taught them in her first class.

Peg thanked Sister Mary Therese for her kind words and walked over to the vase of red roses Jeff had ordered. She took the white flower out of her hair and replaced it with a red rose. She grinned, winked, and said, "This is indeed a special day."

When the show was over, Jeff received a call from the network president. He congratulated Jeff on his engagement and apologized for the heated phone call. He told Jeff that he was looking forward to working with him. The ratings were starting to come in, and it was their most watched show in more than two years. He mentioned that William had tried to call him as he walked out of the studio, but he refused to take the call.

Jeff thanked him for the kind words, and he and Elliott met up with the rest of the family for breakfast.

The show continued to remain in the number one spot. By the third month, Jeff was the star of the morning team. He liked being on top of the world and was immersing himself in all aspects of the show. His goal was to be the best, and he wasn't going to let anyone—or anything—stand in his way.

Soon, the clouds from one of those storms that Calvin had warned him about began moving in. Jeff was too busy and preoccupied to notice that it was beginning to get dark outside.

CHAPTER 16

Winter Melody

Jeff became totally immersed in his job, and the ratings and his desire to be the best became the only things he lived for. He would spend long hours after each show preparing for the next one. His driving force, although much appreciated by the top network brass, was causing tension with the other hosts. They began to resent his prima donna attitude. His attention to detail and demands for absolute perfection for each show became an obsession. He never turned down social gatherings and accepted all the invitations to private parties and dinners that were given to him. The more time Jeff spent socializing, the further withdrawn Elliott became.

Home soon became just a place for Jeff to sleep and change his clothes. He became the face of the show and would offer to fly to other areas of the country to cover news stories that were of national importance.

Jeff's production crew always traveled with him. Patrick, his trusted producer, was the leader. Patrick understood how Jeff worked and ensured that everything was up to Jeff's expectations. He would take the heat when something went wrong. Jeff and his team were always given the best sought after assignments.

One evening, Jeff brought Patrick home with him to go over a few details for the next morning's show. Elliott wanted to be hospitable and attempted to have some conversation with him. After a few minutes, it became evident that Patrick was not interested in anything Elliott had to say. While Elliott was talking, Patrick got up from the table, went over to the living room, and sat down next to Jeff.

Elliott saw how Patrick was looking at Jeff and how he always agreed with everything Jeff said. Elliott suspected that Patrick wanted this relationship to go beyond a business relationship. After a few minutes of watching Jeff and Patrick, Elliott rolled his eyes, got up, and put the leash on Jake. Without saying a word, he took Jake out for a long walk.

When he and Jake returned, Patrick had already left. Elliott took it as a perfect time to sit with Jeff and talk to him like they used to.

Jeff said, "Why did you leave without saying anything? Patrick was offended."

Elliott said, "Good. I'm glad he was offended. You offended me by bringing that son of a bitch into our home. Jeff, you must realize that Patrick wants more than a job with you. If you don't see it, then either you are extremely naïve or you want to go further with him. Everything about him is phony, just like his annoying smile and laugh. You need to open your eyes."

Jeff laughed and said, "You are crazy, and you need to grow up. And *you* are stupid if you think that about Patrick. He is a great guy, and he is indispensable on my team. You don't have any idea what I go through every day to prove myself to everyone at the network. I will run anyone over who gets in my way. Do me a favor and keep your mouth shut about Patrick."

Elliott got up and went to bed.

Jeff sat in the dark for a long time. He was pissed that Elliott would even suggest that he and Patrick were having an affair. Jeff understood that he needed to push and fight for everything to be the best at his job. If Patrick could help him get there, then so be it.

Even with everything he had going for himself, Jeff was unhappy. The more this feeling persisted, the harder he worked. He wanted to confide in Elliott about how he felt, but he feared that Elliott would see him as a failure. Jeff's first winter in New York was a circle of confusion, and he was afraid to stop and catch his breath.

Elliott was quiet and withdrawn during the first three months. He was uncomfortable around Jeff's new friends, especially Patrick. He knew very little about the broadcasting business and did not have a desire to learn more. He felt out of place whenever he was around them. It became easier to stay home and let Jeff do the entertaining. Night after night, he was home alone, while Jeff was parading around the city, kissing the ass of anyone of importance. Elliott decided he needed a diversion from his lonely existence. He decided to take the New York bar exam. Studying for the exam kept him occupied during Jeff's absence from home.

Dinner for Two?

One day, knowing that Jeff would be home that evening, Elliott made Jeff's favorite dinner. He wanted the two of them to try to enjoy an evening alone. The next morning, he would be taking the exam, and he wanted to tell Jeff all about it. Cooking dinner and studying took up most of his day. When everything was done, he set the table, opened the wine, and waited for Jeff.

When Jeff arrived home, Patrick was with him.

Elliott said, "I made dinner for the two of us. You didn't tell me Patrick would be here."

Jeff replied, "I didn't realize I needed to check in with you before I invited anyone over to my home. Patrick, have a seat. Elliott will fix us both a plate of food and a glass of wine."

Patrick said, "Thanks, Elliott. This taste good."

While they were eating, Jeff and Patrick discussed the next morning's show and made plans for future shows.

Elliott ate alone in the kitchen. When he was finished, he said, "I am going to bed. See you tomorrow."

Jeff responded, "Hey, I have two suits that need to get dropped off at the cleaners. You need to take them there in the morning."

Elliott didn't respond. Instead, he closed the bedroom door and fell asleep.

The next morning, Elliott took the bar exam. As he was walking home, Jeff called and said, "Why didn't you take my suits to the cleaners as I instructed you to do? Looks like I must do everything myself—just like at work. If I don't do it, then it doesn't get done. I instructed you to do one simple thing, and you couldn't do it. Now what am I supposed to do? Wear the same damn suit two days in a row? Thanks for nothing."

Elliott said, "First of all, don't ever instruct me to do anything. I don't work for you. From now on, you need to instruct Patrick, or anyone else on your team, to do your stupid errands for you. Secondly, you need to show me respect in *our* home—not just yours. You ask me before you invite someone over, just as I would do with you. It's called respect. You better hurry. The cleaners close in an hour. I hope you make it there on time."

After the call, Elliott decided not to tell Jeff about the bar exam. The excitement was gone.

Should I Stay?

Elliott's daily routine included walking Jake and the occasional trip to the store. His appearance began to change. He seldom got his hair cut, only shaved once a week, and wore the same T-shirt and sweatpants every day.

He learned early on to never question Jeff about his job and to avoid complaining about Jeff's long hours and absence from home. He felt like he did in high school when Jeff became the football star—and he became just a friend. The thing that bothered him the most was that he and Jeff never talked about their wedding or found time to make plans. He feared that Jeff only proposed to him to anger his father. He was beginning to feel that they would never get married.

Elliott started wondering if living that way was worth it. He wondered if he made a mistake selling his home in Phoenix. He wanted to do whatever he could to stay and fix his relationship with Jeff, but he believed Jeff was becoming a carbon copy of William. He had to face the fact that Jeff might not want to repair their relationship.

He continued believing that Patrick was using Jeff to advance at the network—and to sleep with him. No matter how hard he tried, he didn't trust him around Jeff. Elliott did some investigating and discovered that Patrick, who was a very good-looking man, would only patronize the finest gay establishments and always hung around men with plenty of money. As hard as it was for Elliott, he tried to talk to Jeff again about Patrick.

Jeff refused to listen. He said, "Don't do or say anything that could fuck up my job at the network."

For Christmas, Jeff had to travel to Georgia to cover an important story, leaving Elliott alone for the holiday. There was shooting in Texas two days before New Year's Eve, and Jeff went to cover it.

Elliott kept it all to himself. When his mom or Darlene called, he would tell them everything was great and that he loved New York. The last thing he needed was for Darlene to say that she warned him that this would happen. Elliott's first winter in New York was dark and lonely. He needed to scream as loud as he could, but he couldn't find the strength to do it.

William's Defeat

January was ending, and the presidential primaries were only a couple of weeks away. William seemed to be on television every day. He was in a race with nine other Republicans for the nomination. Jeff's stunt with Elliott during his first show didn't seem to hurt William in the polls. It appeared that his base of supporters viewed William and Laura as the victims.

William continued his campaign of morality and Christian values. He never mentioned Jeff in any of his speeches and avoided answering questions about Jeff whenever a reporter asked him. The night of the Iowa caucus was a turning point in the campaign. With all the polls predicting that William would win, he came in third. That was a major blow to him politically and personally. He had never lost an election and didn't know how to respond.

His campaign manager strongly urged William to contact Jeff and arrange for the family to be seen together. That would send a message that they had repaired any differences they had. It would also show that William had tolerance for the LGBT community. The campaign needed to pull out all the stops.

One evening, not long after William's defeat in Iowa, a member of William's staff came to Jeff and Elliott's apartment with a message for Jeff.

Elliott answered the door, and when he discovered who the visitor was, he said Jeff was busy and didn't have time to talk to him.

The guy said, "I can see Jeff in the other room. Move your gay ass out of my way."

Jeff ran to the door. "What did you just say? Elliott isn't moving away from this door, and neither is my gay ass. Whatever you came here to say, you can say it from out there in the hallway."

"William wants to arrange a meeting with you."

Jeff said, "Absolutely not. I will never stand next to him and help the son of a bitch win. In fact, tell him that if he bothers me again, I will join forces with the Democratic nominee. I have a lot of things I could talk about. I don't think he wants me to do that. So, please leave my home— and stay the fuck away from me and Elliott."

It was the first time in months that Jeff and Elliott were home together and having a conversation that consisted of more than two or three words. It felt good to both, but as luck would have it, duty called. Jeff needed to leave on another trip.

Is Patrick Going with You?

The call came from the network later that evening. There was a major political situation in France, and the network wanted Jeff to leave immediately in order for him to broadcast live the next day.

As Jeff was packing, Elliott asked if Patrick was going with him.

Jeff answered, "Of course he is. He is my producer. Why would you ask a stupid question like that?"

Elliott replied, "No reason. I'm just asking. I can't believe you thought it was a stupid question. I guess I must be careful about what I ask you from now on."

Jeff replied, "No, just don't ask me stupid questions."

"Fuck you!" Elliott said. "Don't ever call me stupid again. If you do, I will be out of here so fucking fast. I won't ask you anything from now on."

Before Jeff could react, the doorman called and said they had a visitor who wanted to come up. Patrick had all the camera equipment ready, and the driver was waiting in the van to take them to the airport.

Jeff said, "Elliott, I hope it's okay that I didn't ask you in advance if Patrick could come to our home tonight. Don't worry. We won't be here long."

When Patrick arrived, Elliott was pouring himself a glass of wine in the kitchen.

Jeff asked Elliott to pour one for him and Patrick.

Elliott said, "The bottle is in the kitchen—get it yourself."

Jeff went up to Elliott and whispered, "Go fuck yourself."

Elliott laughed, stared directly at Patrick, and said, "Excellent idea. I will have to do that since you won't do it—at least not with me."

Jeff turned red and looked ready to explode.

Patrick stood there with a phony smile on his face.

Elliott said, "Have fun in France, boys. I hope you have an exciting time."

Jeff kept his mouth shut.

Patrick said, "I think this will be a great trip and a fantastic show for the network."

Elliott wanted to tell him to go fuck himself, but he resisted the urge to respond.

After Jeff and Patrick left, Elliott sat alone in the living room and drank glass after glass of wine. *This way of living needs to end. It may be time to leave. I need to try to fix this mess one more time. Tomorrow afternoon, I will call Jeff in Paris and apologize. I hope Jeff will too.*

Two Situations

The morning after Jeff left for Paris, Elliott received a call from Heather. She was hysterically crying and could barely talk. She managed to tell Elliott that Darlene was in trouble. "She is extremely sick. She has breast cancer, and it may have spread. The doctors want to do surgery tomorrow. It's the only thing that will save her. Please come to California. We can't do this alone! We need you here. Please come! Darlene is at USC Medical Center in Los Angeles, and she is scared as hell."

Elliott said, "I am on my way. I will be there as soon as I can." He immediately called the doorman to make arrangements for Jake. One of the perks of living there was that they would take care of pets while a tenant was traveling. He booked a one-way ticket. He didn't know how long he would be there and didn't know if he even wanted to come back. He packed his suitcase, and in a few hours, he was on a plane to California. It never occurred to him to call Jeff.

Because of the time difference, Jeff arrived in France late in the afternoon. He hurried to the news station and was briefed about the news he needed to report. He and his team went into action and prepared to broadcast a live show that would be seen throughout the world.

When the newscast was over, Jeff and his team headed to the hotel. They needed to get a few hours of sleep before they had to do another live broadcast. Jeff took a shower, and he kept thinking about Elliott and how they had talked to each other the night before. He began to understand why Elliott was reacting like that. It was a response to the way he had been treating Elliott since the move. Jeff got out of the shower and tried to call Elliott without any luck.

He was only wearing a pair off boxer trunks when Patrick knocked on his door. He had a bottle of wine and some croissants. "I thought we could both use a couple of glasses of wine after that long trip." Patrick never asked if he could come in. He just walked over and sat down on the couch. He remarked that Jeff looked great wearing only a pair of underwear, and he gave Jeff a swat on his ass.

Jeff made a joke and sat down next to him.

As they were drinking their wine, Patrick suddenly reached over and gave Jeff a kiss on his lips while grabbing Jeff's crotch. For a moment, Jeff didn't react. He didn't know if he should reciprocate. All he knew was that he liked the attention. He started kissing Patrick. Suddenly, Jeff pushed Patrick away, stood up, and shouted, "What the fuck are you doing?"

Patrick said, "I see the way you and Elliott behave around each other. It's no secret that you two are probably on the verge of breaking up. I can make you happier than he ever did. I want to be with you."

Jeff yelled, "I am engaged to Elliott. You don't know anything about him and me. Who the fuck do you think you are? You are crazy to think I would leave him for you. Elliott and I are not breaking up. I have no intention of hooking up with you or anyone else. Now get the fuck out of here before I hurt you!"

Patrick unzipped his pants and said, "You know you want this. Even if you and Elliott are not breaking up, what harm will it do? Elliott never needs to know. It will be our secret."

Jeff grabbed the croissants and shoved them down Patrick's underwear. "Now, as I said, get the fuck away from me. Elliott was right about you. I have some advice for you, dude. When you get back to New York, you need to look for a new job. Your time on my team is over." Jeff opened the hotel door and shoved Patrick into the hallway.

All alone in his hotel room, Jeff started to hyperventilate. He was trying to catch his breath while crying at the same time. He couldn't believe what had just happened. Most off all, he couldn't erase the guilt he was feeling. It was not just about kissing Patrick. It was about how he had treated Elliott ever since they moved to New York.

He tried calling Elliott again, but there was still no answer. Jeff didn't get any sleep that night. He couldn't stop thinking about what a fucking asshole he had been. He needed to fix things, but he wasn't sure he knew how.

The next morning before he met up with his team, Jeff took a taxi to Calvin's old nursing home. He walked through the cemetery, found his grandfather's grave, knelt on the wet grass, and placed his hands on the headstone. Kneeling there all alone, he poured his heart out, hoping to find the answers.

He took a taxi back to the hotel and told his team that he had a family emergency and needed to go back to New York immediately. He told them they would be able to handle the rest of the assignment until a replacement anchor showed up.

Patrick tried to apologize, but Jeff told him to save it. He didn't want to hear it.

Elliott arrived at the hospital a few hours before Darlene was scheduled for surgery.

Darlene said, "You look like fucking hell. What happened to you? You're a mess!"

Heather hugged him, thanked him for coming so quickly, and told him how terrible he looked.

The nurse came in and gave Darlene an injection that made her extremely tired. Shortly after, they took her to the operating room.

Heather said, "They think they can get all the cancer with this surgery. It was discovered during a routine physical for the post office. It was like a bomb went off in our faces when the doctor told us. Now, what the hell is going on with you?"

Elliott walked over, closed the door, and said, "I am losing him, and I don't know what to do. He has become a stranger. I don't even recognize him anymore. He is not the person you remember. I know he is having—or wants to have—an affair with his producer. They are always together. He doesn't talk to me anymore. We just exist in that fucking apartment. I am sorry, Heather. I know you don't need to hear this shit right now. I just needed to talk to someone about it. I will figure it out somehow."

Jeff arrived back in New York and hurried back to the apartment. As he was entering the building, he noticed the doorman walking Jake. He thought it was strange that Elliott would not be walking the dog. He waved and ran up the stairs. As soon as he entered the apartment, he realized Elliott wasn't home.

The place was in disarray with dirty dishes in the kitchen and towels on the bathroom floor. It was not like Elliott to leave the place a mess. It looked as if he just packed up and left. In their bedroom, Elliott had left one of the closet doors open. Jeff noticed that one of Elliott's suitcases was missing. He started to panic, thinking that Elliott had left him. He ran downstairs to find the doorman. He was told that Elliott had left in a hurry yesterday and was going to California.

Jeff ran back into the apartment and tried calling Elliott again. This time Elliott answered.

"I am home," Jeff said. "Why aren't you here?"

Elliott started to explain about Darlene.

Jeff said, "I understand. I will find a way to get to California as soon as I can."

Elliott said, "You don't need to come if you don't want to. It's not a big deal. I am here for the girls, and that's all that matters right now. I am sure you have other things, with other people, going on that are more important to you. Do what you want. I don't care." He hung up.

Heather said, "Dude, that wasn't cool. You come in here looking like crap and crying on my shoulder that you don't want to lose him. Then you talk to him like that? You need to grow up and act your age. Did you ever consider that you could possibly be as big an asshole as he is? It is time to stop playing the victim and take some responsibility yourself."

Elliott's face turned three shades of red. "What gives you the right to talk to me that way? How dare you do that?"

Heather said, "You gave me the right when you started complaining about how miserable your life has been. As a lawyer, you should know that once you open a subject, it becomes fair game for cross-examination."

The nurse came into the room and told them that if they continued being loud, they would have to leave.

Elliott stood up and said, "Fair enough, Heather. You told me what was on your mind, and I respect that. I apologize for bringing my problems with me when the only thing that matters right now is Darlene. From now on, I will keep my fucking mouth shut and my calls with Jeff private."

Heather broke down and began crying. "Stop it. Damn it. Just stop it! Don't you realize that my wife is in surgery? That's my wife in that damn operating room. What will I do if I lose her? She is my life. They must fix her and make her well again. She is so damn scared, but she won't show it."

Elliott hugged her and said, "I am a goddamn fool for coming in here and complaining. Thanks for being so honest with me. There is nothing we can do until she is out of surgery. Let's go get some coffee. I think we have a long wait ahead of us."

Heather said, "Thank God we are married. Can you imagine the hell we would have gone through if we weren't married? I wouldn't have been allowed to be here with her or make any decisions on her behalf if something happened. Now I have to deal with the fucking insurance company and find out what they won't cover."

After several hours of surgery and several more in the recovery room, Darlene was brought back to her room. Her surgeon explained to Heather and Elliott that he was confident they had removed all the cancer. "For the next several weeks, Darlene might have to undergo extensive chemo treatments. She will probably be sick and weak."

Heather asked, "When will we know about the chemo?"

"We must wait for the pathology report before a decision about chemo can be made. I will supply you with a detailed list of instructions that Darlene needs to follow if she starts chemotherapy."

Still out of it, Darlene told the doctor that Heather and Elliott would make sure she followed all his instructions. Before she faded back into a deep sleep, she told him not to come back until he showered and cleaned himself up. "You look worse than I do, dude."

Heather invited Elliott back to the condo for the night. Before they left, she made sure the nursing station had their contact numbers in case something happened during the night.

Elliott took a long shower, and Heather unpacked his suitcase and ironed a shirt and a pair of shorts for him. She let Kathy know that Darlene's surgery had gone well.

Kathy told Heather that she would be there tomorrow evening and planned to stay for a few weeks.

Elliott called his mom to let her know that Darlene was out of surgery, and Luke stopped by to check up on them. Becky had her hands full with Mark and Alexis, their new daughter. Both children had colds, and Becky didn't want them to spread it to everyone.

Heather fixed them a chicken, kale, and lettuce salad along with organic dressing and some wine. While they were eating, Heather said, "You need to call him. You need to let him know you need him here with you."

Elliott said, "Maybe I don't want Jeff to come."

Heather yelled, "Are you fucking crazy? Of course, you want him here! There is one thing about you that I know. You can say whatever you want and talk out of your mouth and ass, but the truth of what you are feeling always shows in your eyes. You have never been able to hide that. Your eyes are telling me that you want Jeff here next to you. That's all I am going to say about this subject. The ball is in your court."

He took his phone out and called Jeff, but Jeff didn't answer. "Maybe he is out with Patrick. If he is, then the hell with him. I will keep trying to call him."

In the morning, Elliott walked over to Jeff's old barber and got a shave and haircut. He was beginning to look like the Elliott everyone loved. He tried calling Jeff again but had no luck. He was starting to panic. He was caught between staying to help his best friend and going back to New York to find Jeff. After he caught his breath, he decided to keep calling. If he didn't reach Jeff that day, he would go back to New York tomorrow.

After breakfast, they went to see that Darlene.

She was sitting up and trying to eat. "That's better, Elliott. You are beginning to look like someone I used to know. Now you need to work on those bags under your eyes."

Elliott called her a bitch, kissed her, and glanced at the mirror. "I love you, girl, but you must still be feeling a bit groggy. I don't see any bags."

The nurse came in and told Darlene that she needed to get out of bed and walk around to avoid blood clots.

Elliott took one arm, and Heather took the other, and they slowly walked down the hall and into a beautiful room that led to an outside sitting area.

Elliott received a text message.

Heather said, "Is the text from Jeff?"

"No," he said in a quiet voice. "I think it's time we get Darlene back to bed."

Jeff Arrives

When they walked back to Darlene's room, Jeff was sitting in the room with Jake.

No one said a word.

Jeff got up and helped Darlene back into bed.

Jake jumped up on Elliott and tried to lick his face.

Jeff said, "Elliott—" Heather stopped him.

She said, "If you two are going to argue, you need to do it somewhere else. Darlene doesn't need this, and I don't want to hear this shit."

Jeff said, "I have no intention of arguing. I want all of you to hear what I have to say. Elliott, contrary to what you think, I do want to be here. It is a big deal to me. I left Paris in the middle of a story to get back to New York to be with you. Had I known about Darlene, I would have come directly here. I panicked when I thought you left me. I chartered a private jet yesterday to get here. So, you see, it is a big deal to me. Darlene, I am so sorry you are going through all of this. I should be the one who is sick—not you. It isn't fair. I want both of you to know that you don't need to worry about anything. You need to get better, and Elliott and I will take care of everything else."

Elliott said, "Is there still a you and me? It's been a long time since it felt like we were still together."

Jeff shut the door. "I can't blame you for feeling that way. I have felt the same way too. I rushed into that job in New York, and in the process, I rushed you too. It was wrong to do that to the both of us. I got lost trying to be perfect. I tried so hard to show everyone that I could do it all. In the process, I forgot about us. I took you for granted. I forgot that we are perfect together, and that's all that matters.

"I can't understand why you stayed around and took all the shit I threw at you. I am such a goddamn fool. In many ways, I am just like my father—and I hate that. I was afraid you would see me as weak if I failed on that fucking show. I called you stupid, and that was wrong. Elliott, you are not stupid in my eyes. You never were, and you never will be. There were a couple of times I wanted to punch you in your beautiful face, and I am sure there were many more times that you wanted to do the same to me. I couldn't blame you if you did. I am not ready to give up on us. I hope you feel the same.

"There is one more thing that I need you to understand. You were so damn right about Patrick. I can't understand how I didn't see it. I am so sorry I didn't listen to you. Patrick did come on to me in Paris. We were alone in my hotel room, and he kissed me. I hesitated for a few seconds, and then I kissed him back. When I realized what I was doing, I stopped and threw him out of the room. It went no further than that stupid kiss. I told him to find a new job, and he is through with my team. I am ashamed of myself, and I hope you can forgive me. I need you to understand that this is the truth. I am so sorry, Elliott. I want to read you something. We both read this together a long time ago. I didn't understand it then, but now I know what it means and why it was written for both of us. 'There will be storms that blow through our lives. Don't allow those storms to destroy you. Let them make you stronger and bring you closer together.'"

Elliott said, "I remember. Calvin wrote that in the letter before he died. He must have understood life better than we do. He knew we would need this. I stayed because I wanted to stay. It wasn't easy. There were times I thought about leaving, but I am glad I didn't. You are right. Together, we are perfect—and I don't want this to be the end of our story. I know there are many more chapters for us to write, and I want to write them with you.

"As for Patrick, I already know you didn't sleep with him. He must have felt guilty at what he tried to do with you in Paris, and he sent me a text. Perhaps he was trying to save his job and thought I could help. He is a fool if he thought that. He confessed that he has always been extremely attracted to you. He told me how you got in his face when he put the moves on you. He saw in your eyes how much you love me. He knew he crossed the line and wanted to apologize to me. There is one thing I know for sure. I didn't trust that son of a bitch from the day I met him. I couldn't stand it when he came to our home. I hope I never have to see him again. Now, Jeff, what do you want for us going forward?"

Jeff said, "I hate New York, and I hate my job. I am tired of trying to impress all those goddamn idiots who think the world revolves around them. I want us to be together, living where we both want to be, not just somewhere because of a stupid job. I often think about coming back to California. We were always so happy here—but only if that's what you want. If not, you name it, and I will go wherever you want us to live. I need to get away from the broadcasting business. I can't do it anymore. At first, I loved all the attention, but I don't love it anymore. Broadcasting was a decision I made to get back at my father. I realize that now. The more he was against it, the more I was for it. I am tired of fighting with him. I am tired of fighting with myself. You might think I am crazy, but I always wanted to teach at a high school. Most of all, I would love to coach a high school football team. That has always been my passion. I miss football so much."

Elliott said, "Jeff, I will make you a deal. We can move back here to Los Angeles. If it's teaching and football that you want, then you need to go after that. Don't do it for me. You need to do it for you—and nobody else. I want to open my own law practice and go back to working with the LGBTQ community. I have learned a few more life lessons since those days, and that will help me help others You don't know how much I missed that while we were in New York. So, do we have a deal?"

Jeff hugged him and said, "Of course we do!"

Elliott kissed Jeff and exclaimed, "Welcome back. I missed you. Oh, and by the way, I hated New York as much as you did. Possibly even more."

Darlene had pushed the morphine button a few times and was in a fog. "My God, this could be a soap opera. Get your act together—or I am changing the channel. By the way, you should try some of this morphine."

That evening, they ordered pizza and hung out at the condo.

Jeff said, "I love the way you girls decorated it. I didn't think lesbians knew how to decorate with accessories."

Heather threw a pizza crust at him and said, "I love you and your humor. We even have a table saw and power tools in the garage."

Elliott said, "My God! Jeff look! Your parents are on TV."

William, with Laura at his side, announced he was dropping out of the presidential race. He looked like a defeated old man. Laura, on the other hand, looked happy.

Jeff said, "Good—he got what he deserved."

The Sun is Shining

In the morning, Elliott opened all the blinds and said, "It's been a long time since I have seen so much sun shining through the windows. I am glad the sun still shines."

Jeff said, "Heather, you should go to the hospital alone. You and Darlene need to be alone for a while. We can go later. Besides, Elliott and I need some alone time."

Heather said, "Please, just make sure you change the sheets when you're done."

Jeff said, "What makes you think we are going to do it on the bed?"

"That's disgusting! You better stay off my couch."

Before Heather left for the hospital, she said, "If you guys move back here, I am sure you will want to move back into this place. Will you give us enough time to find another place to live. It's not going to be easy."

Jeff grabbed her and said, "You couldn't be more wrong. We have a deal, remember? This belongs to you and Darlene. We will find a new place. I think Elliott and I will be checking into a hotel this evening. We need to make room for Kathy. She will be arriving later today. Elliott just talked to Peg, and she will be driving up and staying for a few days."

As soon as Heather left for the hospital, Elliott said, "Jeff, you were a total asshole in New York, but I wasn't any better. I want you to know that I understand what you were going through. I wish you had talked to me about it sooner. Let's never go through that again. We need to talk to each other—no matter what."

Jeff said, "I hope you know how sorry I am for what I put you through." He pushed Elliott down on the couch and smiled. "Heather will never know."

Peg arrived that afternoon and said, "Elliott, what's with the bags under your eyes?"

"Stop it!" he yelled. "There aren't any. Jeff, please tell me I am right."

Jeff said, "I am not going to question your mother. You told me she is always right."

Peg started to laugh and said, "I talked to the girls, and they put me up to it. Now let's be serious for a minute. I know it has not been an easy time for either of you. Are you both all right?"

Elliott said, "Yes. It's all worked out, but we will probably both be unemployed in a few days."

Peg replied, "Great. A deadbeat son and a soon-to-be deadbeat son-in-law. That's what I always wanted. I don't think you guys have to worry much. Something tells me you have a dollar or two around here somewhere."

Jeff laughed and said, "You were right, Elliott. She is never wrong."

They packed up their belongings and told Peg they would meet up with everyone at the hospital.

Peg said, "Great! I need to pick up Kathy at LAX. and then go see Darlene."

Elliott asked Peg if she could keep Jake for a few days.

"Of course. He is my buddy. I love taking care of him. It looks like he lost some weight in New York."

After Elliott and Jeff checked into the Beverly Hilton, Elliott wanted them to go shopping for a few pairs of jeans and some shirts.

Elliott called Darlene to check up on her.

She said, "I am starving and can't stand hospital food. I need some of my favorite junk food soon—or I will scream."

Elliott said, "I have it handled. We will see you later. Hang in there, kid!"

As soon as they arrived at the hospital, Darlene smiled and said, "You remembered! You brought me my favorite dinner! Kentucky Fried Chicken—with all the fixings."

Kathy said, "I guess she's finally getting better!"

CHAPTER 17

Partners Again

Jeff and Elliott agreed that they needed to approach the move back to California in a much different manner from the way they handled the move to New York. They did not want to hurry and make snap decisions. Every detail needed to be thoroughly discussed and agreed on.

Jeff contacted his lawyer to have him start the process of getting released from his network contract. While he was off the air, his absence from the show was explained with a short announcement that he was on an extended assignment. The network's first response was to offer him more money and an agreement that he would not have to travel as much.

Jeff wanted out, and he asked Elliott for advice. He wanted to know if it would be advisable to talk to the network.

Elliott spent several hours looking over Jeff's contract to see if he could find any loopholes to end the agreement. "It wouldn't hurt for you to talk to them. We need to go back to New York anyway. Let me arrange to have a face-to-face meeting with the network. I should probably be the one to do the negotiations and serve as your legal counsel. I have worked on this this type of negotiation many times in the past. It appears that your attorneys aren't fully on board. This negotiation should have been handled in a much timelier manner. They could be dragging this out for as long as they can to bill you more and more."

"How can you act as my attorney in New York? You aren't licensed to practice law there."

Elliott smiled and said, "Yes, I am. I passed the New York bar exam and received my license while you were away on all those work trips."

"Why did you keep it a secret from me?"

"You never asked. At the time, I didn't think you cared. I had planned to tell you about it one evening. I worked all day to prepare you a dinner with the hope that we could be by ourselves and talk. It didn't work out well for us that night—so I kept it to myself."

"Damn. I remember that night. You had the table set and everything ready when I got home, and I brought Patrick home with me. We ate in the living room. I feel like a damn fool."

Elliott said, "I think there were many things we didn't tell each other during that time. I never want to go through that bullshit again. Now call your lawyers and dismiss them from any further negotiations. I will contact the network's attorneys and schedule a meeting for next week."

Patrick Again

The first stop in New York was their apartment. It still was as messy as Elliott had left it. They needed to get everything packed and shipped back to California.

Elliott stood in the living room and said, "It will be a relief to finally be done with this place."

Jeff said "Thank God we didn't buy it."

Elliott mentioned, "Do we really need to ship all this shit back? Some of it has been moved from Cleveland to Phoenix to Los Angeles and then all the way here. Why don't we sell it and buy everything new for our next home?"

Jeff hugged Elliott and said, "Great idea! All we need to do is pack our clothes and personal stuff. While we are here, we can hire an estate liquefier and get rid of all of it."

"Or we can donate all of it to a LGBTQ organization that helps homeless teens."

Jeff said, "That's a great idea, Elliott. Let's do that!"

They stopped for a martini at an upscale gay bar on the Lower East Side before dinner.

When Jeff went to the restroom, Elliott heard a familiar voice.

Patrick was standing there with his fake smile. He tried to hug Elliott, but Elliott backed away. Patrick said, "I'm surprised to see you here. Where is Jeff?"

"I am right here," Jeff said. "I just stepped away for a few minutes."

Elliott said, "I've got this, Jeff. He is right here with me, Patrick. Why do you ask? Are you surprised we are still together? Take a good look at Jeff. He is the man you can never have. Don't think you can come up to me with your fake-ass smile and believe I have forgotten what you tried to do.

"Let me explain something, and I hope you fully understand me. I would have been hurt if I found out that Jeff had sex with someone else, but I would have forgiven him and gotten over it. I would have been devastated if I found out he had sex with a lying, phony bastard like you. I know Jeff would never do that with you. You are so far down the scale of class. You are probably at the bottom of the barrel. Jeff would never lower himself to fuck someone like you. You are a total has-been. You're like yesterday's news. Do yourself a favor. Start acting like a man and less like a whore. Perhaps then you can find someone who wants to fuck you. Now, please walk the fuck away from us before I do something we will both regret."

Patrick never lost his smile as he turned and walked away.

Jeff looked at Elliott and said, "Dude, I am so impressed and turned on by how you handled that. Way to go, babe!"

As they were leaving the bar, Jeff ran into a reporter from Jeff's New York show. The guy had quit his job and left without saying goodbye to anyone. "Was that Patrick?"

"Yeah. That was the son of a bitch," Jeff said.

"I thought it was. He is the reason I quit working for the network. He kept making advances toward me. He was always touching me. He even followed me into the restroom once and wanted me to have sex with him. I kept complaining to human resources. I told them I knew I was not the only one getting harassed—and that Patrick was creating a hostile work environment. Do you know what they told me? They told me to ignore it. After all, gay boys will be gay boys. I quit that day. Is he still working for the network and on your team?"

"Yes," Jeff said. "He is still at the network, but he is not on my team. I fired him a few weeks ago. Also, I am in the process of leaving the network and moving back to California."

"That's a huge move. I hope you will be happy. I never got the chance to thank you for everything you taught me. What I learned from you is helping me at my new job. Good luck."

Jeff said, "Thanks. Do yourself a favor. Don't let your new position get in the way of your life. It is not worth it."

Elliott said, "Would you be willing to come forward and testify about how you were harassed and how the network reacted to your complaints?"

"Name the place and time, I will be there."

On their way back to the apartment, Jeff said, "Why did you ask him that question?"

Elliott said, "It was just something I wanted to know. I like to know all my options before I go into negotiations. It was lucky that we ran into him tonight."

Negotiations

On Monday morning, Jeff and Elliott arrived at the network's office for their scheduled meeting. The network was stalling and refusing to let Jeff out of his contract. Elliott told them that a clause in the contract allowed the network to terminate employment if they felt it was in the best interests of the show. "Remember when Jeff challenged that clause, and how you insisted that it remain in the contract? Now you have to live up to it. You need to understand that keeping Jeff on would not be in the show's best interests."

They didn't budge. After everyone returned from lunch, they countered with an offer that Jeff could pay a substantial penalty for breaking his contract—and then he would be free to go. They would not allow him to work at any network for the remainder of the two years left in the contract.

After a few minutes, Elliott told them he appreciated their offer, but he had a counteroffer. "You will release Jeff immediately without any type of penalty or restrictions. In fact, you will pay for Jeff's moving expenses."

The network attorney laughed, "That is unacceptable, and we decline your offer."

Elliott said, "Well, I hoped it wouldn't come to this, but listen carefully as I explain why I believe you are going to accept our offer. You have someone working in your organization who has been sexually harassing employees. This has been reported to human resources and been documented on several occasions. Management has failed to address this in a proper manner and has placed the blame on those who have reported it. My guess is that your company didn't care because this was a 'gay issue.'

Jeff has been harassed by this individual and feels that he cannot continue working in such a hostile environment. You either accept our offer—or my client will go public and expose your lack of judgment in handling these complaints. He will also bring with him everyone else who was harassed and ignored by you. There is one more stipulation. The network must immediately terminate the employment of the individual responsible for the harassment. There will be no further negotiation on our part."

After a brief discussion, the network president told his attorney to accept the offer. The matter was closed.

When they got back to the apartment, Jeff said, "You're remarkable."

Elliott said, "The network would have released you without any monetary penalty if we had pressed the issue. The only thing they would have possibly held on to would have been the two-year restriction clause. They needed something that they could call a win."

Jeff asked, "Why did you decide to go in the other direction?"

"If the term sexual harassment came up, I knew the network would give in immediately. If word got out that the network didn't consider gay harassment a serious matter, they knew all kinds of lawsuits would be filed against them. We would have been first in line to file ours. It was also my way to ensure that Patrick would be fired. He had that coming. My only regret is that he wasn't there to hear it coming from me. And I do intend to send you a bill and get paid for my services."

Jeff laughed and said, "That's cool. Let me take out my wallet."

Elliott smiled. "That's not your wallet you're taking out, but I do take all forms of payment—and that one is better than cash."

When they finished, Elliott said, "Paid in full."

The next morning, they got in touch with an organization that would take all their donated furniture. All that was left to do was box up the few items they kept and the rest of their clothing and personal papers.

The doorman would have the boxes shipped back to California.

Elliott took one last look around, walked over to the living room wall, and took down the picture that Calvin had sent them. "We almost forgot this."

Jeff placed it safely in his carry-on bag. "Come on. Let's get the hell out of here and go home."

They both started laughing.

Elliott said, "Great—except there's one problem. We don't have a home to go to.

Jeff said, "How about that? We are two homeless, unemployed, good-looking men, flying first class back to California. No one would believe us if we told them we were unemployed and homeless."

On their way out of the building, they thanked the doorman for everything. He said he would miss them and would really miss Jake.

Elliott handed him three hundred dollars. "This is for taking such loving care of Jake."

Home Again

Darlene received the good news on her first post-op visit with her doctor. Based on the pathology report, it was determined that the cancer was a less aggressive type than what was originally diagnosed. She would not have to endure more than three weeks of chemo. Radiation therapy was also ruled out.

She was feeling much better, and the pain was subsiding. Being home was what she needed. She convinced Heather to go back to work. Kathy was there and would look after her during the day. It was time for Darlene and her mother to have some deep conversations. They had always been open with each other, but now they enjoyed their talks more than ever.

One afternoon, Darlene said, "You should leave Ohio and move to Los Angeles. I feel bad that everyone close to you is now living in California—and you are all alone."

Kathy said, "I have been considering that for a while. It might be the right time to move. Don't get your hopes up, Darlene. We will just look around and see what options are out there. If I find the right place, I will decide."

Darlene put a plan in motion. She called Peg and asked her to call Kathy and try to push her over the top.

Peg said, "I will do one better. I will drive up this weekend and take her out to look at houses or condos."

Darlene said, "Please bring some weed. We may need that to help her decide."

Peg drove up, took Kathy out for lunch, and asked if she really wanted to move.

Kathy said, "Yes, I am ready."

That afternoon, they found the perfect apartment near the girls' condo—and Kathy put down a deposit. She said, "I can't believe I am doing this, but it feels so damn good."

Peg said, "I will help with the moving arrangements. Darlene doesn't need to worry about that. She needs to get better."

When Darlene heard the news, she took Peg aside and said, "How much weed did it take to convince my mom to move?"

Peg said, "None. I still have what I brought with me. Can I use your kitchen? I guess I have some baking to do tonight."

Jeff and Elliott started living in a hotel. After looking at countless houses, they finally found one in Brentwood. It was a four-bedroom ranch in a gated community. It had a beautiful pool along with a walled-in backyard that was perfect for Jake. It was only a couple of years old and had been kept up to perfection. They knew it was the right place. They showed it to Peg, and she fell in love with it immediately. They put in an offer and received a call that it was theirs the next morning.

One afternoon, as they were driving around West Hollywood, Elliott noticed a storefront for rent on Santa Monica Boulevard. "Jeff, park the car. I want to look at that building."

After standing on the sidewalk for several minutes, Elliott said, "I want to rent this space. This is the perfect location for my law practice. I can picture my office right here with my name on the door."

Jeff hugged Elliott and said, "Of course you need to rent it. The place is perfect."

Elliott received a call from Becky about the wedding. She was working as an event planner at the Four Seasons in Beverly Hills. Jeff and Elliott had booked the reception room for the second week of August. Becky needed to get their final approval for the arrangements.

The three of them spent the better part of that afternoon going over menus, flower selections, and seating arrangements. For Beverly Hills, it would be considered a small wedding. They would be sending out ninety invitations to family and close friends. Elliott was guessing that eighty or so guests would show.

Becky warned him that he could be wrong and suggested planning food and seating for one hundred. "There is always someone who brings along more guests than what they RSVP'd. Better be safe than sorry." She showed them several videos of local and national musicians and singers, and they fell in love with a local band with a beautiful young lady as the lead singer. Jeff asked Becky to secure the band immediately. Once the wedding plans were complete, they treated Becky to lunch in one of the hotel's restaurants.

All the darkness and drama of New York was behind them, and everything in their lives seemed to be falling into place.

CHAPTER 18

The Rainbow after the Storm

The week of their wedding started out with plenty of last-minute details that needed attention. Of the ninety invitations that had been sent out, all but three responded that they would attend. Two responded that they would not attend, and one didn't respond at all.

Becky said, "That's rude. All they had to do is check the not attending box and throw it into a mailbox."

Elliott suggested that it could have been lost in the mail and might show up later. He assured her that it was no big deal.

Becky wouldn't drop it. She kept going on about how she hated rude people.

Again, Elliott asked her to forget about it, but she wouldn't drop it. He explained that he knew why they didn't respond. The person had called him a few days earlier and explained why they would not attend. "Please don't bring it up anymore." He showed her the name and made her promise to not tell anyone, especially Jeff.

Several out-of-town guest would be arriving a few days early. Jeff made sure they all had accommodations in the hotel.

On Wednesday, Elliott and Jeff had their final fittings for their tuxedos. While they were there, they got into an argument because Elliott started second-guessing the tuxedos they had selected. He kept looking at other ones.

Jeff said, "Please stop it. You need to focus your attention on where it is needed."

Elliott walked outside and pouted for a few minutes. When he came back in, he hugged Jeff and said, "I want to apologize. I guess I am more nervous than I realized."

Becky and the hotel baker were finalizing and approving the decorations for the cake. She also scheduled a meeting with the hotel chef about the menu for the reception and the wine list.

On Thursday morning, Peg showed up at the hotel to have breakfast with the boys. While they were eating, she handed them an envelope. It was a check to cover the cost of the wedding. She said it was from her and Dan. "We saved it all these years for you and Becky. I gave Luke and Becky their share when they got married—and now it is your turn."

Jeff and Elliott said they could not accept it. They had everything covered.

Peg grinned and said she would not take it back. "If both of you don't need it for this wedding, then please find some other beneficial use for it."

Elliott knew she was finished discussing it. "We will figure it out," he said as he gave her a kiss on her cheek.

Becky was on the phone as she joined them at the table. She was yelling at whoever was on the other end and trying to explain that she had ordered white and red roses for the table settings and not several different colors. "Just get the damn order correct!"

Elliott said, "You go, girl. You should have been a lawyer."

She laughed and said, "No thanks. One lawyer in the family is more than enough. Tomorrow morning, both of you need to pick up your tuxedos. Here are the key cards for your rooms for tomorrow night."

Jeff looked at the keys and said, "These rooms are on opposite sides of the hotel."

"That's right! Neither of you will see each other until the wedding—starting tomorrow evening. Elliott, your out-of-town guests will stay on your side of the hotel, and Jeff, your guests will be with you. So, you won't be doing anything with each other tomorrow night. I don't care what you do tomorrow night with your guest, but you need to show up on time on Saturday. I don't care if you have the worst hangover ever—you will both be there on time. Darlene will oversee Elliot, and Heather will be with Jeff. Any questions?"

Both quickly replied, "Nope!"

"Good! Don't fuck it up."

Peg laughed and said, "Becky, you scare me, and I would not dare fuck anything up. It's wonderful to see my two children who have lives of their own—but still are so important in each other's lives. Your father would have been proud of both of you."

On Friday afternoon, after Jeff and Elliott returned from the tailor, they kissed each other and went to their respective rooms.

Soon, a few of Elliott's college friends and his best friends from Phoenix began arriving.

Darlene had arranged for them to go out to dinner and then hit a few bars. She looked and felt better than she had in months, but Elliott asked her not to overexert herself. She laughed and said, "Honey, I will drink you under the table tonight. After all the shit you have put me through all these years, I plan on just letting go and having a fucking enjoyable time."

Jeff's friends from the LA TV station and a few friends from college went to Santa Monica. Heather instructed them, "We will have dinner at the pier and then hit all the bars along the oceanfront. The limos will be waiting for us in front of the hotel at six thirty."

Becky and Luke dropped the kids off with Peg and Kathy at the girls' condo, joined up with Darlene's team, and then found their way to meet up with Heather's team.

When the celebrating was over, Elliott had a deep feeling that his life would be complete. He was gay and proud of it, and in a few hours, he would be a married man.

Jeff sat in his hotel room and looked out the window. He was, for the first time in his life, completely at peace with himself. He couldn't wait to be married to Elliott and begin the next chapter of their lives together. His only regret was that no one from his family would be attending his wedding. He had reconciled with that a long time ago, but he wished it all could have turned out differently.

You May Both Kiss Your Husband

On the morning of his wedding, Elliott woke up feeling like he had been run over by a train. He knew that he should have stopped drinking much earlier and should have refused that last round of tequila. After he called room service and ordered plenty of coffee, he turned on the shower and let the hot water rain down on his pounding head.

He jumped out of the shower and quickly drank two cups of coffee before he remembered that he had an appointment to get his hair cut. He hurriedly put on a pair of shorts and T-shirt and ran down to the barber shop in the lobby.

Becky was finalizing the last-minute details. She looked him up and down and said, "You look much better than I had expected. Remember to be here at three o'clock—and don't be late."

Jeff was up early. He didn't have a hangover and was eager to begin the most important day of his life. He called Elliott to see how he was.

Elliott said, "Much better now—thanks to the coffee and ibuprofen."

"I love you."

"I love you too."

They would not see each other again until the wedding.

Heather stopped by Jeff's room to make sure he was up and brought him coffee and muffins. As they were eating, Jeff told Heather that he was proud that she would be standing next to him during the ceremony. "You, Darlene, and Elliott's family are now my only family. My parents lost out on that privilege by their own choice years ago. I don't even hate them anymore. I feel sorry for them. They are two lonely, sad people. They made their life, and I have made mine." He handed Heather a small wrapped gift. "I want you to have this. It's a token of my appreciation for your friendship." Inside the package was a gold necklace with a beautiful diamond in the center. "You are my one diamond friend, and I hope you never forget that."

She hugged him and thanked him with a kiss. "Ditto, my friend," she said with a smile.

After his haircut, Elliott went back to his room. He was surprised to see Darlene waiting for him in the room. She told him, "Becky let me in."

"You look almost presentable."

He said, "Thanks for last night. I had a wonderful time. It was nice to hang with my friends from Phoenix. Thanks for planning the evening."

As they were finishing the last of the coffee, Darlene said, "I can't fucking believe this day is finally here. It's been one hell of a ride."

Elliott said, "There was a time in New York when I thought this day would never happen, and there was a time in high school when I thought I would never see Jeff again. I am lucky, and I know it. You were there with me all along, and I will never forget that." He handed Darlene a gift.

She opened it and found a beautiful gold bracelet. On the back, it was engraved: "Best Friends Forever." She said, "Forever, dude, and don't ever forget it." She started laughing and said, "Don't worry! Just because you are married, I will still be around to kick your ass when you need it. You need to be downstairs and ready by two thirty."

He said, "No. Becky said three."

Darlene said, "Two thirty to be safe. I will be waiting for you in the lobby."

Jeff would be standing in front with Darlene, Heather, and the judge. Elliott would escort his mother to her seat and then join them on the stage.

Jeff looked perfect in his white tux as he took his position next to the girls. He was amazed at how great Elliott looked and couldn't stop smiling. It was the first time Jeff had seen Peg in a beautiful designer dress and not a colorful, loose dress. He noticed that she didn't have a flower in her hair. As Elliott took his place beside Darlene, Jeff walked down to Peg, handed her a red rose, and gave her a kiss.

When Peg placed the rose in her hair, Jeff said, "Now, we are ready to begin."

Heather was wearing a short, white sequined dress. Around her neck was the necklace Jeff had given her.

Darlene was wearing a white silk pantsuit. Her new bracelet sparkled in the light streaming down from the skylights.

Sister Mary Therese, who was honored to be invited, walked onto the stage and explained that even though her church didn't sanction this union, she did. "It is okay to go against the rules sometimes and follow what is in your heart. That is what Jesus taught us, and that's what is happening here today. I know God will bless this union. I have known these two men since they were in grade school. If ever any two people belonged together, it is these two."

The judge said, "Now, let us begin what you have all been waiting for." He asked Jeff and Elliott to face each other. "I understand that both of you have a few words you want to say to each other. Elliott will start first."

"Jeff, I promise you my love always. I have always known that we were meant to be here on this day and every day after. When I look into your eyes, I forget the world around me. All I see is love. For me, there is nobody in the world but you. You are the one love of my life. You have made me a complete and happy man. I love you."

Jeff took hold of Elliott's hands. "Elliott, all through those times we were not together, the thoughts I had of you guided me. When I was scared, those thoughts comforted me. When I was hurt, they helped me get better. I have loved you since that first day of school, and that has never changed. It has only grown stronger. I am nothing without you. With you, I am on top of the world. I loved you, then, now, and forever."

The judge said, "Do you, Jeffrey Stephan Ryan, take Elliott as your lawfully wedded husband?"

Jeff said, "I do."

"Do you, Elliott Dominic Romano, take Jeff as your lawfully wedded husband?"

Elliott smiled, placed both of his hands on Jeff's, and said, "I do."

They were asked to exchange rings.

Darlene handed Jeff's ring to Elliott, and Heather handed Elliott's ring to Jeff.

The judge said, "These rings are a symbol of your unbroken love for each other. A love that no person or law can ever deny you. I now pronounce you both legally married. You may now each kiss your husband."

Looking into each other's eyes, they kissed for what seemed like a couple of minutes.

Everyone was standing and clapping, and Becky was crying.

Peg gave them her famous grin and a wink.

Elliott and Jeff took in all the happiness and congratulations that their guests where showing them. These two men, in their own separate journeys of space and time, had made it to this day. They had long ago accepted that their minds were not wired wrong. They accepted that their hearts did not beat in an abnormal manner. They knew who they were, but hearing the judge speak their full names while looking into each other's eyes, and when they spoke their vows, they now understood that for the first time, they were totally free.

It was not an imitation of life. It was a validation of their lives. Their commitment to each other was real, and no one could ever take that from them. It was their emancipation. They broke free of any demons that were still lurking in the corners of their minds. The simple act of hearing their full names while saying their vows solidified all the abstract visions and colors within their minds. The colors represented their pride, acceptance, and freedom. They walked down to greet everyone, shake hands, and receive kisses. It was time to have a party.

The Reception

Becky had outdone herself, and the room looked magnificent. There were dozens of white and red roses in beautifully designed crystal vases. The tables were covered with pristine white satin tablecloths, red and white china, crystal glasses, and perfectly polished silverware.

At the end of the dance floor, the band was already performing. The guests were served by six gorgeous men who were impeccably dressed in black tuxedos and white gloves.

The dinner consisted of dill salmon and filet mignon, cooked to order. California wine was served to everyone except the wedding party. They were served wine that Jeff had shipped over from France. The wine was from the winery next to the nursing home where Matthew and Calvin had lived.

During dinner, Darlene and Heather stood up to offer a toast. Darlene told everyone how proud she and Heather were to be friends with Jeff and Elliott. She shared a few details about things Elliott did back in high school, which embarrassed him to no end. She spoke about how she has come to accept "the rich, spoiled one" as her dear brother. She assured everyone that Jeff was not spoiled and had a warm, good heart. "As for the rich thing, I'll leave that up to all of you to figure out. All I know is he does nothing on a budget."

They all laughed, and Jeff turned red.

Heather held up her wineglass and wished them good luck.

With dinner over and the wine flowing freely, the band announced that it was time for the first dance. Elliott had selected "When You Tell Me That You Love Me" by Diana Ross. He heard it at a concert in Phoenix and fell in love with it. The lyrics said everything he ever wanted to tell Jeff.

As the band started the music and the singer began with the first lines, Jeff and Elliott started their dance. Soon, Darlene and Heather joined them along with Becky and Luke. Elliott left the dance floor to escort Peg onto the floor. On the way to the dance floor, Peg convinced Sister Mary Therese to join them.

While they all were dancing, a FedEx delivery woman walked in with a package for Jeff. While standing with his husband on the dance floor, Jeff opened it. Inside was a vintage gold watch. On the back of it was inscribed: "Happy Birthday, Dad. Love, Laura." There also was a letter from his mother.

Jeff,

I want to thank your new husband for inviting me to your wedding. I didn't think it would be appropriate for me to show up. I didn't want to spoil your special day. When I received the beautiful invitation, I called Elliott and had a long talk with him. He is a remarkable man. In a way, I think I have always known that. I am truly happy for both of you. Please don't be upset with him for contacting me. As for the watch, it belonged to my father, your grandfather. It is one of the few possessions of his that I have kept all these years. I want you to have it now. Perhaps one day, when or if you are ready, we can sit and just talk. I would welcome that. Take care of Elliott. He loves you so much.

Love,
Mother

Jeff couldn't stop crying. He looked at Elliott and said, "Thank you! I could never be mad at you for doing this. But why couldn't she have come?"

Elliott said, "One step at a time, my love. One step at a time."

Darlene ran up to the microphone and announced that it was time to cut the cake. With everyone around the table, she handed them the silver knife.

Jeff and Elliott cut the first slice together and gave each other a taste of the first slice. When it looked as if they would smear each other's face with the cake, they quickly turned and rubbed the cake on Darlene and Heather's faces.

Everyone besides Darlene was laughing.

Elliott looked at her and said, "Come on! You should have seen that coming. You know me better than that. I would never be seen in public with cake on my face."

Heather laughed and said, "Darlene—once a queen always a queen."

The girls then took some cake and rubbed it in Jeff and Elliott's faces. Darlene said, "I thought you knew me better than that—I got you!"

After all the guests left besides Peg, Becky, Luke, Kathy, and the girls, Elliott said, "I have something I want to show everyone. It's not far from here. Get in your cars and follow us."

They drove to West Hollywood and stopped in front of a building on Santa Monica Boulevard. There was a sign on the outside of the building: "Elliott Romano, Attorney at Law." He invited them all inside to see his new office. They had champagne to toast the new business.

Jeff and Elliott thanked them all for the beautiful day and all the work they put into their wedding.

Peg asked them where they were going on their honeymoon.

Jeff said, "Nowhere. We are staying in our new home tonight." He took Heather aside and whispered that he and Elliott were going to fuck like high school kids that night. "We are going to christen the new house."

On their first night as a married couple, Jeff and Elliott had to sleep on the floor. Most of the furniture they had ordered was delayed. The only thing that arrived on time was the massive dining room table and chairs.

They wrapped themselves up in a blanket on the living room floor, and Elliott said, "Sleeping on the floor is perfect. Why would we have wanted it any other way? Nothing has been conventional for us—why start now?"

They kissed each other good night.

CHAPTER 19

Full Circle

On a warm Friday evening, Elliott, Darlene, and Heather found their way up the bleachers to their seats. Elliott remarked to the girls that it was the perfect way to celebrate his and Jeff's first anniversary.

Darlene said, "I feel like I'm back in high school."

Elliott joked, "Don't you wish."

The home team was announced and ran onto the field. "Ladies and Gentlemen, the home team coach: Jeff Ryan!"

Jeff ran on to the field. He stopped, looked up into the bleachers, and saw Elliott in a pair of jeans that fit him perfectly and a new yellow sweater. For a moment, he was fixated on Elliott's smile. Elliott was waving back at him while enjoying how Jeff's eyes were shining from the overhead lights.

It was the school's first game of the year.

Elliott noticed that it looked like his high school football field—but there was no stage for a dignitary to stand on and make a ridiculous speech.

Jeff looked sexy in his coaching uniform and led his team to victory. It would be the first of many victories that would land the school at number one for the season.

After the game, Darlene and Heather said they were heading home.

Jeff said, "No way! We are going to celebrate together. There is a pizza shop just down the street from here. We can walk there and pig out on some pizza and beer."

Darlene said, "You guys can walk—Heather and I will drive."

As they were walking, they passed a small Catholic grade school and stopped.

Jeff said, "Brings back memories for me."

Elliott replied, "The best memories. I will never forget that day, and for me, every day that we are together is like that first day of school."

The girls were already seated when they arrived. Darlene had ordered two pizzas that she hoped everyone would enjoy and a pitcher of beer. "Don't worry, Jeff. I ordered a veggie one just for you."

They ate, drank, laughed, and told stories from days gone by.

Elliott handed Jeff a small gift-wrapped package. "This is for you. I have waited a long time to give it to you."

Jeff opened it and said, "This is the necklace I wanted to buy at the mall when we were in high school."

Elliott smiled and said, "Yeah, it was supposed to be your Christmas gift that year. Better late than never."

Jeff kissed him and thanked him.

Darlene smiled and said, "Remember how I told you to never give up hope? You never know what the future will bring."

Heather gave a toast to celebrate Jeff and Elliott's anniversary.

Jeff said, "When I look back, at times, I can't believe all the shit the four of us went through."

Elliott said, "I often think about the same thing. We were the lucky ones. We, for whatever reason, figured it out. I had my family on my side to guide me. Jeff, you had resources—and you were smart enough to do it on your own. Even with all that, we still had a tough time finding acceptance. I worry about all the kids who don't have family or money to help them. Just think about it. At this very moment, there must be countless young gay and transgender teenagers who are struggling for their lives while trying to come to terms with who they are. Without a support system, they find themselves in a dark, lonely place. I wonder how many of them won't make it out of that place. Yeah, we are the lucky ones."

A New Adventure

Elliott received a text message. "Mrs. Sidley needs to meet with us at my office tonight."

Jeff smiled and said, "Wow! That was fast."

Darlene said, "Who the hell is Mrs. Sidley?"

Elliott replied, "I guess you need to come with us to find out."

Jeff looked at Elliott and asked if he was sure he wanted to pursue this.

Elliott said, "I am all in. How do you feel about it?"

Jeff smiled and said, "I can't wait! Together, we will be good at this. Let's go. We won't know until we give it a try."

Mrs. Sidley was waiting outside when they pulled up to Elliott's office.

Darlene said, "That lady is not alone."

Elliott replied, "We know. That's the reason we are here."

Mrs. Sidley introduced herself to Darlene and Heather as a county social worker. She also introduced Juan and Candace. Juan was fourteen and had been living on the streets for six months after his parents disowned him when they found him in bed with another boy.

Candace was thirteen and came from a broken home. Her mother abandoned her family, and her father threw Candace out when she announced that she was gay.

They all went inside, and Mrs. Sidley asked Juan and Candace to wait in the outer office.

Jeff asked Darlene and Heather to stay with the kids.

Elliott, Jeff, and Mrs. Sidley went into Elliott's office and closed the door.

Mrs. Sidley apologized for asking them to come at such a late hour. Even though they had discussed helping one child, both teenagers were put in her custody by the juvenile court. They had been arrested for stealing from Whole Foods. They would have to spend the night in juvenile detention if she couldn't find an appropriate place for them to stay. Since Jeff and Elliott had already been cleared by the courts to foster a child, they were the first ones she thought of, and she was hoping they would consider fostering two.

Mrs. Sidley said, "These kids need help. I can't, in good conscience, send them to that terrible juvenile home. They will get lost in the system. They are good kids at heart."

Jeff said, "We have never raised any child—let alone two. I am willing to give it a try, but the final approval needs to be Elliott's."

Elliott looked through the office window at the kids and said, "You need to see this, Jeff."

Juan was sitting behind Elliott's desk. He seemed timid and lost.

Heather was braiding Candace's hair, and Darlene was scolding the young girl for using foul language.

Elliott looked at Jeff and said, "They need us."

Darlene knocked on the door and told them that she and Heather would be willing to help. "Candace needs a woman's perspective at this age. Mrs. Sidley give them two days. These two will make sure Juan is the best-dressed kid in all of Los Angeles."

Mrs. Sidley asked Darlene if she and Heather had ever considered filling out an application to foster a child.

Darlene confided that they had often talked about it.

Mrs. Sidley said, "Until you are approved, Candace will have to be in the care of Elliott and Jeff—if they agree to take her."

"Of course! Elliott and I will take both into our home."

Life had come full circle for Elliott and Jeff. Perhaps all the pain, anger, and shame they had gone through were life lessons they needed to experience in order to help others navigate their own journeys of acceptance. It was their turn, and they knew it was their duty to use the love they discovered for each other on that first day of school as proof that no one should ever deny who they are or who they love.

That night was the beginning of the next chapter in the lives of four friends who found each other when they needed a friend the most. They knew they would always need each other.

Heather and Darlene spent that night at Jeff and Elliott's house.

Jake jumped onto Juan's bed and stayed there all night.

As soon as Juan and Candace were asleep, Jeff, Elliott, Darlene, and Heather went outside, sat by the pool, and had a glass of wine. There wasn't much conversation. There was, however, a tremendous feeling of peace and love. After all the bullshit of life, love was all that mattered. Love had conquered all.

Jeff went over to Elliott, picked him up, walked to the pool's edge, and tossed him in—fully dressed. "I always wanted to do that to you. Happy anniversary. I love you."

Elliott reached up, grabbed Jeff's leg, and pulled him into the water. "Happy anniversary, my love!"

Heather and Darlene were laughing—until Jeff grabbed Darlene's foot, and Elliott grabbed Heather's foot. At the same time, they pulled the girls into the water.

All four of them were standing fully clothed in the pool and laughing their asses off. They were celebrating more than Jeff and Elliott's anniversary. They were celebrating their love and friendship for each other, which had survived so much over the years. That night was for fun. Tomorrow would be the first day of their next chapter.

No matter what was ahead, they knew they would get through it. They were survivors.

The End.

Printed in the United States
By Bookmasters